"You are enemy."

"Me?" Barlow said in surprise. "Your enemy? How the hell do you figure that, hoss? I ain't even seen you—or your people—before this."

"You and your friends, you attack our village."

"Like hell I did, hoss," Barlow snapped. He had no idea where these Comanches had gotten such a notion. "Like I said, I ain't never seen none of you before you come for me just a little bit ago. Hell, I ain't ever been in this land before."

"Enough!" Slow Eagle roared. "You will die for what you did to The People. The more you deny, the longer your death takes."

Barlow tensed. He knew he could easily take these three men, no matter how good they were as warriors. But what would that get him? That would bring the rest of the warriors running and, while he knew he was good and a hell of a fighter, he could not take on ten, twelve, maybe fifteen warriors all at once. Especially not when he was unarmed.

Wildgun
Winter Hunt

Jack Hanson

JOVE BOOKS, NEW YORK

WINTER HUNT

A Jove Book / published by arrangement with the author

PRINTING HISTORY
Jove edition / November 2002

Copyright © 2002 by Penguin Putnam Inc.

Visit our website at
www.penguinputnam.com

ISBN: 0-515-13408-2

A JOVE BOOK®
Jove Books are published by The Berkley Publishing Group, a division of Penguin Putnam Inc., 375 Hudson Street, New York, New York 10014.
JOVE and the "J" design are trademarks belonging to Penguin Putnam Inc.

PRINTED IN THE UNITED STATES OF AMERICA

10 9 8 7 6 5 4 3 2 1

1

TAOS HADN'T CHANGED much in the couple of months Will Barlow had been gone. It was the same dusty brown place, the adobe buildings drab except for the occasional colorful door or window sash and the ubiquitous *ristras* of bright red chili peppers. Caballeros still walked the streets, preened and on the prowl, though they did seem a bit less cocky now than had been the case. And the señoritas were still there, wearing their short dresses, their shoulders bare, their hair long and silky. Seeing them made Barlow's spirits rise a little from the depths of despair at having lost his young daughter, Anna, for good.

Anna had been taken by the Umpquas up in the Oregon country when she was just a baby. Barlow had tracked her for almost five years, until he finally found her living with a Mexican family in San Diego. Though he wanted more than anything to take her with him, to bring his daughter to her grandparents in the Willamette Valley up in the Oregon country, he could not bring himself to do so. The Moraleses were the only family Anna had ever really known, though she had not been with those people all that long. They provided a safe, stable environment for the girl, one in which she could live healthily and probably happily.

It was the hardest thing Barlow had ever done, but he finally acquiesced and allowed the family to keep the child. It was with a heavy heart, however, that he—along with his

Shoshoni friend White Bear and his giant Newfoundland dog, Buffalo 2—had ridden out of San Diego.

When he did, he was rootless, and no longer had a purpose to life. He debated with White Bear about where to go and what to do, but the Indian—who had been raised by a English family in Missouri and spoke their language with a decidedly British touch—had no answers. White Bear wanted to return to his people, whom he had not seen in several years, but he could not just abandon his friend. They had been through too much together for him to just ride off leaving Barlow to fend for himself in his state of melancholy.

Finally White Bear had suggested they return to Taos. It was there they had discovered that the family Anna was living with had moved to San Diego. And it was there they had been conscripted to lead General Kearny's Army of the West to wrest California from the Mexican people. And while the two men had no real ties to the town, they had had a wonderful time with a couple of señoritas while they were there. White Bear figured that Barlow might perk up a bit after a few sessions with the delightful Rosaria Carrillo, who had entertained the former mountain man quite well during his stay in Taos.

Barlow gave it a little thought. He had nowhere to go, really. He could go to the Oregon country and explain to his in-laws that he had found Anna but had left her with a Mexican family. But he didn't feel he could face that now. In fact, he was not sure he could ever face the task, though he knew he would have to sooner or later. His late wife's parents deserved to know what had happened to their granddaughter. But that was for later, he decided. For now, he would go to Taos, where he thought he might be able to drown some of his sorrow in fiery *aguardiente*. Or between the thighs of some hot and willing señorita.

"Taos it is, my friend," he said quietly, trying to work up a smile. He succeeded only a little.

So they had turned east, crossing the dangerous Colorado River, skirting the gigantic canyon—which they had almost stumbled into on the trip west—and making their way through the pine-forested mountains and eventually onto the high, windswept desert plains, the home of the Navajo Indians. They were not bothered on the trip, which surprised them only a little. When they were heading to California, they had defeated some Mohave Indians who had attacked them. The Mohaves wanted nothing more to do with white men—or other Indians—for the time being. The Navajos, while a large tribe, had seen the many soldiers passing through their land and figured it wiser to keep the peace for now, rather than run the risk of having the white man's army come and destroy them.

There were more mountains then, higher ones, as they crawled up the San Juans through Wolf Creek Pass. As they did so, they could feel the first brush of winter, although that season was still a month or so off. Up here, however, it started early, and the travelers rode through some snow flurries more than once.

Finally, they were riding into Taos. The sky was a brilliant, cloudless blue, although the temperature couldn't have been much more than sixty degrees; not enough to give one a chill, but cool enough to serve as a reminder that winter was not that far off, and of how harsh winter in this high country could be.

The only real difference that Barlow could see in the drab town of low, flat-roofed adobe houses was the number of American soldiers strutting around. Many of the troops looked with contempt at the new arrivals making their way to the plaza. The soldiers also seemed to view the town's Mexican residents the same way.

"Bloody friendly bunch of blokes, wouldn't you say?" White Bear said.

"Ass wipes, every goddamn one of 'em," Barlow snarled. He had no liking at all for soldiers, not after the run-ins he had had with some of them here and on the trail to California, as well as enduring Kearny's overbearing and patrician ways.

The dog, Buffalo 2, growled his assent.

The señoritas, however, gazed at them with much more warmth than the soldiers. Indeed, many offered glances that were pure invitation. Barlow's spirits rose minutely. *Maybe this wasn't such a bad idea,* he thought.

They stopped in front of a cantina they had visited before, and alit—Barlow from the big, black mule he called Beelzebub; White Bear from his piebald pony. Each brought his rifle with him in a move so practiced that neither realized he was doing it. Buffalo 2 plopped his behind in the dirt and raised up little dust storm as his tail swished back and forth.

Barlow stood for a moment, smacking the dust out of his large-brimmed hat by strongly whacking it on a thigh. He still wore buckskins, in the manner of his days as a beaver trapper in the Rocky Mountains: worn, fringed pants that were thick with grease and blood and smoke; a matching shirt and a pair of worn moccasins that likely would not last more than a few days on him, though he seemed not to notice or care.

White Bear wore no hat, though he did have a couple of feathers dangling from his long, loose hair. He, too, wore buckskins: shirt, breechcloth, leggings and moccasins.

Under the watchful eyes of a few soldiers—whom the two men and the dog ignored—they entered the dim, cool cantina. The place was unpretentious to the point of being spartan—just a few tables and a makeshift bar on a dirt floor. The adobe walls were unfinished, giving the cantina a musty, earthy smell that mingled with the stench of spilled whiskey, sweat, unwashed bodies and urine. Since it was windowless, sputtering candles broke the gloom only a little, their acrid smoke mixing with that of pipes and cigarillos.

The two men stopped at the bar and laid their rifles atop it, out of the way but near enough to hand in an emergency. "Some Lightnin', hoss," Barlow said to the bartender. "And two glasses."

The barman, a small, thin, nervous individual with a narrow face and slim mustache, eyed the two warily for a few moments, as if trying to decide whether to serve them or ask them to leave. At Barlow's questioning raised eyebrows, the bartender shrugged and went to get the bottle and glasses.

He slapped them on the table and turned to head away, but Barlow stopped him. "I need some water, too. In a bowl, if you got one."

"*Agua?*" the bartender asked, surprised.

"*Sí.* For my dog." He snapped his fingers and Buffalo 2 stood on his hind legs, his front paws resting on the bar.

"Right away, señor," the surprised bartender said, scurrying off.

As Barlow filled the two crockery mugs with some of the locally made Taos Lightning, a voice came from somewhere in the room: "Injins ain't allowed in here."

Barlow and White Bear ignored the voice. Barlow nodded when the bartender handed him an old pot full of water. He bent and placed it on the floor, where Buffalo 2 quickly began slurping the liquid up, splashing out nearly as much as he drank.

"I said, Injins ain't allowed in here," the voice repeated, this time louder and with a bit more vehemence. On his third time, Barlow and White Bear slowly turned and leaned back against the bar, each with a glass in his hand. "You addressin' us, hoss?" Barlow asked politely, though there was an edge to his voice.

"Yeah, I'm talkin' to you, you dumb son of a bitch." The man stood and glanced around at his fellows, pleased at his witty repartee. "Git that goddamn Injin of yours out of here and tell him to take the damn dog, too."

"Who're you calling a goddamn Injin, you bloody twit?" White Bear inquired, polite as could be.

"You, you goddamn fool," the man snapped after getting over his shock. He wore an American military uniform, albeit one that had seen better days.

"You must have me mistaken for someone else, old chap," White Bear said evenly.

"You sure as hell look like an Injin," the soldier said, again looking around for approbation on his wit.

"Looks can be deceiving, old chap." Some of the politeness had dropped out of White Bear's voice, though it was still calm and reasoned.

"What's that supposed to mean?" The trooper seemed confused.

"Just what it says," White Bear retorted. He couldn't believe a soldier—or anyone, for that matter—could be so stupid. "It means that things aren't always the way they bloody seem." He smiled, though there was little humor in it. "Take yourself, for example," he continued, voice smooth and even. "You appear to be a bloody soldier, a man not old, but no bloomin' youngster either. And yet, you seem to not have the brains that God gave a turnip." He held up his glass in a mock salute and turned back to face the bar.

The solider clumped toward them—White Bear facing the bar, Barlow still facing away from it, watching. The man was big—a bit over six foot tall and weighing nearly two hundred pounds. His shoulders were wide, tapering to a slim waist. As he neared, Barlow could see the soldier had three stripes on his sleeve, and he wondered how someone so stupid could become a sergeant in the army. As the soldier drew near, Barlow shifted his glass from his right hand to his left.

"I said, boy," the soldier snapped, grabbing White Bear by the shoulder and trying to jerk him around to face him, "that no goddamn Indians are allowed in here."

White Bear spun, much faster than the soldier had expected, and he took a step back. Next to Barlow, Buffalo 2 growled softly and watched warily.

The sergeant paid him no mind. Instead, he glared at White Bear and said tightly, "Now, boy, are you gonna walk out that door, or am I gonna have to toss you out on your ass?"

He moved a step closer to White Bear, and in the act jostled Barlow's drink, spilling a little.

"Hey, hoss, watch what you're doin'," Barlow protested. "This here *aguardiente* don't come free, you know."

"Shut your hole, you Injin-lovin' son of a bitch," the sergeant snapped, giving Barlow only a cursory glance.

Barlow calmly set his drink on the bar. He was several inches shorter than the soldier was, but broader in the chest and shoulders, his massive torso thick with muscle. He grabbed the soldier by the back of the neck, half spun him and then slammed his face into the top of the bar.

The soldier groaned but did not pass out. Barlow pulled his head up and forced it around to look at him. "I think you should be a good little feller, hoss, and go on home. Seems to this ol' chil' that you've had a mite too much to drink and are gonna have a mighty powerful hangover come mornin'. You mess with us again, you won't ever see another mornin'. That clear, hoss?"

Barlow helped the sergeant shake his head. Then he pulled him all the way up and gave him a shove toward the door, accelerating his pace with a moccasined foot to the man's rump. The soldier staggered out.

"You get that kind of thing often?" Barlow asked the bartender as he turned to face the bar and pick up his drink.

"Too often, señor." He smiled, more friendly now that he knew these two men were not like the soldiers. "Those *americano soldados,* they theenk they own everything here now." He shook his head in annoyance. "They push people around, make trouble for us. Damn *pendejo*—cowardly and stupid—*soldados*."

"Well, he's gone now," Barlow said.

"*Sí,*" the bartender agreed. "But he will be back. Today, tomorrow, sometime. And he weel be with amigos then. If you are wise, you weel not be here when they come back." He walked off, muttering imprecations against American soldiers.

Barlow almost grinned in amusement at the man's annoyance, but he could understand it. He drained his glass and then refilled it. White Bear did the same. They both drank in silence for a few minutes, before putting their glasses down. Barlow jammed the cork into the bottle and threw a couple of coins on the bar. Grabbing the bottle in one hand and his rifle in the other, he said, *"Adios,"* before heading for the door, White Bear and Buffalo 2 right behind him.

The two men mounted up and rode out of the plaza through a small alley, and then wove down several small streets. They stopped at Viuda Garza's house and knocked on the door.

The old Widow Garza answered it, and smiled broadly, overjoyed to see them. "Come een, come een," she said excitedly, stepping back out of the way.

2

VIUDA GARZA TOOK them back to the room they had shared when they spent time in Taos before. It was a cramped place, but neither Barlow nor White Bear was so fussy as to complain about it. When Viuda Garza turned up the oil lamp to light the room, the men saw that it had not been changed—still two small, creaky beds with straw ticks and covered with fine blankets, and nightstand between the beds on which sat a washbasin and pitcher with a towel folded next to them and homemade lye soap on the towel. A crucifix hung on one wall.

"Bueno?" Viuda Garza asked anxiously.

"Ah, *sí,* señora," Barlow said. *"Muy bueno."* The room could have been prisonlike and they would still be happy with it. Not so much for the room, but to be able to eat Viuda Garza's cooking.

The old widow was all smiles again. She had hopes of encouraging one of these young men to warm her bed for an evening, though she knew the chances were slim. Still, an old woman could dream, she always thought.

"Hambriento?" she asked.

"What?" Barlow asked. He had heard the word before, but it was a couple of months ago, and he could not remember it's meaning. *"Que?"*

Viuda Garza made eating motions, saying *"hambriento"* over and over.

"Ah, hungry?" Barlow asked.

"Sí, sí," the woman said, pleased that she had gotten her message across.

"Sí," Barlow said with a grin. *"Muy hambriento!"*

Viuda Garza grinned, showing a surprisingly full set of teeth for a poor woman in her late fifties. Then she hurried off toward the kitchen.

Barlow, White Bear and Buffalo 2 entered the room, which could barely contain the three of them if they were not lying down. The men tossed their possible bags on the beds and sat. They were glad to be off the trail, and happy to be in one spot for a little while with no obligations hanging over them.

As the aroma of spices drifted into the room, Barlow rose, poured some water from the pitcher to the washbasin and washed his face and hands. Then he splashed some water on his hair. "Ah, that's a sight better," he said as he whipped his head back, sending a small shower around the room.

Buffalo 2 barked to let his master know he did not think very much of such a thing.

There wasn't room when Barlow was finished and lying on his bed, for them both to stand at the table at the same time, so White Bear got up and washed the trail grime off his face. Then, he, too, stretched out on his bed, waiting.

It wasn't long before Viuda Garza was calling to them, and the two men, followed by the big dog, hurried to the kitchen. Though the kitchen was cramped and close, it seemed airy to the visitors after their short time in the tiny bedroom. They sat on high-backed chairs at the scarred wooden table and dug into tamales and spicy soup and tortillas and goat milk. Neither man liked the latter but said nothing so as not to offend their gracious hostess. Instead, each looked up, smiled and said, *"Muy bueno, señorita. Muy delicioso!"*

Viuda Garza beamed in pride—and hopefulness.

Finally sated, Barlow sat back and belched in appreciation. He hadn't felt so good in a long time. Not to say that he felt good; just that he was not as melancholy as usual. He didn't think he would ever be truly cheerful again. Not after having lost his wife and infant son to the Indian attack in which Anna was kidnapped. And not after he had had to leave the little girl behind in San Diego. He knew that was the right thing, but it still did not comfort him much.

"What now, old chap?" White Bear asked.

Barlow shrugged. He was content for the moment to just sit here and dwell on the wonderful repast he had just had.

"I say we go out and find some bloody women to share our beds with tonight, old chap," White Bear said with a gleam in his eye.

Barlow considered the suggestion for some moments, and then decided it was a good thing to do. He nodded and pushed himself up. "I wonder if Rosaria and Inez are around," he mused as they headed toward the room to get their guns. They would as soon go outside without their clothes as without their weapons.

"That would save us a bloomin' heap of trouble in finding some new women," White Bear responded. "But they bloody well may be married by now." He didn't really care either way. Inez was wonderful, but he had nothing against exploring another woman.

They stopped at the cantina where Rosaria and Inez had worked. Barlow had purposefully not gone there when they had ridden into town earlier, because he was not sure how White Bear would feel about it.

The two pushed through the doors and stepped inside. They heard a couple of squeals and, before they could do much, were catching two women who had run up and launched themselves onto the two men. Barlow and White Bear caught them without losing their balance, and hugged them tightly. Buffalo 2 danced around, barking, unsure whether his master was being attacked.

Finally Barlow set Rosaria down on her feet. Grinning widely, he pulled her to him again, holding her close to his massive torso, much to the annoyance of most of the patrons in the cantina.

"Will you stay long here?" she asked after taking a step back to gaze up at his face.

Barlow shrugged, though he was still grinning. "I got nowhere else to go, so I might be here a spell."

"Muy bueno!" Rosaria gasped in delight.

"Can you leave here?" Barlow asked eagerly. He couldn't wait to get her undressed and in his bed. She was a fine looking woman, even finer than he had remembered: short and slim with skin the color of burnished copper, deep-set dark eyes that flashed fire when she was being passionate, generous lips and a thin nose. Her hair was pitch black and lustrous. It hung loose around her shoulders. And her body. Lord, he remembered her body well—breasts the same color as her face, with big, very dark areolas and thick nipples, a gentle slope of her belly leading to the lush tangle of black curly hair that hid her womanhood. He was getting hard just thinking about her.

"Not yet," she said in accented English. She spoke English better now, he noticed. "But soon."

"Damn!" Barlow muttered with more vehemence than he wanted her to hear, but it was out and he couldn't take it back.

She smiled at him, though, and said, "Sit. I weel bring you something to drink."

Barlow nodded, walked stiffly to an open table and plopped into a chair. Buffalo 2 came and lay on the dirt floor next to his chair, and White Bear took a chair on the other side. This way both men could keep an eye on the patrons, lest someone object to Mexican women consorting with an American and an Indian.

But no one bothered them, though they did receive plenty of angry or annoyed stares. Rosaria and Inez brought a bottle of whiskey and two glasses to the table. As she set the bottle down, Rosaria bent over and whispered in Barlow's ear, "It won't be long, *hombre grande*." Then she was gone again.

She was true to her word. After less than an hour—an immensely long hour for Barlow—she and Inez marched up to their table. "We are ready, señors," Inez said. Both women were smiling brightly.

A short walk brought them all to Viuda Garza's, and they headed straight to the small room. The lantern was still glowing brightly. "Buffler, go lay down," Barlow commanded.

The dog did as he was told, his bright dark eyes sad though understanding.

Barlow turned to Rosaria. In his haste and eagerness, he almost tore her dress off of her. But she slowed him down, grabbing his big hands in her small ones. "We have time," she said quietly.

"But . . ."

Rosaria placed a slim index finger to his lips, silencing him. She helped Barlow tug his shirt up over his head and they dropped it on the floor. Rosaria knelt and tugged his pants down. His hardness, freed of its confinement, sprang proudly out in front of him, right in Rosaria's face. Though he could not see it, she smiled when she gazed at his strong member. She opened her mouth and slowly slid her lips around the tip.

Barlow sucked in a breath and then groaned as pleasure surged up his manhood and straight to his brain. He was vaguely aware that despite the smallness of the room, White Bear and Inez had managed to get their clothes off and tumble onto the bed, where they were kissing and moaning.

He forgot about them completely as Rosaria's mouth, lips and tongue worked magic on his hardness. Her hand came into play, lightly massaging his sack. He groaned again, unable to hold off any longer. "Rosaria," he croaked, "I'm . . ."

But she already knew, and was braced for the flood that came seconds later. She held on, almost choking, but managed. And when he had finished spurting, she started working on him again with her lips and tongue. It took perhaps fifteen minutes, but she coaxed his staff to life again.

Finally she stood and smiled up at him. "Now we take our time, no?" she said coyly.

"*Sí*, señorita," Barlow responded lustily. "*Sí!*"

Rosaria slid easily and quickly out of her dress, letting it fall to the floor, and then lay on the bed on her back, her legs open, her womanhood beckoning him. He smiled into the dimness and got on the bed, too, kneeling between her legs. Leaning forward on his hands, he brought his lips down and touched them lightly on Rosaria's forehead, her closed eyes, her nose, her lips. The trail of light kisses continued down her neck and through the valley between her breasts. Without pausing for a break there; he kept on going, his lips leaving a damp feathery path down her belly, past her navel and . . .

He abruptly stopped, scaring her. But he only spun around and started working his way up her body from the other direction, starting at her tiny toes. As he neared her womanhood, her hips began to shift and gyrate in anticipation.

But again he confounded her by bypassing her pleasure spot, moving north again. This time, however, he lingered long at her breasts, nipping at her tight nipples, sucking them into his mouth and then pulling back, letting them ease out.

Rosaria moaned. Her hips lifted as she tried to find some contact on his body where she could rub her special spot. But he was out of reach. She moaned again, half in passion, half in frustration.

Barlow moved away from her breasts and started down her stomach again, tonguing her navel for a moment as he neared the garden of her womanliness. Then he leaned back, sitting on his shins, back straight. He slipped his big hands under her firm but soft-skinned buttocks and easily lifted her up to his mouth.

Moments after his tongue had invaded her secret place, Rosaria was writhing, screeching, overcome with the passion. It was all Barlow could do to hold her against his mouth as she rode the waves of rapture to new heights. Only his great strength allowed him to keep her from flying out of his hands.

When she had finally calmed herself a little, he began his tender manipulations of her womanhood again, licking, sucking. Rosaria quickly felt the heat rising in her again, and once more she galloped along the trail of passion that engulfed her.

Now he needed her, however, and when she had come down from those lofty heights of lust and passion, he gently placed her buttocks back on the bed. Then he moved up between her legs, bent forward and leaned on his hands, one on each side of her head. The tip of his manhood touched the gates of her femininity and she shuddered with pleasure. She reached down and, with her tiny hand wrapped around his hard member, helped him breach those gates, until he was entirely sunk into paradise.

They each lay there for a few moments, not moving, just enjoying the intensity of that simple act. Then he began to move, slowly drawing himself back until he was almost out of her pleasure place, and then sliding it home again, gently. He gradually picked up speed and increased the power of his thrusts. Rosaria's body shook with the intensity of it, and she clung to him, her short, ragged nails cutting thin furrows in his wide back. Her legs swept up around his lower thighs and she thrust herself up at him as he plunged into her.

Their rhythm swiftly synchronized and they pounded at each other in a primal dance of lust. More than once, Rosaria screamed in passion as surges of pleasure swept over her again and again.

Rosaria could feel Barlow begin to tense, and she threw her arms around the back of his neck and held on tightly.

Like a crazed buffalo, Barlow pounded into her again and again. Finally he snuffled loudly, rammed himself deep into her and stayed there. His back arched and the muscles of his neck tightened as he was swept away by the power of his orgasm. He relaxed a bit, eased out and slammed home again, holding there again as he continued to quake with his release.

Ever so slowly he began to come down from the summit he had achieved, and he finally collapsed on the bed beside Rosaria. She turned to face him. "You're something—" he started, but a hand over his mouth cut him off.

"Don't say anything," Rosaria whispered.

"But . . ."

"No need. We know."

He smiled and kissed her. "You're right, woman." He sighed, enjoying the lingering passion that still roamed through his body, and enjoying the feel of Rosaria's hot body against his own. Still clutching her close, he was soon asleep.

3

ROSARIA'S SLEEK, SENSUAL body did a fine job of keeping Will Barlow's mind off his despair for a couple of days. He couldn't seem to get enough of her; nor she him. But eventually they had to get out into the world again, and Barlow did not look forward to that time. He just knew trouble would be waiting for him. Trouble always seemed to find him, no matter how hard he might try to stay out of it.

When he, Rosaria, White Bear, Inez and Buffalo 2 went outside, they were nearly blinded by the sunlight after several days inside the dim bedroom.

"Waugh!" Barlow growled. "This don't shine with this ol' chil' no how."

Shading his eyes with a hand, White Bear grunted in agreement. "Makes this bloody chap want to go back inside and not ever come out again."

They strolled down the street, their eyes quickly adjusting to the brightness, then walked arm in arm with their women as they meandered around the plaza. They drew an inordinate number of hostile stares, from both Mexican people and American soldiers. Neither side liked the idea of señoritas consorting with Americans—and the Mexicans, at least, considered White Bear an American. But the former mountain man and the Shoshoni were a bit too fierce looking for anyone who was sober to take action against them. In addition, there was the huge dog to contend with, and he looked more savage than the two men.

The two couples ignored the unfriendly eyes cast at them, and instead just enjoyed each other's company. Still, Barlow and White Bear were wary, as they always were.

They dropped the women off at their homes, with plans to meet again later. Then the two men headed for a cantina, where they sat sipping fiery whiskey from crockery mugs and casting savage glances at whoever dared to look at them. They thought it somewhat humorous to frighten these peasants, who cared not a whit for them to begin with.

So it went for the next several days—nights of frenzied abandon with Rosaria and Inez, days wandering the Taos plaza or spending time in one cantina or another, most afternoons enjoying the delicious meals Viuda Garza made for them and trying to fend off the old widow's feeble but obvious attempts at seduction.

The activity was enough to keep Barlow's mind off of Anna's loss to some extent, though there were times when, for some unknown reason, the despondency over the situation rose up inside him and almost made him ill. When it swept over him, he became nearly impossible to be around, even for a close friend like White Bear, or a woman like Rosaria, with whom he had been so intimate so many times. The others mostly just left him alone in those times, though White Bear often had to work hard to keep Barlow from doing something foolish, until he became himself again, and all would go on as before.

They did manage to stay out of trouble, however, at least for a while, but the two men both knew it could not last. Life was not that simple for them. They were not well liked, either by the soldiers or by many of the Mexicans, which made avoiding trouble difficult. Even worse, watching the way the troopers treated the Mexicans did not sit well with them. The way the American soldiers treated the women was especially galling to Barlow.

And that sensibility was what eventually caused trouble for Barlow and White Bear.

The two were sitting one evening in the cantina where Rosaria and Inez worked, waiting for the two women to finish up so they could head back to their room at Viuda

Garza's. Barlow was coming out of one of his depressions, so he was still edgy. Plus he had had a fair amount to drink, though he could not really have been said to be drunk.

They were minding their own business, until their attention was drawn to a group of six soldiers who had boisterously entered the cantina. It was obvious that most, if not all, of them were well on their way to becoming drunk. As Barlow and White Bear sat there sipping at their whiskey, puffing on pipes, they kept a wary eye on the soldiers. Both knew instinctively that trouble was about to rear its head, and they waited patiently for it to erupt.

The troopers loudly demanded whiskey, and when it was brought to them, they refused to pay, insulting the cantina's owner in the process. At his table, Barlow shook his head and growled in annoyance. He knew he would tangle with these soldiers sooner or later. He started to rise, but White Bear pulled him back into his chair.

"Let it be, old chap," the Shoshoni said quietly. "This isn't our bloody fight."

"The hell it ain't. Old Fernandez has been mighty friendly to us when a lot of others hereabouts haven't been. He deserves to be paid for his goods."

"I agree, old chap, but let's let it sit awhile. They might change their bloomin' minds and pay eventually."

"That ain't likely," Barlow snapped.

"No, it bloody well isn't. But those chaps appear to be well into their cups, and might pass out soon. If that's the case, Fernandez can just take his money off them."

"I reckon you're right, hoss," Barlow agreed, though he was not happy about it. As he settled back into his chair, he realized that he needed to get into a fight. It had been too long. It was not pleasant knowing that, but it was a fact.

Minutes later, two of the soldiers grabbed Rosaria and Inez by the arms and dragged them onto their laps at the table at which they sat. The two women struggled, but the other troopers crowded around them. The ones holding them tried to both kiss them and shove their cotton peasant blouses down.

"Now, old chap," White Bear said harshly as he rose, "it's our fight."

" 'Bout time you realized that," Barlow said roughly. He,

too, stood up. Next to him, Buffalo 2 pushed to his feet and growled softly. Barlow looked down at the big Newfoundland and smiled harshly. "Yep, ol' hoss, it's time to do something about them ass wipes over yon."

The two men and the dog marched toward the soldiers, who were beginning to succeed in kissing, undressing and fondling the two women, who fought as well as they could. But they were no match for the half dozen burly soldiers.

Two of the soldiers had Inez on her back on the table now. Her blouse was pushed down, exposing her full breasts. One of the troopers was holding the struggling woman down, while the other was roughly shoving her skirt up. One other soldier still sat, holding the thrashing Rosaria. The three others stood around, eagerly watching the progress of the solider about to penetrate Inez. They were unaware of Barlow, White Bear and Buffalo 2 walking up behind them.

Without warning, Barlow grabbed two of the soldiers, each by the back of his neck, and with a powerful jerk cracked their heads together. He released them, and they slumped to the dirt floor, not unconscious but out of the fight, for the moment anyway, groaning in pain.

"I don't think these señoritas want your attentions, boys," Barlow said flatly.

"Piss off, shit ball," the one holding Rosaria said, his hand squeezing one of her naked breasts. "They like it jist fine, don't you, sweetheart?"

Rosaria cranked her head around as best she could and spit in the soldier's face, then released a string of Spanish that no one but she and Inez could understand, though they all knew she was not complimenting the soldier on his handsome looks and gentlemanly demeanor.

"You goddamn whore," the soldier snapped. He stood, shoving her to the floor as he did and kicking her in the side. "Spit on me, will ya, bitch?" he snarled. "I'll show you, goddammit." He moved to kick her again, but Barlow stepped up and pounded him in the face with a mighty fist. The trooper fell back, knocking over the chair and rattling the table enough so that one of the glasses of whiskey crashed to the floor.

The other soldier who was standing moved toward Barlow, but Buffalo 2 sank his teeth into the man's thigh. The soldier doubled over in pain and tried in vain to pry the dog loose.

White Bear stepped up and grabbed the soldier by the back of the shirt near the neck and the back of his trousers at the waist, and as Buffalo 2 released the man, Barlow shoved him forward. The man smashed head first into the wall and slid down it, moaning once before he lost consciousness.

Barlow and White Bear turned their attention to the two soldiers accosting Inez on the table. The two seemed transfixed by what was happening to their fellows, but they finally moved. The one holding the woman grabbed a whiskey bottle by the neck, whirled and swung it at Barlow, who was nearest him, figuring to surprise him.

Barlow ducked the bottle and grabbed the man's arm as it whooshed by his head. He slapped a big paw on the soldier's back and jerked the arm as hard as he could.

The soldier screamed as his shoulder muscles tore loose of the bones and ligaments. Barlow let him fall, but before he could turn, the soldier he had punched slammed into his side and back, driving him into the table, which rocked severely but did not fall over. However, the glasses and bottles went sailing off, landing with a rattle on the floor or hitting against the wall.

Inez was no longer there, White Bear having grabbed the soldier who was on top of her by the throat and jerked him up and away from her. Then he proceeded to punch and kick the man mercilessly, not giving the soldier a moment to collect himself and fight back. The soldier's now flaccid manhood flopped about, since he had had no chance to stick it back into his unbuttoned pants before White Bear was on him.

Buffalo 2, barking and snarling, bounced around, prepared to save his master or his master's friend if necessary. But the big Newfoundland's help wasn't needed.

The two men whose heads Barlow had cracked together had managed to get to their feet and were heading for the door as fast as their wobbly legs would take them. The one with the separated shoulder was crawling out of the way, having almost been stepped on when his companion slammed into Barlow. Then he got up and, clutching his arm tightly to his side, followed the two others out of the cantina.

The soldier who had tackled Barlow got his arm around the big man's throat and started to squeeze. With an effort, Barlow straightened, trying to pry the man's hands free. But the soldier had too good a grip on him. Not panicking, Barlow turned and shoved the man backward at the wall. Bits of adobe sprinkled to the floor as the soldier's back smashed into it. His grip loosened but did not break.

Barlow, finding it a bit easier to breathe now, took a step or two forward and then pushed backward forcefully, slamming the soldier against the wall again. The trooper's hold around Barlow's neck broke.

Barlow calmly turned to face the soldier. "You are one dumb son of a bitch," he said evenly.

"Piss off," the soldier snarled, apparently unable to come up with any other comeback. His face showed his fear, however.

"Not only dumb as a dirt floor," Barlow responded matter-of-factly, "but damn unfriendly, too." He shook his head, then suddenly slammed the heel of his hand into the soldier's forehead. The trooper's head snapped back, hitting the wall. His eyes grew dull and unfocused.

Barlow grabbed the soldier's throat in his big, powerful hands and began to squeeze. The soldier's tongue lolled out.

"That's enough, old chap," White Bear said, walking up and placing a hand on one of Barlow's arms. "You don't want to kill the bloody bastard."

"Yes, I do," Barlow replied coolly, not loosening his grip any, though not increasing it either.

"That'll cause no end of bloomin' trouble, old chap," White Bear said reasonably.

Barlow shrugged, unperturbed by the thought. "I been in trouble before, hoss."

White Bear muttered something in Shoshoni, then said in English, "We don't need the bloody army after us, old chap. We might be bloody good fighters, but we can't take on the whole bloomin' army."

Barlow sighed. "I reckon you're right, hoss," he said in resignation. He had never taken his eyes off the soldier's face, though, and now said to him, "I ever catch you molestin' a woman again, hoss, I'll slice your nuts off—if I can even find the shriveled up little things—and shove 'em up your ass. You got that?"

The soldier said nothing, but his eyes remained wide.

Barlow pulled the man's face toward him, then slammed the back of his head into the wall once more, just for good measure. Then he let go of the soldier, who slid down the wall until he was sitting on the floor, his head cocked at a funny angle.

Barlow turned to Rosaria.

She had pulled her blouse up, covering herself. She looked a little shaken, but she was, for the most part, calm and poised. She smiled at Barlow. *"Gracias, mi hombre grande,"* she said, stepping up to place a small, soft hand on one of his stubbled cheeks.

"Da nada, mi bonita señorita—It was nothing, my beautiful señorita," he replied graciously.

White Bear and Inez moved up alongside them. The woman looked none the worse for her experience at the soldiers' hands, though her eyes still reflected fright. For the most part, though, she was composed—and fully dressed.

"You señoritas want to go to your homes?" Barlow asked. "Or go back with us to our little hideaway at Viuda Garza's?" He, of course, hoped they would choose the latter, though he would understand if they preferred the former.

The two women conferred for a few moments in their native language, then Rosaria said, "We'll go with you."

Barlow was relieved, but still asked, "Are you sure? After what you just been through . . ."

"Eet was not so bad," Inez replied.

Barlow nodded. Since Inez had gotten the worse treatment of the two women, and she was calm about it all, he figured they would be all right. "Then let's git goin'," he said jovially.

He stopped at the bar. "This going to cause you any trouble, Señor Fernandez?" he asked.

The cantina owner shrugged. "Maybe, señor. But I weel just blame it on the *loco americano,* eh?"

Barlow laughed. "That should satisfy anyone who comes

around askin' you about this," he said. *"Adios."*

As the four, accompanied by Buffalo 2, walked out of the cantina, Barlow gave no more thought to the soldiers or the damage he had caused.

4

A COMMOTION OF some sort started Buffalo 2 growling, which woke Barlow and White Bear. The former was up in an instant, still naked, leaving a frightened Rosaria in the bed, the sheets pulled up to her chin. He turned up the lantern a bit and took the couple of steps to the doorway just as it burst open. Barlow reached out and grabbed the barrel of the rifle that had poked through the doorway and yanked it forward. The young soldier holding the weapon flew into the small room and slammed into Barlow, who was braced for it and did not move.

Before the soldier could gather his wits, Barlow flung him to the ground. "Watch him, Buffler," he commanded.

The big, black-furred Newfoundland moved just a bit and straddled the fallen soldier, his snarling muzzle only a couple of inches from the trooper's scared face.

Another soldier tentatively began entering the room, and Barlow punched him full in the face, knocking him back out the doorway, where, apparently, he fell against a fellow trooper, who managed to keep the both of them from falling.

"Bloody damn fools," White Bear muttered. Since there was so little space in the room, he remained in bed, but was propped up on one elbow. Inez cowered behind him.

"That's factual," Barlow responded. He shook his head in disbelief. The soldiers had made a big mistake in trying to get him and White Bear here in their room at Viuda Garza's.

Only one man could get through the door at a time. In fact, the troopers had had to stand outside the door in single file because the hallway was so narrow. Besides, even if more than one could have gotten through the door at the same time, there was no space for maneuvering in the room itself. Not with the one soldier on the floor, the big dog hovering over him and Barlow's bulk taking up a lot of space.

"You boys best be on your way," Barlow called out, "lest you get my blood boilin'."

"Come on out of there, you," one of the soldiers said. "You and that savage you consort with."

"If we don't?" Barlow asked sarcastically.

"We'll have to come in and get you." The soldier's voice was not as sure as it had been a moment ago.

"You saw what happened when you tried that, hoss. Didn't work too well, did it?"

"Then we'll jist start shootin' in there," the soldier went on, once more bold. "It'll like to kill you two as well as those two strumpets you got in there."

"First one gonna die'll be your amigo here, hoss," Barlow said diffidently. "My dog's hankerin' to make a meal out of him right now."

"You all right, Ogilvie?" the soldier outside yelled. When he got no response, he yelled again, "Ogilvie? You in there?"

"Best answer him, hoss," Barlow said calmly. "Before your amigo out there shits his britches."

"The dog?" Ogilvie said in a wavering voice.

"He won't hurt you just for talkin', ol' hoss. Only if you try to git up."

"I'm all right," Ogilvie shouted. "But this damn dog's got me pinned to the floor here and is lookin' like he's ready to tear me to shreds with his teeth and claws."

Barlow could hear a couple of soldiers murmuring, and he assumed they were trying to figure out their next move. "Look, boys," he said, "I'm right sorry we whupped your amigos last night. But they asked for it, the way they was treating the señoritas. You comin' over here to get vengeance ain't so smart."

"It was up to me, peckerwood, I'd just wait outside till you come out and then drop you with a rifle ball," the soldier said harshly. "But Major Heckendorf wants you arrested and thrown in the jail till he can hold a trial, and then hang you two all legal-like."

"Arrest me? Us?" Barlow said, surprised. "For whupping a couple of his precious soldier boys?"

"That would've been bad enough," the soldier said bitterly, "but you went and killed Corporal Cudahy."

"Weren't none of them boys dead when I left there last night," Barlow said, annoyed more than anything by this turn of events.

"Well, he was dead when some of the other boys got there, because we heard there'd been some kind of ruckus."

"Well, I'm plumb sorry to hear that," Barlow said, not too contritely. "But him and them others started it all with tryin' to molest them women—our women. And then attackin' us when we pointed out the error of their ways."

"Don't matter none who started it. Not to me, anyway. Major Heckendorf wants you arrested and tried for the killin', so I aim to bring you in."

"That might not be so easy as you might be thinkin', hoss," Barlow said evenly, though annoyance was beginning to creep into his voice.

"I can wait," the soldier said firmly.

"Good. 'Cause I aim to spend a bit more time in here with the lovely señorita Rosaria."

"Me and my men will be waitin' outside the house. For as long as it takes. We'll arrest you as soon as you step outside, which you're gonna have to do sooner or later."

"I reckon we will have to at that," Barlow reasoned. "Eventually."

"We'll be there." There was a pause. "And if you don't come along peaceably, I'd just as soon shoot you down," he added. "Even if that means gettin' the major's balls in an uproar."

"Well, we can't have that now, can we?" Barlow said dryly.

"All right, then, Barlow, we'll be waitin' on you and your Injin pal."

"What's your name, hoss?" Barlow suddenly asked.

"Kendall. Sergeant Marty Kendall." He paused again. "If

we're done jawin'," he finally added, "send out Private Ogilvie."

   "I think not, hoss," Barlow said, smiling into the dimness.
"I think that ol' chil' is jist fine right where he is. We'll
give him back to you when we get outside. Till then, he's
stayin' here." Barlow kicked the door shut and turned toward the bed, which was against the wall to the right of the
door. With an effort, he pulled part of the bedstead in front
of the door, so it couldn't be opened. Then he climbed into
bed with Rosaria and pulled her close to him, his mouth
searching for hers.

Barlow finally rose and pulled his clothes on. He sat on the
bed while Rosaria, Inez and White Bear got dressed, one at
a time, then he got up, pushed the bed away from the door
and opened the door a crack. There was no one in the small
hallway. "Señora Garza?" he called. "Are you out there?"

   "Sí, Sí, señor," the old widow said, poking her head into
the hallway from the kitchen.

   "You all right?" Barlow asked suspiciously.

   "Sí."

   "And you're alone?"

   "Sí."

   "Bueno. We're hungry. We need some of your good food,
comprende—understand?"

   "Sí, Pronto." Viuda Garza grinned and withdrew back
into the kitchen, where she was most comfortable.

   "Hey, mister," Private Ogilvie croaked, "can you get this
damn dog off me?"

   Barlow laughed. The young soldier must've had an interesting couple of hours, flat on his back with Buffalo 2 standing over him, or, like now, lying on him, listening to Barlow
and White Bear making love to the two women. "Buffler,"
he called, "leave him be now, boy."

   The dog rose up and let the soldier slide out from underneath him. Ogilvie sat up and then used his feet to push
himself backward across the floor until his back was against
the wall. "Thanks," he said, his chest still hurting from
having more than two hundred pounds of dog parked on it
for the best part of three hours.

   Buffalo 2 lay back down where he had been, but this time

he was resting only on Ogilvie's ankles. He licked his lips and let out a sigh.

It was not long before Viuda Garza called out to them, and the five people and one dog filed out and went to the kitchen, where they sat at the old wood table.

"You mean I get to eat, too?" Ogilvie asked in surprise.

"Sure," Barlow said flatly.

Ogilvie looked at him in wonder. The man was minutes away from being arrested and thrown into jail, facing a murder charge in a court run by soldiers, and yet he seemed perfectly at ease, unconcerned.

"Dig in, boy," Barlow said. "Lest you don't get any."

Barlow and White Bear ate heartily, Rosaria and Inez daintily, and Ogilvie worriedly. He had never gotten quite used to the food these Mexicans ate. It was all too spicy for him, and consisted of strange things that he sometimes could not identify. Still, for Mexican food, what the old woman had prepared was quite good, and he partook of more of it than he might have elsewhere.

Finally they all sat back, sated. Barlow pulled out his small clay pipe, filled it and lit it from the candle on the table. White Bear rolled a shuck cigarillo.

"You are in trouble, señors?" Viuda Garza asked, the creases in her face worsened with worry.

"*Sí,*" Barlow answered. "We got into a ruckus with some of the soldier boys last night," he added, wondering if she understood anything of what he was saying. "Now the commander—the *jefe*—wants to talk to me 'n' White Bear about it."

Viuda Garza nodded. She had not understood much, but she was astute enough to figure out that whatever it was that the soldiers had come for her two boarders about, it wasn't good.

Barlow at last knocked the ashes from his pipe into his hand, dumped them into the beehive fireplace in a corner of the room and stuffed the pipe through two slits in a heart-shaped piece of leather he wore around his neck.

While Rosaria and Inez kept Ogilvie occupied by asking question after question, Barlow and White Bear took Viuda Garza back to their room and showed her their weapons. "As soon as we're gone," Barlow said slowly, wanting her to understand, "you take these guns and you hide them for us. *Comprendo?*"

The old woman nodded.

Each man secreted a knife on him under his clothes, then made sure they each had their big knives and their tomahawks. They knew they had to have some kind of weapons for the soldiers to take from them. They all headed back to the kitchen.

Barlow grabbed Rosaria in mock gruffness and pulled her to him. He kissed her hard, then said, "You and Inez stay here until after we're gone—with all the soldiers. Then you two head for your homes."

"And stay there," White Bear added.

The women nodded.

Barlow clapped his floppy old hat on his head, looked at Buffalo 2 and said, "You stay here, Buffler. Watch over them women."

The dog cocked his head to the side as if trying to understand.

Barlow looked at Private Ogilvie. "After you, hoss," he said. He was not about to go out the door first, knowing that the soldiers would love to just shoot him down and tell Major Heckendorf that he and White Bear had tried to resist and had had to be killed.

The troops snapped to alertness when the door opened, and they nervously aimed their rifles at the house.

"Go easy, boys," Ogilvie said as he stepped out first. "Put your guns down. They're comin' and won't resist, unless . . ." He shrugged, knowing that his fellow soldiers understood.

"Where's your guns?" Sergeant Kendall asked.

"Left 'em behind," Barlow said easily. "I figured we wouldn't be needin' 'em when we talk to the major."

"You ain't gonna need 'em ever again," Kendall muttered. "Private Ogilvie, since these bastards've been holding you against your will, you have the honor of relievin' these two skunks of the weapons they are carryin'."

Ogilvie felt odd about taking the big knives and tomahawks from Barlow and White Bear. After all, they had not treated him all that badly. In fact, except for the dog sitting on him, he had been treated pretty well. Of course, it had been hard listening to them making love with the women, but that wasn't all that bad. He decided somewhere during the meal they had all just eaten, while he had a chance to really look at the women, that he would have to investigate Mexican women. Most of the men held them in contempt, but Ogilvie had been able to see that they were intelligent and fun loving. And, if their moans, groans and screams were any indication, they were wonderful lovers.

"Sorry, boys," Ogilvie said as he relieved Barlow and White Bear of their weapons.

Barlow shrugged. He knew the soldier had no choice.

"All right, you two," Kendall said, lowering his rifle in a silent threat, "let's move out."

As they all started to walk off, Kendall suddenly shouted, "Halt!" When they did so, he went and stood directly in front of Barlow, less than a foot away. "Where's that goddamn mongrel of yours?"

"Mongrel?" Barlow said with raised eyebrows.

"You know what I mean, knothead. That big goddamn mutt you always have runnin' around with you. The one that kept Private Ogilvie prisoner in there."

"You mean Buffler?" Barlow said, knowing he was irking Kendall.

"Is that the critter's name?" Kendall said huffily. "Then, yes, if that's the one."

"He's inside," Barlow said evenly. "I told him to stay there."

Kendall's eyebrows rose in surprise. "And it listens to you?" he asked in wonder.

"Yep."

"That true, Private Ogilvie?" Kendall asked over his shoulder.

"Yes, Sergeant."

Kendall continued to stare at Barlow, who returned the gaze calmly. Then the sergeant turned and ordered them to march on again.

5

THE TWO PRISONERS were escorted into the office of Major Rupert Heckendorf. The military commander for the area had commandeered a small hacienda for his own use, evicting the once-prosperous Mexican family. He now sat behind a plain wood desk that was fairly clear of debris, except for two sheafs of papers, a bottle of ink, nib pen and a large blotter. An American flag behind him glowed in the light from the window to the major's right. Above the flag, centered on the wall, was a painting of President Polk. Two chairs were up against the wall across from the big window.

All signs of the previous occupants had been removed. There were no crucifixes, statues of the Virgin Mary or votive candles, none of the trappings of many Mexicans' deep Catholic faith.

The major himself was an impressive figure. At least what could be seen of him was. He had a big head, almost perfectly round, with a large, florid nose befitting such a huge skull. A mass of wavy blond hair cascaded over his ears and neck. Thick, matching eyebrows bristled wildly over a pair of shockingly blue eyes, and a thick mustache of the same color and consistency drooped heavily under the prominent nose. His uniform coat was draped over the back of his chair, and the white linen shirt he wore was sharply creased. His hands and forearms rested on the desk top.

Barlow and White Bear were told to stop three feet in

front of the desk. There were no chairs, so they were not invited to sit. Heckendorf glared up at them, his blue eyes boring into theirs. The two prisoners stood, staring benignly back at the military man.

Finally Heckendorf cleared his throat, then said, "You two swine are in serious trouble." His voice seemed to rumble up from somewhere down in the pit of his stomach. "I hereby officially place you under arrest for the murder of a soldier of the United States Army, one Corporal Tommy Cudahy."

Neither Barlow nor White Bear reacted to his harsh statement.

"You will be confined to the local jail, under the watch of my troopers until I can put together a trial, at which I will preside. After said trial, you will be executed at the earliest possible time."

Again, neither prisoner reacted.

"Don't you have anything to say?" Heckendorf demanded, scowling even more, if that was possible.

Barlow shrugged. "Not much to say, hoss," he commented flatly. "You've got your mind made up. Hell, I don't even know why you're plannin' to have a trial, since you've already decided our guilt and sentence."

"Everything will be done legally, and by the book," Heckendorf rumbled, leaning back, his weight making the chair creak a little.

"Buffler shit," Barlow said. He managed to contain the smile he felt surge forth at the shocked look on Heckendorf's face. "Any trial you convene for me 'n' White Bear will be a sham, Major. There ain't a damn thing legal about it."

"It is entirely legal, dammit," Heckendorf snapped, eyes glittering in rage. "This area is under military jurisdiction, which means the army is the law. All very legal and proper."

"I don't give a hoot how much authority you have—or think you have, hoss. If you put us on trial for killin' one of your goddamn soldiers—one who was tryin' to rape a woman, no less—it'll be a sham, nothing more."

"Rape?" Heckendorf bellowed, as if the loudness of his voice would wash away the accusation. "Not one of my mine, sir. None of my men would do such a thing."

"Then either you're a goddamn idiot, or you don't know your men very well," Barlow retorted, growing angry. "The six of them critters was trying to force their attentions on two women, who didn't want no part of those drunken worms. All me 'n' White Bear did was to—"

"Enough!" Heckendorf roared. "I will not sit here and listen to you spout your vicious lies about my men." He paused, composing himself. "So, off you go to the jail, sirs. I don't expect it'll take more than a couple of days to assemble a trial for you." He paused, then looked at Sergeant Kendall. "Take them away, Sergeant," he said. He leaned forward, resting his arms on the desk top again, watching intently as Barlow and White Bear were marched out the door.

The jail was a small, old one-room adobe house a few blocks off the plaza. The house had been abandoned for some time, though it had not been all that great of a house before that. Its adobe walls had a decided tilt toward one side, and the roof looked unstable. The two windows had been walled in with fresh adobe until only a slit across the top of each let in some air and a little light—when the sun was in the right position.

"Well, old chap," White Bear said when the soldiers had left, locking the door behind them, "this doesn't look very bloody good."

"Reckon it don't, hoss," Barlow said nonchalantly. He started walking around the small interior, testing the walls to see if any of them had some give that might provide a way out.

"You seem mighty bloomin' calm about all this, old chap." White Bear wasn't really nervous, but he was annoyed at being in this predicament.

"What's to worry over, hoss?" Barlow responded, continuing his search.

"Well, the fact that we're bloody well going to get hanged in a few days, for one."

Barlow stopped and looked across the dark room at his friend. "You really intend to be around here long enough for that goddamn soldier boy to stretch our necks?"

"You have something in mind, old chap?"

"I do," Barlow said flatly. "Gettin' the hell out of this hole long before Heckendorf gets a chance to hang us."

"I thought you might say that, old chap." White Bear grinned, though Barlow couldn't see it in the gloom. "Well, I was bloody well *hoping* you'd say something like that. You have a plan?"

"Not yet." Barlow returned to his exploration of the makeshift cell, hands prodding the adobe. All the while, he hoped a scorpion or other poisonous critter wasn't lurking in a small crack in the wall somewhere. "But I reckon I'll come up with somethin' before that reptile gets his rope out."

"I sure hope so, old chap."

"You could help here, ya know, hoss," Barlow said. "The sooner we find a way out of here, the sooner we'll be out of the clutches of that shit pile of a major."

"If you insist, old chap," White Bear said with a sigh that was not really a statement on the task ahead.

Barlow continued to concentrate on the west wall, while White Bear began probing the south wall, each taking his time. They were in no rush, and they wanted to be thorough. Finding a weak spot might be their only way out, and they did not want to miss it by hurrying for no good reason.

Eventually they moved on, Barlow to the north wall, White Bear to the east. "You checked the door, didn't you, hoss?" Barlow asked after a few minutes.

White Bear didn't think that deserved a response, so he said nothing.

Barlow stopped for a moment and looked over at his friend, just a dim figure in the dark structure. Then he smiled. Of course, White Bear had checked the door. He went back to work.

They finally stopped at the sound of soldiers coming. When the door creaked open, letting in a wide shaft of light, the two prisoners blinked at the unaccustomed brightness. While they were doing so, two armed soldiers entered, one stopping on each side of the door. Another entered with two plates. He set them on the floor a few feet from the door. He went back outside and then returned with two large tin mugs, which he placed next to the plates. As he straightened, he said hatefully, "Enjoy your meal, boys." Then he turned and walked out.

The two guards edged toward the door and backed out, one after the other, never lowering their rifles or taking their eyes off of the prisoners. Then the door slammed shut and the key clanked as it turned the lock.

With the light gone, Barlow and White Bear could not see their dishes, so they shuffled toward them on hands and knees. As they drew near, they could make out the outlines of the dishes and cups. Then Barlow saw a fair-size rat inching toward the plates. He reached down into his pants and untied the knife that he had tied so that it dangled down the inside of his thigh near the knee. With a snakelike move, his hand darted out, impaling the rat, nailing it to the dirt.

Barlow pulled his knife out of the rodent and wiped the blood off on his pants. Then he picked the rat up and tossed it into the darkness of a rear corner. "We might need that little critter if these boys don't feed us so well, hoss," he said, as he and White Bear sat.

White Bear just grunted and picked up his dish, which had a spoon on it, stuck under the food. He took a mouthful and winced. "What in the bloody hell *is* this?" he wondered aloud.

Barlow took a tentative bite, and almost spit it out. "I think it's buffler shit mixed with goat entrails and boiled up in bear piss." He paused, thinking. "Might have a few bites of some kind of meat in it, too. Most likely somethin' left over after a groundhog died and was eaten on by a coyote for a while and then got left in the sun for a few weeks."

"Well, old chap, as long as we know what it is," White Bear said sarcastically. He spooned some more into his mouth. It was just as rank and foul as the first spoonful had been. But it was sustenance, and that was what mattered right now.

Barlow dug into it, too, almost sickened by its odor, but knowing that they had to keep up their strength for when they escaped. And they would escape; there was no doubt whatsoever about that in Barlow's mind. After half the food or so, he picked up the tin mug and hesitantly sipped from it.

"Drinkable, old chap?" Barlow asked.

"Barely," Barlow responded. "But it's better than the damn vittles."

"At least that's bloody something," White Bear groused.

They finished their meal in silence. Fortunately, the soldiers had not taken their tobacco, so after they finished they lit up using one of their small supply of matches—Barlow his pipe, White Bear another cigarillo, relaxing as much as they could in the dank cell.

The two men spent the rest of the afternoon finishing their exploration of the room, and finally sank down, backs against one wall, frustrated.

"This does not bode bloody well, old chap," White Bear noted.

"Ah, hell, hoss, we only been in here a few hours. It'll be at least a day or two before Major Humpback there can get up enough men—and enough balls—for a trial. So we got plenty of time to find us a way out of this." He looked over at his friend. "You seem to be mighty glum about this, hoss. Somethin' eatin' at you?"

"Getting hanged bothers me, old chap."

"Damn, White Bear," Barlow said, a little concerned about the Shoshoni, "we've been in a hell of a lot tighter spots than this before, and you never acted so melancholy about it. We've even been in the *calabozo* before and made it out without a whole heap of trouble. What makes you think we can't do it again?"

White Bear shrugged. "I don't know what's wrong, old chap." He paused and sighed. "I think it's just my being more of a Shoshoni all of a sudden. You know us people— see too much in spirits and believe too much in medicine. Well, I think my medicine's gone bad, Will. Real bad." In his seriousness, he had discarded his somewhat affected English accent and phrasing surprising Barlow, who had never heard him speak other than that way.

"What makes you think that?" Barlow asked, curious and apprehensive.

"I had a dream the other night," White Bear said quietly. "In it were some signs that . . . well, they meant something to me."

"What were they?"

"If I tell you, it'll be bad for me. And maybe for you,

too." He shrugged, knowing he should be able to explain it
better but also knowing that he couldn't. "Anyway, even
though it was not a vision, really, there were certain things
that I was supposed to do to make sure my medicine stayed
good. I . . . I . . . Well, I failed to do a couple of those
things."

"So you think you're medicine's gone bad and you're
doomed? Is that it?" Barlow asked, surprised. He had never
seen White Bear being quite so Indian, and it perplexed him.

White Bear nodded glumly. "I don't see any way out of
this."

"Buffler shit, ol' hoss."

White Bear looked at him in shock and anger.

"Jist relax, hoss," Barlow said gently. "I don't mean to
make light of your beliefs, but we been through so much
and overcome it all—and we've done so without your
dreams, visions or omens. Or medicine." He shifted, turning
so he could look directly at White Bear. "And we don't need
any of those things now, neither, hoss. You jist git your
mind off'n them things, and we'll overcome this just like
we've done all those other hard doin's."

"I don't know, Will . . ."

"C'mon, old chap," Barlow said with a broad smile, "shed
this bloody gloom and get on with things."

White Bear offered up a small, lopsided grin. "I'll try, old
chap. I'll bloody well try."

"A man cain't ask no more'n that of another." He stood
up and stretched. "Well, hoss, I reckon it's time for some
robe time." He grimaced. "Even though we ain't got any
robes." He stretched out on the ground, trying to get comfortable.

A few feet away, White Bear did the same.

The two lay there in the dark, listening to the thunder
ripple through the mountains outside, and being dazzled by
the quick, blinding shafts of light that snuck in through the
windows whenever lightning struck.

"Christ, jist what we need now—a goddamn rainstorm,"
Barlow growled. Then he drifted off to sleep.

The rain awoke Barlow, and he sat up, knowing that something was strange, but unable to figure it out right away.

Then he realized he was getting wet. He looked up and caught a large, fat raindrop right between the eyes. He swiped it away, wanting to jump up and shout with joy, but that would not be wise, he knew. Instead he turned and looked toward White Bear. The Shoshoni was still sleeping soundly. Barlow could not see him, but he could hear him quite well. He smiled and edged up to his friend.

6

"WAKE UP, HOSS," Barlow hissed in excitement. He shook his friend urgently. "C'mon, hoss, wake up."

White Bear awoke and sat up, groggy. "What in the bloody hell do you want, old chap?" he snapped. He had been dreaming that he was back with his band of Shoshonis, hunting buffalo, the wind whipping through his hair, the scents, sounds and feel of it washing over him. He was annoyed that he had been torn so abruptly from that pleasant scene.

Despite his excitement, Barlow noted with great relief that White Bear was back to being "English" again. "I found us a way out of here," he said eagerly.

White Bear's eyes widened in the dark, the small amount of white reflecting brightly for a moment in a burst of lightning. "How?"

Barlow pointed up, but White Bear could not see it. Then another bolt of lightning gave him a second of illumination, and he saw Barlow's arm.

"The roof, hoss. The roof," Barlow said enthusiastically.

"The roof?" White Bear was still trying to get his mind working. "How . . . ?"

"I was woke up by the rain," Barlow said with great excitement.

"So?"

"The rain's coming through the roof, hoss! It means

there's got to be some holes up there. If there is, we can get out of here."

White Bear sat there silent for some moments, the dream all but forgotten, as he mused about the likelihood of escape. Then he nodded in the darkness. Realizing right away that Barlow could not see him nod, he said, "That sounds bloody good, old chap. When should we take our leave from this bloomin' hell hole?"

"No better time like right now," Barlow said. "We can't wait till daylight, of course, and we don't want to wait till tomorrow night, jist in case Major Ass Wipe decides to hold his trial right away."

"Good points all, old chap. Let's go, then."

They both rose, and White Bear took hold of Barlow's shirt, as the former mountain man led him toward where he had been sleeping. They looked up, and could see a slightly less dark spot in the blackness. Even though the roof was only eight feet or so, the faint light spot was barely discernable with the eyes. But the rain still dripped through. "How're we going to go about this, old man?" White Bear asked.

"Let me think on it a minute." He paused, calculating. "I'll hold you up whilst you make us a decent-size hole in there. One big enough for us to get out."

"Bloody good," White Bear said. He could see the sense in it. Barlow was stronger than he was and would be able to hold his slighter body up a lot better than he could hold Barlow's bulk in the air for however long it took to scrape out an escape hatch.

"All right, then. Climb up on my shoulders," Barlow ordered.

"That's no good, my friend. I'd have to crouch too much, which would be uncomfortable for me, and make your job a lot harder. The roof isn't all that tall."

"Damn," Barlow muttered. "Well, I reckon I can make like a stirrup with my hands and let you stand there as best you can."

"Might work, old chap. But how about this—would you be able to bear my bloomin' weight while bent over? Then I could stand on your back."

"Reckon I could do that." He paused. "Long's you don't take all goddamn night to get the job done."

"I'm every bit as eager to get out of this bloody hell hole as you are, old chap. Now, bend at the waist." He had pulled his knife out from where he had hidden it under his shirt, and he stuck the blade crossways in his mouth.

After several aborted attempts, Barlow finally said, "Hold on, ol' hoss. Let's try it this way." He got down on all fours. "Climb on, amigo." When White Bear had gingerly done so, Barlow used the great power in his thick, powerful legs and pushed up. When he stopped, he braced his arms with his hands on his thighs.

White Bear took a moment to get his balance, since Barlow's back was not completely flat, but he finally managed, with one moccasin wedged a bit into the top of his friend's belt. It was not comfortable, but it was enough to steady him, and he didn't plan to be there that long.

With his knife and his hands, White Bear tore away at the crumbling adobe of the roof right next to one of the vigas—crossbeams—sending a shower of debris down on the back of Barlow's head. The white man said nothing, though he did grunt once or twice when a particularly large chunk of mud hit him.

Rain began to pour steadily in through the hole, drenching them both within minutes. But, as they hole widened, they got a little bit of light despite the clouds. It wasn't much, but it was better than nothing.

"How's it goin' up there, hoss?" Barlow wheezed. This was not a comfortable position and White Bear was not exactly a lightweight.

"Almost done, old chap," White Bear said, ripping more frantically at the roof. He knew that despite Barlow's great strength, he could not hold out much longer in the position he was in.

Finally the Shoshoni jumped down. "What do you think, old chap?" he asked as he began trying to brush the mud off his face, hair and shirt.

Barlow straightened with a little effort and kept going, stretching his spine, hands bracing his lower back. Then he looked up. "I reckon I can get my big ass through there," he commented.

"Good," White Bear responded. "Because you're going up first."

Barlow turned to his friend, whom he could see only as a blurry glob in the darkness. "You sure about that, hoss?"

"Bloody well right I am."

"I'm a heap heavier'n you, amigo," Barlow said. "You sure you can support my weight?"

"A lot bloody easier than I can sittin' up there on the roof trying to pull you up."

Barlow could see the wisdom in that. White Bear was strong enough to lift him far enough and long enough for him to clamber up on to the roof, and Barlow had the arm strength to be able to reach down and haul the lighter man up after him. "You ready?" he asked.

"As I bloomin' ever will be, old chap." He moved a step up and laced his fingers together, making a cup of his hands. "Up you go now."

Barlow slipped his moccasined left foot into his friend's hands. "Go," he suddenly said, as he pushed off the ground with his right foot. At the same time, White Bear surged upward, grunting as all of Barlow's two-hundred-plus pounds pulled at his shoulders, legs and back.

Without hesitation, Barlow got his right foot on White Bear's shoulder and reached up at the same time. He got a good grip on the viga and pulled himself up, swinging his left leg over the log roof beam. Then he was lying facedown on the thick wood pole. The rain pounded on his back. He stretched out his arms. "All right, hoss," he said, "your turn."

White Bear grabbed his friend's big, callused hands and felt himself being lifted. In moments he was up far enough that he could grab the viga with one hand. Barlow let him go and he slapped the other hand on the wood. As Barlow squiggled back out of the way, White Bear pulled himself up to his chin, then straightened his arms until his midsection was even with the beam. He swung a leg up and over the log and sat up in the pouring rain.

"I do believe we're free of that bloody place, old chap," he said, breath coming hard.

"That we are, hoss." He squinted into the rain at his friend. "You ready to move on?"

"Bloody well right I am."

Within seconds they had maneuvered to the edge of the roof, eased themselves off it until they were hanging by their arms and hands, then dropped the last foot or so to the ground.

"Viuda Garza's?" White Bear asked. "For our weapons?"

"Yep. And Buffler. But the major's office first. I aim to get my tomahawk and knife back. I'd feel right nekkid without them once we git out of here."

White Bear didn't know if that was the wisest thing to do, but he said nothing. He would not usually be worried about such a thing, shrugging off the risk. But he was still not certain that his medicine had improved any, despite the ease of their escape.

They crept through the darkness to the major's office, which also was serving as the officer's home. Heckendorf slept in the living quarters at back. The two stopped across an alley from the house and watched for a little while, but there seemed to be no guards around.

Barlow went first, slipping up and testing the door. To his surprise, it was not locked. As he stepped inside, White Bear hurried to catch up to him. They quickly found their weapons in a storage trunk to one side, and slid the knives into sheaths and tomahawks into their belts.

"That's better," Barlow said, comforted by the familiar feel of the weapons.

They scurried out, closing the door behind them, then hurried as fast as they dared through alleys and small streets, alert for any patrols. But the American soldiers had gotten complacent, because there had been no real trouble from anyone in quite some time.

They finally squatted just outside Viuda Garza's front door, keeping in the shadows, knowing they could not be seen unless someone was just a few feet away. The rain would cover up any sounds they made.

"Buffler," Barlow called in a hissing whisper. "Buffler. C'mere, boy."

Moments later he heard a soft whine on the other side of the door. He smiled, rose and opened the door. The big Newfoundland sniffed at the two men suspiciously, assuring himself that they were really his master and his master's friend. Certain, he showed his delight at seeing them. His tail wagged so hard it made his whole back end wriggle wildly. He happily licked Barlow's hands, then White Bear's, all the while whining softly in happiness.

"You miss me, boy?" Barlow whispered as he kneeled and let the dog lick his face.

"Quien está allí?" a voice suddenly said in the dark. "Who's there?"

"It's us, señora," Barlow said hastily. "Will Barlow and White Bear."

The old woman hesitantly stepped into the small ante-room. When she saw they were really who the voice said they were, she smiled and put the old pistol she had carried into a pocket of her voluminous robe. *"Buenas noches,"* she said with a smile, pleased to see them. *"Dónde has estado?"* [Where have you been?]

"The *calabozo*," Barlow answered.

Viuda Garza showed no surprise. She had suspected as much when the soldiers had marched her two boarders away from the house that morning.

"Tienen hambre?" [Are you hungry?]

"Sí, señora," Barlow answered. "What they gave us to eat was horrible. Ah, *comida repulsiva*," he added after some moments' thought, trying to figure out the words to use.

"Come," the woman said. "I cook. You eat." Her English had not improved much, Barlow realized as he followed her to the kitchen. On the other hand, his Spanish was even worse.

Barlow didn't know how she did it, but in what seemed to be a mighty short time, she had a variety of spicy dishes on the table, and the two men were wolfing down tamales, frijoles, a kind of a chili stew, pieces of chicken mixed with peppers and Lord knew what else, all wrapped up in warm tortillas. And coffee, of course.

When they finished, they sat back to finish another cup of coffee more slowly. They couldn't take the time for a leisurely smoke, however. And as soon as they had drained their mugs, they stood.

"Muchas gracias, señora," Barlow said. "But we have to go now. The soldiers will be after us at dawn."

Viuda Garza did not understand all of what Barlow had

said, but she knew what he meant all the same. She would be sad to see the two men go; she was sure she would never see either of them again.

"Where are our guns?" Barlow asked.

"I get." The white-haired old woman turned and went off, deep into the house. She returned minutes later with Barlow's muzzle-loading rife and single-shot pistol, as well as his small, five-shot Colt Paterson revolver and White Bear's rifle, pistol, bow and quiver of arrows.

"Señora," Barlow said. He gave the woman a hug that for a moment she thought would crush her. Then he turned and headed for the door.

White Bear gave her a bright smile and a nod of thanks before following his friend outside. They turned to the adobe stable a few yards from the house. It was in poor shape after some years of neglect, and Barlow had a few moments of regret that he had not gotten around to trying to fix the place up for the old woman.

Inside, they quickly saddled their mounts, but before Barlow could haul himself up onto Beelzebub, White Bear grabbed his sleeve.

"Have you given any bloody thought to where we're going, old chap?" he asked.

That stopped Barlow cold. He had been so focused on just getting free that he had not even considered where he— and White Bear—should go once they were out. "Can't say as I have," he admitted.

"Well, we had better bloody well think about it now. Before we get out of this bloomin' barn and wind up back in the jail because we were runnin' about trying to figure out what to do."

"Damn, you're an annoying son of a bitch when you get practical, hoss," Barlow groused. He paused. "Got any ideas?"

"Not straight off," White Bear admitted. "I suppose going west is out of the bloody question."

A picture of Anna flashed through Barlow's mind. If they went to California, even if they didn't go to San Diego, he knew he would not be able to stay away from his daughter, and that would not be good for either one of them. "No, that won't do," Barlow said, melancholy settling over him.

"East doesn't seem all that bloomin' wise either, old chap. Nothing that way but Comanches."

They fell silent, thinking. Suddenly, Barlow blurted out, "South. We'll head for Santa Fe."

White Bear's eyes raised in question. "Is that smart, old chap?"

Barlow nodded. "Them soldier boys are going to think we've gone north, heading up into the mountains where the army has no jurisdiction, even if they could find us. They'll never think to look south."

"Bloody brilliant, old chap."

7

IT STOPPED RAINING sometime before dawn, though sunrise was hard to see because the cloud cover was still thick. Barlow and White Bear did not stop, however. They just kept plodding along the muddy path, their clothes dripping.

The rain spit at them on and off during the day, never very hard, but with annoying consistency. The two men and the dog finally stopped at dusk, managing to find a dry spot in a small copse. They managed to get a fire going and warmed up some of the food Viuda Garza had insisted they take with them. They were glad now that she had done so.

They ate, then smoked quietly, too tired to want to converse. While they fed themselves, Buffalo 2 wandered off. He was soon back with a dead rabbit clenched in his powerful jaws. He flopped down near the two men and began noisily to tear the rabbit to shreds and gulp down the chunks.

They turned in as soon as they had finished pipe and cigarillo, burrowing deep into their robes against the biting chill that had come along with the cold rain and the wind.

The clouds were breaking up in the morning, but it was still quite cold. "Winter's comin' soon," Barlow said offhandedly as they ate their meager breakfast.

White Bear grunted in agreement. "I don't bloody well like the thought, either, old chap," he said.

"More bad medicine?"

White Bear glanced sharply at his friend, trying to decide if Barlow was mocking him. "Maybe," he said, still unsure, but willing to give his companion the benefit of the doubt.

"You sure you ain't takin' this thing a bit too far, hoss?" Barlow questioned.

White Bear ignored it. He felt odd about these rather new—and decidedly unusual—feelings, and he did not like Barlow making light of them, which he was sure now that his friend was doing.

Barlow shook his head. He couldn't understand this new side of the Shoshoni, and it disturbed him. Except at the very first, when Barlow had just met White Bear in the Shoshoni's village far to the north, the Indian had never shown much of his nativeness. And it seemed mighty odd to Barlow that such a thing was suddenly raising its head.

They quickly broke camp and saddled the animals in silence. There was no need to talk. Besides, both men were uncomfortable with the invisible wall that had sprung up between them. Each rode with his own thoughts—Barlow's mind dwelling on his lost Anna; White Bear thinking about his newfound feelings of being a Shoshoni.

As the sun rose and the clouds fully dissipated, the temperature climbed somewhat. It created an eerie landscape as the sun gleamed through the moist air. And with it rose the two men's spirits somewhat, and they relaxed, especially after seeing a large, brilliant rainbow. Though their conversation was spare through the rest of the day, at least they were speaking to each other.

They spent another night camped on the trail, but early the next afternoon they rode into Santa Fe. As with Taos, Santa Fe had changed little in the few months the two men had been away, except for the American soldiers. Residents still flocked to the large church that dominated the plaza. Vendors still sold their goods and wares. Children still played, their boisterous activities covering them with mud in the plaza. Men still took siestas under the porticos of the cantinas and shops that ringed the plaza.

"Well, it don't look like Major Humpback has sent anyone down here lookin' for us," Barlow commented as they rode through the plaza and kept on going.

"It's too soon for that, old chap. Especially if, as you

bloody thought, they went looking for us to the north."

"Wonder how long it'll be before they catch on."

White Bear laughed, the first time he had done that in a long time. "From what I've seen of the bloomin' soldiers, they might not ever catch on, old chap."

"That would be a nice thing, but I doubt much that it'll happen. Even those damn fools'll figure it out sooner or late."

"I suppose you're right," White Bear said, sinking into despondency again.

A few blocks away, they came to the house they had rented the last time they were in Santa Fe. It was even more rundown than it had been before, but it was still empty. So they rode to the cantina that the proprietor also owned and made arrangements to stay at the house indefinitely. While at the cantina, they downed several full glasses of whiskey, and then, with a slight glow on their insides, they headed back to the house.

When they went inside, they found that the place was a mess. What furniture there was in the front room was covered with a thick layer of dirt, and cobwebs hung from the walls. The few knickknacks that remained were scattered across the floor. The fireplaces—one in the main room, one in the fairly large kitchen—had not been used since the two men left, so they would have to be cleaned out before they could be safely used again. Weeds grew out of the adobe walls in several places, as well as the dirt floor. The whole inside had a musty smell, worsened by the rain of two days ago.

Each man checked his own bedroom. Barlow found that the wooden bed was still covered with a goose-down tick and several warm blankets, though they were coated with dust, as were the nightstand and bureau with a washbasin and ewer. The small *horno*—the ubiquitous adobe fireplaces that also served as ovens—was also in need of a serious cleaning.

"Damn," Barlow growled when he and White Bear met up again in the front room. "This goddamn place is gonna take a heap of cleanin'."

"Well, I'm not about to do it, old chap," White Bear said. His gloom had increased. The mess in this place was just more bad medicine, he thought. "I can sleep in the dust."

"Reckon I can, too," Barlow said with a sigh. He brushed away some cobwebs hanging in his face from the ceiling. "What about you, boy?" he said, petting the Newfoundland on the head. "Can you live in this dusty ol' place?"

The dog woofed his acceptance, and Barlow grinned a little.

The men went outside and got their sparse belongings, which they carried into the house and dropped on the floor almost out of the way. Then they returned outside and unsaddled and tended the mule and pony, putting them in the adobe barn behind the house. Outside the stable, they leaned back against the wall, waiting for hay to be delivered. They had made arrangements for it when they were at the cantina.

Before long a wizened Mexican came along, walking beside a cart piled high with fodder. The cart was pulled by a scrawny burro that looked about ready to keel over. As the man and cart neared, Barlow could see that the elderly man was not in much better shape than the animal. He was short and thin, with a scraggly white beard clinging to a narrow chin. Rheumy, colorless eyes stared out from under a thick brow. His hair was very thin, his clothes worn and tattered.

The cart creaked to a halt as the old man muttered something in Spanish. The burro stopped, too tired, it seemed, to even shake its head or tail to get rid of the insects that buzzed around it.

"Habla inglés?" Barlow added.

"Some," the old man replied.

"Good. Take the cart right on in there and dump that hay along the back wall." He hooked a thumb in the direction of the stable.

"Sí, señor." He slapped the burro on the rump, and the long-suffering animal lurched forward, straining to get the small cart moving forward. The two disappeared inside, then returned a few minutes later and stopped again. The man turned to face Barlow, who nodded and handed him some coins. The old man looked at them, and his eyebrows went up. "This is too much, señor," he said in halting, heavily accented English. He held out his hand with the coins in it.

Barlow took the man's small, frail hand in his own big, powerful ones, and he folded the man's hand up. "Keep it, señor," Barlow said quietly. "You've earned it."

Eyes almost filling with tears, the old man turned and headed off. The cart still creaked, and the burro still looked like it was on its last legs, but the old man had something of a spring in his step, and his back was straight.

Barlow and White Bear headed for the house, but stopped just as they got to the door when they heard female voices shout, "Señors!" in a singsong tone.

They turned and broke into grins as Natividad and Lupe hurried up and straight into embraces from the two men. "You're not angry that we are here?" Natividad asked Barlow.

"Hell no. It's plumb pleasurable havin' you here. Want to come inside?"

"*Sí,*" the two women answered in unison.

"The place is a mess," Barlow said, trying to make it sound like an apology.

"We will fix that, Will," Natividad said. Her English was better than he remembered it, though her accent was still thick.

"That can wait," Barlow said, voice thick with lust.

They all entered the house, and stopped. "Is the bedroom as bad as this?"

"Afraid so, little one."

"Then love weel have to wait, señors," Natividad said firmly. "We cannot make love in all this dirt."

Barlow nodded rather glumly. While he was pleased that the women had volunteered to clean the place, he did not like the idea of waiting before taking the lusty señorita to bed. "What should we do meanwhile?" he asked.

"Go get some food," Natividad ordered. "We weel have to eat soon, and there is nothing here. Is there?" She looked up at Barlow in question.

"Don't expect so," Barlow mumbled.

"Then go." She pointed a long, slim finger toward the door.

Barlow nodded. Then he suddenly grinned, grabbed Natividad, pulled her close and kissed her hard and long. She melted in his arms, and gave back as good as she was receiving, her tongue darting into his mouth, teasing his, then retreating, only to renew the loving assault moments later.

Finally they broke apart. Barlow looked fondly down at the woman, as if trying to memorize the beauty of her face: her dark, flashing eyes; sensuous lips; slim nose; smooth, unblemished skin. "You clean fast, you understand?" he said. His lust was strong, and he wanted nothing more than to toss Natividad down on the floor, tear her clothes off and plunge his rampaging lance into her.

"I weel. You hurry back."

He nodded, and he and White Bear headed out. The late afternoon was fairly warm, the sky clear and blue. After the chilling rain of just two days ago, it was odd, but very welcome.

Rather than saddling the animals again so soon after putting them away, Barlow and White Bear walked toward the plaza, Buffalo 2 at Barlow's side.

"You know, old chap," White Bear said, seeming to force the Englishisms, when they stopped at one stall to buy some peppers, "we might want to keep out of sight for a while."

"Why?" Barlow asked, looking at his friend in surprise.

"Well, if the bloody soldiers figure out that we headed down here, as you seem to think they will, then finding us won't be so bloody hard, now, will it? How many chunky white men are accompanied by a Shoshoni warrior dressed the way I am, and a bloody monstrous-size dog?"

"Reckon there ain't but one group like that, hoss." He thought about it as they walked to another vendor for some beans. Once he really put his mind to it, he realized that the soldiers would easily find them. It was inevitable. Not that they were so smart, but someone from Santa Fe was bound to mention the odd little group of white man, Indian and dog in Taos. There were always military couriers moving between the two towns carrying messages. It was impossible that some soldier in Taos would not mention the search for him and White Bear. And, he knew, the trooper from Santa Fe would ask what they looked like, and he would be told, and then he would tell the Taos man that he knew where they were. He could expect just a few days, a week at most, before they would have to start worrying about it, and making plans to leave. But it would have to come, and soon.

"You're right, amigo," he said. "We'll get us enough food

to last us for a number of days. Then we can stay inside
that ol' lodge of ours for a while."

"Then what?"

"Then we had best figure out where to go and what to
do." Barlow explained his thoughts about the soldiers and
their inevitable discovery of the fugitives. "Till then, though,
I ain't gonna worry about it. I just aim to enjoy the pleasures
Natividad can provide."

White Bear grunted agreement, even more certain now
that his personal medicine had gone bad, and that he would
come to a bad end if he didn't do something to right it. And
soon.

The two men headed into a store that sold pretty much
everything they would need in one place. Buying small
amounts from vendors would take too long, and would not
get them enough goods to hold them for a few days.

While Barlow picked out the items needed and saw them
packed in crates, White Bear went off to find the old man
who had delivered the hay earlier in the day. He found him
and hired him to take all their purchases to the home. There
was too much for the two of them to carry, and after their
earlier conversation, both men were reluctant to call too
much attention to themselves by showing more people
where they were staying. They were sure the old man would
not give them away, even if the soldiers thought to question
him.

Barlow, White Bear and Buffalo 2 got out of the plaza
via the nearest street, and then kept to smaller streets and
alleys as they made their way back to the house. They
waited outside for the old man and his burro cart. When he
arrived, Barlow and White Bear unloaded the goods and
brought them into the house. Once again, Barlow paid the
old man more than he was used to getting. The old man
beamed, and offered profuse thanks.

Barlow was surprised at how much the two women had
accomplished in so short a time. But he was happy about it,
since Natividad started tugging him toward the one bedroom
just about the instant he put down the last of the food packages.

8

AS HE HAD been the first time he was away from Natividad for a little while, he was amazed at the thrills and desire this fireball of a woman brought out in him. He could not figure it out. She was no more beautiful than Rosaria, or many of the other women he had been with. She was no more shapely; her breasts were no bigger or firmer than the wonderful Rosaria's. Still, she managed somehow to hold him in thrall even just standing there fully clothed. He decided it did not matter why; he just accepted it as a fact and put it from his mind.

Barlow allowed her to tow him to the bedroom, which was chilly after having had no heat in it for some time. He would have to get some firewood and start a blaze in the small *horno* pretty soon. But, he thought as Natividad stopped, turned and pulled his head down to kiss him hotly, that could wait.

"I missed you, *mi corazón*," Natividad said as she broke off the kiss and looked up into his eyes.

"And I missed you, little one." He hadn't realized how much until he had seen her running across the short courtyard to him just a little while ago.

Natividad moved back a couple of steps. She kicked off her soft shoes. Then, with a smile, she stared brazenly at him as she began slowly unbuttoning and stripping off her clothes.

Barlow sucked in a breath as her breasts were unveiled—
beautiful, soft, ripe, dusky-colored mounds. The areolas and
nipples—firm and protruding from the cold and lust—were
much darker than the flesh of her breasts, so dark a brown
that they could be mistaken for black in the right light.

Then her belly came into view, soft, smooth, slightly
rounded, with a deep-seated navel.

She continued pushing her skirt down, ever so slowly,
easing it past her full, womanly hips, then revealing the dark
triangle of her womanhood. She let the skirt drop, and stood
there nude, her body—from the top of her slick, long black
hair to the toes at the ends of her long, perfectly shaped
legs—gleaming golden in the candlelight.

Barlow swallowed with difficulty. She was even more
beautiful than he had remembered. Near perfection, he
thought. *"Magnifico,"* he breathed. *"Absolutamente magnifico*—absolutely magnificent."

Natividad smiled at the compliment. "Undress," she ordered in a whisper. "Quickly." She *did* want him, badly. But
she was also getting cold in the chilly room.

Barlow shook his head to break the spell she had him
under, so that he could function. He quickly shucked his
shirt, belt, trousers and moccasins. Standing there a few feet
from her, it was obvious that he wanted her very much.

Natividad stepped forward and gently encircled Barlow's
rigid lance with one hand, while the other went around his
neck and pulled his face down for another deep, tongue-
dueling kiss.

Stepping back, Barlow swept her up in his big arms,
turned and gently tossed her on the bed, where she landed
with a little bounce and a giggle. Her ripe, firm breasts jig-
gled delightfully. She smiled up at him, opened her arms
and spread her legs, waiting for him, wanting him.

He eagerly accepted the invitation, climbing onto the bed
on his knees and edging up between her thighs, until the tip
of his manhood was just touching the gateway to her heav-
enly pleasures. "Yes?" he asked quietly. He wanted to
plunge his stiff shaft right into her, not sure that he could
delay his climax much longer.

"Sí," Natividad said eagerly, nodding enthusiastically.
She reached down and took his hardness in her hand and

tenderly introduced him to the entrance of her velvet sheath.

Once he had breached the opening of her moist citadel, he surged forward, plunging deep into her, bringing forth a groan of pleasure from the woman and a husky hiss from deep in his chest.

Barlow lay there a few seconds, resting his weight on his hands and knees. He pulled his shaft back, then surged forward again, and again, gradually gaining speed and intensity. Pleasure snaked up his manhood, then spread through his body like a gently enveloping fog.

Both of them began to moan. Natividad locked her ankles around the backs of his knees, trapping him in her silken embrace. She grabbed the back of his head and pulled him forward. Her lush lips were parted, waiting for him. Her tongue pushed forth, invading his mouth and capturing his tongue. Her eyes opened briefly so she could stare into his, then closed again, their dark depths hidden but not forgotten by Barlow. Those sparkling orbs were burned into his consciousness.

Barlow pulled his mouth free; he needed air because his breath was rapidly becoming labored. Then he could hold himself back no longer. His hard shaft drove frantically into her sopping womanhood and retreated in a strong, primitive rhythm. The power of it had the old bed creaking, sounding dangerously close to breaking.

Natividad dropped her feet until they were flat on the bed, and she pushed up a little, lifting her buttocks slightly, and so her womanhood, smoothing Barlow's path. She squealed in delight as her climax rose swiftly, then soared over her like a refreshing rainstorm after a long period of heat and drought.

Barlow snorted, and rammed her wildly until his essence exploded from his staff and roared into her, splashing in pulsating bursts, the ecstasy sending waves of fire blazing through them both.

Breathing heavily, Barlow finally flopped alongside of Natividad. He could not speak for some time, as he tried to suck in sufficient amounts of air. He finally began to calm down, and his chest ceased its erratic heaving until it returned to something approaching normal. He looked over at Natividad, who was staring at him, a large smile on her face, her eyes blazing with lust and . . . something he could not decipher.

"I wasn't too soon?" he asked, not too worried. He could tell she had had a good time. He just wanted to make certain it was good enough.

"No, *mi corazón*," Natividad said, still smiling. "It was soon," she added, then paused, trying to think of how to say the rest. Her lack of familiarity with English made some ideas difficult to phrase. "But not too soon," she finally said, pleased at herself.

Barlow smiled at her, relieved.

"And," she suddenly added, rolling onto her side to face him, "you are big, strong. We do it again. Soon. Very soon."

She reached down and stroked his flaccid penis with a featherlight touch.

"Mmmmmmmm," Barlow murmured at the touch. "That'll surely make certain of it."

"Then this should help more," she said softly. She kissed his lips, lightly but with fervor. Then she moved down, planting soft, almost ticklish kisses across Barlow's broad, muscled, scarred chest. Then lower, and still lower. Until she took his soft manhood in her mouth.

He shivered at the delicateness of her lips and tongue as they worked their magic on his shaft, which soon began to rise and stiffen. He looked down at her, amazed again at this woman.

She looked back, her dark eyes smoky with heat and desire. If her ministrations to his manhood hadn't brought him to life again, the look in those sensuous eyes would have been enough to do the trick, he thought. He dropped his head back onto the bed and for several minutes enjoyed Natividad's mouth moving slowly up and down his strengthening, lengthening shaft, teasing it—and him—into a raging mass of desire.

Finally he reached for her, tugging her up toward him.

The rest of the afternoon passed in a blur of carnality, as they hungrily consumed each other with a heat and passion neither had ever experienced before. They eventually fell asleep from sheer exhaustion, but they took up where they had left off as soon as they awoke in the morning.

Finally, though, hunger drove them out of the bedroom. Hastily, and rather carelessly, dressed, they headed out to the kitchen. Barlow let Buffalo 2 out to take care of business, and perhaps hunt for his own breakfast. Then Barlow sat with a cup of coffee while Natividad—a terrific cook, he had found out the last time he had been with her—made them something to eat.

Just before the food was ready, White Bear and Lupe strolled in.

"You look like hell, hoss," Barlow commented. They looked as tired and worn as Barlow felt.

"You're no bloody prize of gentlemanly comportment either, old fellow," the Shoshoni snapped as he plopped himself into a chair.

"You're ever so cheery, too," Barlow noted, looking at his friend in surprise.

"Comes from a lack of sleep, old chap. You should know that."

"I do know that," Barlow said easily. He grinned a bit. "But I thought it all depended on *why* you didn't get enough sleep." His eyes flicked to Lupe and then back to White Bear.

The Indian suddenly laughed. "I suppose you're right about that, old fellow. It was an exhausting, but ever so bloody delightful, night. And you?"

"Our doin's last night shined, hoss, plumb shined," Barlow responded with a wide grin.

Natividad, blushing only a little, began slapping plates of steaming eggs mixed with meat and chilies on the table. Since all were hungry, they ate with gusto, but without much conversation. Many a hot, lusty glance was shot from one person to another, however.

The only time any of the four of them came out of their rooms over the next three days was to eat, dump a chamber pot or let Buffalo 2 out. The two couples holed up in their rooms, making love as often and with as much fervor as they could.

After those three days, however, they were sated—and exhausted. They were also just about out of food, so Barlow and White Bear made plans to head to the plaza and replenish their supplies. They also had to get some more wood for the fireplaces.

Natividad and Lupe decided that while they men were gone, they would resume cleaning, to make the place more respectable, and comfortable.

With Buffalo 2 happily cavorting around them, the two men headed off, this time taking Barlow's mule, Beelzebub, and White Bear's pony. The animals needed a little exercise, and the men were both too lazy and too tired to walk.

As they clomped sluggishly into the plaza, they slowly became aware that they were attracting a fair number of stares. While they were used to being stared at, as unusual a group as they were, this seemed to be far more than normal. And with more malice, Barlow thought.

Barlow looked at White Bear. "You gettin' a strange feelin' about the folks hereabouts today?" he asked before glancing around the plaza again at the many unfriendly faces.

The Shoshoni nodded. "Aye, old chap." But his Englishness was forced.

They suddenly glanced at each other, eyes narrowed in worry and anger. "They know about us," Barlow said, suddenly realizing what the problem was.

"You're right," White Bear said flatly. A sudden stab of iciness pierced his heart. He just knew they were going to be captured at any moment and hanged soon after—before they could escape again. He mumbled under his breath in Shoshoni about how bad his medicine had become, and how he would never now have a chance to make it strong again. The feelings were as strange and discomfiting as they were new.

"We best start movin'," Barlow said urgently, kicking the big black mule into a trot.

They hurried through buying some food, and bought far less than they had thought to; their plans had changed drastically, though they were not yet sure how, or what they would do. They just knew they could not stay in Santa Fe much longer.

They tossed the sacks of supplies over the mule and horse, climbed aboard and galloped toward the house, taking a roundabout way in case they were being followed. Leaving the animals saddled, Barlow and White Bear hauled the supplies inside and slammed the door.

Natividad turned toward Barlow, a big smile on her face, which froze and then fell off, to be replaced by a frown when she saw him. "What ees wrong?" she asked.

"I think word has gotten out that me 'n' White Bear are wanted by the military up in Taos. Which means they'll catch up to us sooner or late. And that means we can't stay here no more."

"Where will you go?" Natividad asked.

Barlow shrugged. "Don't know, little one." He paused. "How's about you make us somethin' to eat whilst me 'n' White Bear figure out what we're gonna do and where we're gonna go."

Natividad and Lupe, suddenly very worried—and heartbroken—nodded and went about their business.

Barlow and White Bear sat at the table. "Got any ideas, hoss?" the former asked.

White Bear had thought about this considerably on the short ride from the plaza back to the house, and had made up his mind. The only trouble was, he didn't know how to break the news to his friend. Over the course of just several years, Barlow had become the most important person in White Bear's life. The former mountain man had saved his life more than once, had shared women with him, had split whatever food and drink he had, no matter how little there was. They had traveled side by side for what seemed a lifetime, and certainly had a lifetime of adventures in that relatively short period. They had faced enemies white, red and brown together; had ridden out snowstorms and avalanches together; had made love to women white, red and brown side by side; had crossed raging rivers, blistering deserts, high mountain passes often choked with snow; sat out drenching rainstorms.

White Bear shook his head. This was probably the hardest thing he had ever done—would ever have to do—but he knew it had to be done, and this was the time to do it. He suddenly cheered himself a little with the thought that perhaps Barlow would decide to join him, though he wasn't sure that he wanted that either.

The Indian took a deep breath, sighed it out and then said, "I'm going back to my people. The Shoshoni."

9

BARLOW SAT THERE stunned for some moments, the words clanging around in his head. He stared at his friend, noting though not analyzing the pained look on the Indian's face. He rubbed rough hands over his suddenly tired face, then sighed. "You sure, hoss?" he asked.

White Bear nodded, not certain words would come out, as bad as he felt. Or if they did, he doubted they would be the right ones.

"Why?" Barlow wasn't sure if he was more angry, hurt or just plain puzzled by White Bear's announcement.

"You remember I told you not too long ago how I thought my medicine had gone bad?"

Barlow nodded curtly, and gratefully accepted the mug of steaming hot coffee that Natividad handed to him.

White Bear accepted his coffee from Lupe and took a tentative sip. "Well, old chap," he said, grimacing at his poor attempt to return to using proper English, "I need to get it back. Almost everything that's happened since I first realized that has been trouble—the fight that got us into trouble, getting thrown in jail; the ride down here; now this."

"Hell, hoss," Barlow snorted, "not everything's been bad. We survived that fight, got out of the jail with little effort, had no trouble on the way here, and you've just spent the past several days with Lupe, who's everything you could want in a woman."

White Bear nodded glumly. "I know all that. But it still doesn't seem right. I keep wondering how long it'll be before my medicine gets so bad that I'll end up going under. And I don't want that happening here in Mexican lands, or even the white man's country back where I was raised." He sighed and sipped coffee, then continued, "Besides, my friend, I don't want you caught up in my troubles."

"Hell, hoss, we been through so many poor times together ain't much can happen now'd make it worse." Barlow glared at the Shoshoni.

"Well, I know that, Will. But . . ." He shrugged, knowing he would never be able to satisfactorily explain it. ". . . I can't believe that. I know that doesn't make any sense, but that's the way of it anyway."

Barlow continued to stare at White Bear, as if trying to see behind the Indian's eyes and into his thoughts. Then he shook his head sadly. He knew he could not change White Bear's mind, and that saddened him. Not only would he be on his own and have to find something to do with himself, but he would also be without the closest friend he had had since he had left home so many years ago. Maybe in his whole life.

He sighed and nodded. "If that's the way of it, hoss," he finally said, voice cracking just a bit.

"It is."

"You certain I can't change your mind, White Bear?" Barlow had to give it at least one more shot.

"I'm certain." White Bear sipped some coffee, then drew in a large breath and released it. "I know this is strange to you, my friend, but . . . I don't know, Will, I just can't explain it. Why this sudden need to return to my Shoshoni roots. It's just there and it can't be denied." He showed embarrassment at the revelations, so he busied himself with drinking coffee, keeping the mug in front of his face.

"All right, hoss," Barlow said morosely. "You're right. I don't much understand it, but I can understand you needin' to follow your ways. They may be different than my ways, but they're yours and you have to live with them." He, too, took some time slurping down coffee. "But I will say, hoss, I'm plumb gonna miss ridin' with you."

"And I with you," White Bear agreed sadly.

"We sure as hell had us a heap of adventures, didn't we?" Barlow asked, a small smile springing onto his face.

"Almost more than I can count." A wan smile spread across White Bear's lips, under the prominent nose. "But I'll remember them all."

"Me, too." Barlow sighed, glanced up and smiled as Natividad stuck a plate of food in front of him. As he dug in, he asked, "When're you plannin' to leave, hoss?"

White Bear took a moment to finish chewing and swallow. "Soon as I can, Will. I don't plan of sitting around here waiting for the soldiers to come knocking at the door here."

Barlow nodded and just continued eating. There was nothing more he could say to his friend. White Bear was bound and determined to go his own way, and Barlow would just have to accept that.

"What about you, Will?" White Bear asked around a mouthful of tamale. "Got any idea of what you're going to do?"

"No notion whatsoever, hoss," Barlow said. He had seen no reason to give it any thought until he knew that the army had found out he was here in Santa Fe. Now that it had happened, he would have to figure something out, and soon. It wouldn't take the soldiers long to find the house where he was staying. Some of them were bound to follow him one day, or, more likely, they would offer a reward or use coercion to get one of the Mexican people to find out where he lived. He had, at most, another day.

He finished eating about the same time White Bear did. The two rose and went through the supplies they had just bought, and separated them—some for White Bear, some for Barlow when he left and some to tide the women over for a day or so.

As they worked, Barlow said, "You might want to wait till dark before you set out, hoss. That'd make it a heap harder to spot you."

White Bear was eager to be on the way, but he saw the sense in what his friend said. He nodded. "Guess I can spare Lupe a little more time," he said with a grin that wasn't too forced. "Might even get some sleep, too."

Soon after, White Bear grabbed Lupe and the two disappeared into White Bear's room. Natividad turned to Barlow with a warm smile, one that offered infinite promise and warmth. While he wanted to get out and start making some plans, he could not turn such an enticement down. He returned her smile, took her hand and led her to his room.

A subdued Natividad said nothing when Barlow slipped out of the bed and threw on his pants, shirt, moccasins and coat. She, too, had heard White Bear and Lupe rustling around a few minutes ago, then silence, and knew what it meant.

Barlow kissed her on the tip of the nose. "Be right back, little one," he said quietly, with an odd hitch in his voice.

She nodded as he headed out with Buffalo 2 at his side. Man and dog were waiting in the cold when White Bear and Lupe, both mounted on the Shoshoni's pinto, rode out of the barn.

White Bear stopped and stared sadly at his friend. "I was hoping to avoid a scene, old chap," he said softly, breaking his gaze with his friend.

"I know," Barlow admitted, even more quietly than White Bear had spoken. "But I couldn't let you do that. We been through too much together to let that happen." He paused, smiling wanly up at Lupe. "Ain't nether of us given over to sentimental displays at partin', but I had to at least tell you adios, my friend."

White Bear considered that for a moment, then nodded. "I'm glad you did, old chap." He tried to keep his face stoic, but a slight tic in one cheek gave his emotions away. He leaned far over and patted Buffalo 2's broad head.

The dog licked White Bear's hand, confused, wondering what was going on, knowing that something was wrong.

"Well, you ride careful, hoss," Barlow said, stepping closer, hand outstretched. "There's a heap of troublemakin' peckerwoods—white and red—'tween here and your village."

White Bear nodded as he shook Barlow's hand. "I'll do that, Will. And you watch your hair, wherever you head off to. There's many a bloody chap will look to take it from you."

That did not require an answer, so Barlow said nothing. He and White Bear stared at each other for a few moments,

before White Bear nudged the pinto into motion. He rode
away, spine straight, not looking back.

Barlow watched for the few moments it took for White
Bear and Lupe to disappear into the darkness, and then stood
there for another minute or so, fighting back his emotions.
Then he turned and headed inside, a confused and worried
Buffalo 2 at his side.

Natividad was asleep when Barlow slipped out of the bed
and dressed. It was still only early afternoon. He knelt and
patted Buffalo 2 on the head. "You stay here, boy, and
watch over everyone." He didn't like leaving the dog behind, but he figured he'd be a lot harder to pick out if the
large, distinctive dog were not with him. After all, there was
no shortage of men wandering around Santa Fe in buckskins. Buffalo 2 whined a bit, but stayed when Barlow left,
mounted Beelzebub and rode off on the big mule. He
stopped just outside the plaza and dismounted. Having tied
the mule to a post, he moved swiftly around the outskirts of
the plaza. He wasn't sure what or who he was looking for;
he just hoped something would strike him as he traveled
about.

He finally walked into a store run by an American trader
who had been doing business there for some years. Barlow
didn't know him well, but had met him.

Fred Lindermeier was surprised to see Barlow. "I didn't
know you was in town, boy," the big, gruff, jovial man said,
shaking Barlow's hand. As usual, his face was flushed.

"Only been here a few days." He grinned, but there was
little heart in it. "Spent it all with a right shinin' señorita."

Lindermeier laughed. "Best way to spend time, I always
say." He paused, running a slablike hand through his thin-
ning gray hair. "So, what can I sell you today, Mr . . . ?"

"Barlow. Will." He did not expect the man to remember
his name. The only reason he knew the store owner's name
was that it was painted on the front of the shop. He grimaced
a little, not liking what he had to say. "It ain't so much that
I need to buy anything," he said. "What I need is some
information." At Lindermeier's raised eyebrows, he added,
"Like if there're any trappin' parties leavin' out from here
soon."

"None that I know of," Lindermeier said, scratching the stubble on his big, square jaw. "You that hard up for money? I could might be able to help you out a bit, maybe see about gittin' you a job hereabouts."

Barlow smiled ruefully. "I wish it was that easy, hoss. Truth to tell, the soldier boys are after me, and I need to light out plumb quick."

Lindermeier's eyebrows rose. "Soldiers huntin' you?" he asked warily. "I don't need no trouble with them goddamn boys. They're enough of a pain in my ass, without askin' for more. What in hell'd you do?"

"Ah, hell, some of them ass wipes up in Taos was trying to have their way with a couple of señoritas . . ."

"That ain't so strange," Lindermeier commented.

"True. But these women happened to be spendin' their time with me and an amigo. So me and my friend, we jist went and discouraged those soldiers' unwanted attentions. In the doin', though, one of 'em went under. The commander up there, well, he didn't take too kindly to havin' a dead soldier on his hands."

"So you took off and come down here?"

Barlow nodded. "Not right off. They arrested us and threw us in the *calabozo*. But me 'n' my friend took our leave of it in the dark of night. We skedaddled right down here."

"You weren't foolish enough to think you could get away from the soldiers here, were you?" Lindermeier asked, surprised.

"Hell no. But I knew it'd get us some time. Now, I ain't sure, but when me and my amigo come into the plaza this mornin' for supplies, we got some mighty odd looks. Stranger than usual, anyway, and I figure the soldiers know we're in town here. They just don't know *where* in Santa Fe we might be. I don't figure it'll take 'em long to find that out."

"So you need to skedaddle in a hurry?"

"Yep." Barlow pulled his old hat off and tossed it on the counter, then scratched his head. "I figure that if some trappers—or, probably more likely, some traders—were headin' out, mayhap I could sign on with 'em. Headin' out with a group would help cover my leavin'. At least some, anyway."

"Might help," Lindermeier said, again running a hand across the stubble on his face. He stood, thinking, then said, "I don't know of any such groups, though," he added.

Lindermeier's assistant, a young, fresh-faced man with an eager look about him, sidled up to Lindermeier and whispered into his ear for a few moments. The shop owner finally nodded, and looked at Barlow. "We might could help you, though, Mr. Barlow, but we ain't sure just yet." He paused, then added, "Can you come back in about an hour or so? By then I should have an answer and know whether I can be of any help."

Barlow nodded. "I can do that." He slapped his hat on, hefted his rifle and started to turn to leave, then stopped. "I'm mighty obliged for the help, Mr. Lindermeier. But I jist got to wonder—why're you bein' so helpful? It ain't like we're bosom friends or anything."

"I got no love for the soldiers, Mr. Barlow," Lindermeier said stiffly, as if he was feeling he had been insulted. "And if I can bite their ass without it causin' me no trouble, then I'm gonna do such." He smiled, realizing that Barlow wasn't insulting him; he was just suspicious, as anyone in his position would be. "And this don't seem to be a time when the soldiers'll cause me no trouble. Leastways no more than usual."

"Why do you dislike the soldiers?" Barlow asked, curious.

"Them peckerwoods have a habit of comin' in here for supplies and not payin' for 'em. It ain't as bad now as it was a couple months ago, but their promises ain't worth the paper they ain't even written on."

"Sounds about right," Barlow commented, remembering his treatment by General Kearny. "Well, I'll be obliged for whatever help you can give me, Mr. Lindermeier," he said as he headed out the door.

Not being fully trusting of Lindermeier's motives, Barlow slipped into an alley next to the store, then took some side streets, weaving this way and that to make sure, once again, that he was not followed. He took a roundabout way back to the house, too, once he had gotten his mule.

Natividad was awake and anxiously awaiting him. She sat at the table, nervously sipping at a mug of coffee and drumming her fingers on the scarred table. She looked up in relief when Barlow came through the door and smiled at her.

Barlow kissed Natividad lightly on the top of the head, and then, the cheek. "Miss me?" he asked.

"Very much," she said, her eyes wide yet with apprehension. "I worried about you."

"I reckon you did. I didn't want to wake you, though. I figured I'd be back before you woke."

She nodded, just relieved to have him back. "So, where did you go?" she asked.

"Down to the plaza, see if I could find some group of trappers or traders leavin' out of here."

"Did you?"

"Nope. Didn't really think I would, considerin' how late in the year it is, but I wanted to see. A Mr. Lindermeier who owns a store in the plaza said he might have a way to help me. I got to go back and see him in an hour or so."

"Do you trust him?" Natividad asked suspiciously.

"Nope. But if he figured on havin' someone follow me back here, he's plumb out of luck. And if he plans to have soldiers waitin' for me at the store when I go back, he'll be some disappointed. I aim to be mighty careful when I go back there."

"Bueno." Natividad rose and ran a soft palm against his scratchy cheek. "You said an hour?" Her dark eyes suddenly grew smoky with desire.

"A little less," Barlow said, closing his eyes and simply enjoying the feel of her hand on his face.

"Still enough time, eh?" She smiled lasciviously. Taking his hand, she led him back to the room they had been sharing.

A bored Buffalo 2 yawned and sprawled out on the kitchen floor under the table with a big sigh.

"I got to go now, little one," Barlow said. He got out of bed and began pulling his clothes on.

Natividad stayed in the bed, her long black hair spread out over her slim brown shoulders. She had the blanket pulled up to her chin. "You be careful, *hombre grande. Comprende?*"

"Sí," he said with a little smile. He kissed her softly and headed out. This time he called Buffalo 2 to accompany him. If there was trouble at Lindermeier's store, he wanted the big Newfoundland with him.

10

ONCE AGAIN, BARLOW took a roundabout way to Lindermeier's store. He tied the mule off in the alley half a block from the back of the store, then moved up the small space between the shop and the next building. He stopped there and watched for a while. There seemed to be a dearth of soldiers in the area, which Barlow found curious. He began to wonder whether a bunch of them were in Lindermeier's waiting for him. He didn't know the shop owner very well, and the man might've seen fit to tell the army about him, despite the hate he claimed to have for the military.

He was going to have to take a chance, sooner or later, however. He couldn't stand here all day. When he found a moment when no one else was around, he slipped around the corner and into the store.

Fred Lindermeier was waiting on two former trappers, whom Barlow knew only in passing. He nodded at them with relief and the two responded in kind, before turning back to their business. Lindermeier called his clerk, Tom McDuffie, and had him take over the dealings with the two trappers. Lindermeier lifted a hinged section of counter and stepped through it before setting it quietly back into place. He jerked his head toward a far corner of the store and headed that way.

Barlow followed, curious, and still just a bit wary.

Lindermeier turned and leaned back against a pile of furs of all kinds stacked almost to the ceiling. "I found a wagon train out of town," he said without preliminary. "It's the last one heading up the Santa Fe Trail for the season, and it's lucky I found them. Most of those boys are long gone. It won't do to be caught out there in the Llano or on the Plains when winter sets in."

"Will they take me on?" Barlow asked.

Lindermeier nodded. "Yep. Man named Seamus Muldoon owns it. He's fairly new to the Trail, so he's getting a late start on headin' back. In part because he was having trouble findin' anyone to go with him to help out. He finally found nine men to ride along. Seems like a mite lot of men for his small wagon train," Lindermeier added with a shrug. "But that's his business, I reckon."

"Where do I find this feller?"

"He said to meet him just after first light three miles out of town along the Trail. You know where that is?"

Barlow shrugged.

"You can't miss it, boy," Lindermeier said heartily. "Starts right over there," he added, pointing, though Barlow did not look, "by the Governor's Palace. The tracks of all the wagons make it pretty clear not far outside of town."

Barlow nodded. "I'm obliged, Mr. Lindermeier. I'm in your debt. If there's any way I can repay you . . ."

"Hell, son, I didn't do much. Just asked around a little bit. And, like I said, if I can bite the army's ass some, I'll do so." He spoke the truth, but he also knew that it was highly unlikely that Will Barlow would ever be back in these parts. Not as long as the army was looking for him. And there was nothing Barlow had that Lindermeier wanted or needed.

Barlow nodded again. He, too, knew it was almost certain that he would never stop here again. But he had to make the offer; after all, he was grateful for Lindermeier's help, no matter how little the shop owner thought about it. He turned to leave, but then spun back. "Reckon I ought to get some supplies now, whilst I'm here."

"Sure. What do you need?"

"Not much. Some powder, lead, caps, jerky, beans and

coffee. Maybe a little sugar. That should do it. I gotta travel light, you know."

Lindermeier nodded, then said, "C'mon with me." He led the way across the store.

The two trappers were just leaving, their arms full of paper wrapped packages. The clerk, McDuffie, held the door open for them.

Lindermeier began grabbing things and slapping them on the counter—several thin, short lead bars that Barlow would melt down to make whatever size bullets he needed; three cans of DuPont powder; several little tins of caps; a couple of pounds of jerky that he wrapped in a piece of rawhide; a cone of sugar; a sack of beans; and, finally, a twist of tobacco.

Barlow paid the man, and stuffed everything into a burlap sack Lindermeier gave him. "Again, Mr. Lindermeier," he said as he turned toward the door, "mighty obliged."

"It's nothing, Mr. Barlow."

With Buffalo 2 at his side, Barlow stood and watched out the window for a bit, once again waiting for the plaza to be empty for a few seconds. Then he was out the door and around the corner. A few minutes brought him to Beelzebub. He hung the sack off his saddle horn and climbed aboard. He rode slowly back to the house, on alert for anyone around him as he meandered through small streets and alleys. But he saw no one who took any interest in him.

At the house, Barlow put Beelzebub in the stable, took off the sack of goods and unsaddled him. Then he rubbed the mule down well and made sure he had plenty of food and water. He needed to make sure the animal was in fine shape, lest he get put afoot out there in the trackless wastes he had heard awaited him along the Santa Fe Trail.

Finally he headed into the house, where Natividad was waiting for him. She looked at him with worry in her soft brown eyes. *"Que?"* she asked.

Barlow reached out, grabbed her gently by the arms and pulled her close. "I'm headin' east with a wagon train of goods for the Settlements," he said quietly.

"When will you leave?" Natividad asked, voice quavering.

"Soon's it gets dark." He sighed. "I ain't supposed to meet

them boys till tomorrow, but I expect I ought to get out of here as soon as possible. The chances are too great of them findin' I'm here. And I want to get you back to your own home, too, so they can't bother you none should they find out you've been with me."

Natividad nodded against his chest. She was unable to speak without tears streaming down her face. She bit her lip, trying to keep the flood at bay. She knew full well that once he got back to the Settlements he would never come back here. And she had had her heart set on keeping him here with her for all time. She thought he wanted that, too. But whether he did or not didn't matter now. He was going—he *had* to go—and there was no way to change his mind. Not that she would have wanted to anyway. Not with the threat of the soldiers being ever present. What kind of life would they have with the army always looking for him? She hoped he would suddenly suggest that she go with him, even though she new that was a foolish notion. She had no experience with such harsh traveling and would be more of a hindrance than a help. Besides, even if she made it all the way, she was certain she would not be accepted by the Americans there. Not if the actions of the soldiers were any indication.

A sob burst forth, impossible to contain any longer, and she clasped her arms around Barlow's thick, powerful middle, holding him as tight as she could.

Barlow let her stay that way for several minutes, then gently peeled her arms from around him and held her at arm's length. "I *will* come back one day," he said softly. He did not know that such a thing would ever be possible, but he hoped saying it would make Natividad feel a little better.

It didn't work. Tears were coursing down her face, dripping onto her thin cotton peasant blouse.

"We still got some time," he said, again in a soft voice. "We can make the last few hours plumb shine, little one."

Natividad nodded. She would like that. Of course, she would like it better if he didn't have to go at all. She sighed. It was probably for the best. She doubted that she would have been able to keep him here for long anyway. He was too footloose to be tied down to one place for too long. She knew that, but she had never wanted to admit it to herself.

"And I cain't leave here without one more of your *muy bueno* suppers." He grinned weakly.

She returned the smile with little emotion behind it. "Food now?" she asked.

"Or . . . later," Barlow responded gruffly. "I have a hunger for *you* right now that must be fed."

She smiled then, almost for real, and followed him into the room they had shared.

More than two hours later, they came out. Barlow was feeling considerably better, though he knew Natividad wasn't. He felt bad about that, and he wished there were something he could do to chase her melancholy away. But he knew that short of his agreeing to stay here forever there was nothing that would cheer her.

Her sadness, however, did not keep her from treating him well—in the bedroom, and now in the kitchen. She made him the best meal she could with the ingredients she had at hand, and sat across from him after she had served him.

"Ain't you havin' none?" he asked, surprised, just as he was about to dig into the thick bean and chili mixture.

Natividad shook her head. "I'm not hungry," she said flatly. Even if she had been hungry, with her rolling emotions, eating now would have done nothing more than upset her stomach. "This is enough," she added, holding up her coffee mug.

He looked at her strangely for a few seconds, then shrugged and started to eat. He couldn't help her, and he needed to eat to make sure he stayed strong and alert.

Natividad watched him shoveling in his food. She could not really figure out just what she found so enticing about this man. Oh, there were a number of mostly superficial things that attracted her—his size, his courage, his strength, despite which he was gentle with her; she loved the way he loved her cooking; she loved the way he made love to her, too. But there was more to this former mountain man than that. She just couldn't figure out what it was. Not that it mattered now anyway, what with him getting ready to leave her in just a short while.

Barlow finally finished and leaned back in his chair with a sigh of contentment. He had never eaten food cooked as well as Natividad made it. He threw his feet up onto the table, much to Natividad's chagrin, and rested his legs there, crossed at the ankles. He slowly filled his pipe and lit it from the candle on the table, saving his small cache of Lucifers. With the pipe in one hand and a mug of hot, sweet coffee in the other, he relaxed, trying to keep his mind off of his having to leave Santa Fe—and Natividad. The thoughts were not pleasant, and he did not want them crowding into his mind right now. That might cause him to start thinking too much, and that could lead to making foolish decisions, like staying here, which would be fatal to him.

Finally he finished the coffee and the pipe. He put the former down on the table, then rose and knocked the ashes out of the latter into the fireplace. He slid the pipe away and turned to face Natividad, who was still sitting at the table. She had not moved, other than to sip at her coffee, since she sat.

"It's time," he said softly, hoping the words did not set her to crying again.

She didn't even look at him; just nodded and continued staring straight ahead.

He stepped up behind her and gently ran his fingers through her hair, from crown to shoulders, loving the silken feel of it. Still, she did not move. He grasped her shoulders gently and tugged her up. "We got to get you home, little one," he murmured into her ear.

Another nod.

Barlow sighed again, wishing once more that he could help her. But he couldn't. It was that simple. If he stayed here with her, he would be caught by the army sooner rather than later, and then he would be hanged. And what good would that do either one of them? If he got out of here, as he was going to do, there was always the chance that he could—would—come back. Natividad Santiago had an immense pull on him, and he would certainly want to return. It would all depend, he supposed, on the military. If the army moved out of Santa Fe, which they were bound to do someday, or if they just forgot about him and his "crime," he decided he would return as quickly as he could.

He turned Natividad to face him. "Look, little one, I got to go. *Got* to. You know that, don't you?"

She nodded, having nothing to say.

"Well, I was just thinkin' that I might be able to come back here one day." He explained his thoughts of moments ago.

Finally Natividad showed some life. "Really?" she asked, afraid to hope too much, but unable to stop herself.

"Yep," Barlow said more forcefully, trying to make sure the doubts that were in his mind didn't come out in his voice. "And ain't that possibility, even if it is mighty small, a heap better'n me just stayin' here and gittin' hanged by them soldier boys, meanin' I'd be gone from you for all time?"

"*Sí*," Natividad answered, brightening a fraction more.

"Then stop your grievin', woman, and send me off with a big ol' kiss for this ol' hoss."

"I can do better than that," Natividad said, some sparkle returning to her eyes.

"You think so?" he asked with a wide grin.

"*Sí, sí,*" she responded fairly enthusiastically. She took one of his big hands in one of her small ones and tugged him toward the bedroom.

She was almost back to her normal bubbly self when they returned to the kitchen a little while later. He grabbed her and kissed her once again. "Time to go, little one," he said with an earnest regret.

She nodded, sadness overcoming her again.

"I'll go saddle Beelzebub, then come back for you."

"You sure you will be back?" she asked, suddenly frightened. He nodded and pointed to his rifle on the table. "I ain't leavin' without that, little one," he said. "And I ain't leavin' without my supplies." He pointed again, this time at the bag that rested on the floor next to the door.

"All right," she said in a mousy little voice that hit Barlow right in the heart.

He left, but returned ten minutes later. "Time," he said, as he entered.

Natividad wrapped a shawl around her shoulders to ward off the night's chill. "I'm ready," she finally said.

Barlow grabbed his rifle and the sack of supplies. Buffalo 2 went out first, his nose snuffling as he drank in drafts of fresh, cold mountain air. He pranced around, enjoying life.

Natividad followed him, and then came Barlow, who closed the door firmly behind him. They walked through the darkness that was broken only by the starlight and into the barn. Barlow hung the sack on the mule, then climbed into the saddle. He reached down. Natividad grabbed the hand, and Barlow swung her up into Beelzebub behind him.

11

BARLOW HEARD THE wagons coming long before they hove into sight. He had gotten to the spot he thought was the right one for meeting Seamus Muldoon and his wagons well before midnight. There was no real cover here, so he just unsaddled Beelzebub. Spreading out his sleeping robe and using the saddle for a pillow, he lay down and drifted into slumber. He was a light sleeper and probably would hear anyone trying to creep up on him. Even if he didn't, Buffalo 2 certainly would.

The wretched, almost painful creaking of the wagons roused him from slumber. He listened for a few moments, and realized it would still be some time before they reached him. So he shut his eyes and tried to go back to sleep. But it was useless. The torturous, excruciating squeal of the wagons would not allow it.

He rose and stretched, shivering a little in the coldness of the predawn. He wished he had some fuel for a fire; some hot coffee would be mighty nice right now. But there were no trees, and if there were much in the way of scrub brush or buffalo chips he could use, he wouldn't have been able to find them in the dark. With no enthusiasm, he grabbed a piece of jerky and sat on the ground, back against the saddle, and sadly gnawed away on it.

The sun was fully up, and Barlow had saddled Beelzebub, by the time the wagons finally came into sight. The closer the wagons grew, the more unbearable the noise became. When it finally came to a stop, the silence created a roaring in Barlow's head.

A short, barrel-chested man of about forty slid off a chestnut horse and, holding the reins, walked toward Barlow, the animal towed behind him. He stopped and held out his hand.

Barlow shook the man's hand. "You must be Seamus Muldoon," he said.

"One and the same." He was a jovial sort, his chubby, round face cheerful, though his eyes were hidden under the shade of a wide-brimmed hat much like Barlow's. "And you are Will Barlow, I presume?"

"I am."

Buffalo 2, who had been lying low behind the saddle, just watching things, stood and walked toward the two men.

Muldoon suddenly looked frightened. He pointed. "Is that beast safe?" he asked, voice aquiver.

"Ol' Buffler? Hell, he's as safe as can be," Barlow said. He paused for effect, then added, "Unless you try raisin' hair on one of us."

Muldoon held out his hand, palm outward, fingers down, and the Newfoundland came up and sniffed at the man's hand, then circled him, sniffing al the while, making sure he was all right. The big dog accepted a few pats on the head from Muldoon before returning to plop down on Barlow's left. Barlow almost unconsciously began petting Buffalo 2.

Muldoon's face showed relief. "Well, Mr. Barlow," he said, "welcome to my little caravan." He named the rest of his men, pointing to the individuals as he did. Each nodded, some grinned, others grunted in greeting. "That tall, lanky feller is Enos Priddle. The Mexican with the red shirt is Ignacio Sanchez, the one in blue is Jorge Gutierrez. The short one with the dark beard is Normand Daigineault, and next to him is José Abrego. Over on the other side is Robert Dunsmore, Lachlan O'Hagin, Carlos Camacho and Tom Kilkenny."

Barlow nodded back at each of them, trying to match each with his the name. Kilkenny was about the same height as Muldoon, though slimmer and much younger. He looked no more than nineteen. Priddle was, as Muldoon had said, tall and lanky, with a bony face and a nose that was considerably off canter. The one with the French name also was about the same height as Muldoon, but was built like him as well, and had a thick, black beard and matching bristling eyebrows. The others all were mostly medium in height, weight and features, nondescript in most ways. It would be hard to distinguish them from each other.

Barlow stuck the butt of his rifle on the ground and leaned on the muzzle. "So, Mr. Muldoon, just what am I supposed to be doin' for you? I don't figure you're gonna let me tag along without earnin' my keep. I wouldn't want it that way anyway."

"I thought you might hunt for us, Mr. Barlow." Muldoon pulled his hat off, revealing an almost totally bald head. He wiped a sleeve across it, more out of habit, Barlow assumed, than any actual sweat. It was much too cool still to work up a sweat, unless one was actually working hard. "Lindermeir says you're an excellent shot and a finer tracker. So I thought huntin' would make the best use of your talents."

Barlow nodded. "Reckon that won't put me out none." He actually liked the idea. It would keep him off on his own much of each day, away from the others. He didn't know these men, and was not about to put much trust in them, at least not for a while.

"Well, then, Mr. Barlow, are you ready to go?" Muldoon asked.

"Reckon so. But I gotta ask you somethin' first."

"Yes?"

"Didn't you bring any grease for the axles on them damn wagons? You can hear 'em miles away."

"I thought the noise would keep Indians away from us."

"Are you *loco*, hoss?" Barlow snapped. "Any Injins hear that and they'll know jist what the hell it is. And they'll be sittin' there waitin' for us. We wouldn't even be able to hear 'em when they attacked neither, 'cause those wagons are so goddamn clamorous."

"But . . ."

"Even worse, hoss," Barlow continued relentlessly, "is that it'll scare the game away for miles around. It's gonna be hard enough findin' buffler and such out on those plains at this time of year without scarin' 'em off with all the goddamn noise these wagons make."

Muldoon nodded without hesitation. "What you say makes sense, Mr. Barlow," he said evenly, as if in thought. "I never thought of that." He turned and called out, "Break out the grease, boys, and slop it on them axles."

"Obliged," Barlow said without apology.

"I aim to get these wagons to Missouri before winter really sets in, and I'll do whatever need be to accomplish that. If makin' huntin' easier helps get it done, I'll make the huntin' easier any way I can."

Barlow was beginning to like Seamus Muldoon. The man had sense and seemed easy to work with, though Barlow could see that he would have a spine of iron when it was needed. It was a good combination—toughness and sensibleness.

The men were soon finished with greasing the wagons, and they set off. The wagons were still noisy, but compared with the way they had been, it was as close to silence as they could expect. Barlow sat on Beelzebub off to one side, watching the wagons roll by. There were nine of them, with one man driving each one. They were far smaller than he had expected. Most of the wagons he had seen coming into Santa Fe from the States were huge. But these were barely bigger than large carts. Each was pulled by four mules and was well packed with Mexican silver, wool and woollen garments, thick blankets and more.

Behind the wagons were six extra mules and two horses, tied together and roped to the last wagon. Ahead of them all rode Muldoon, sitting proudly on his chestnut horse.

Barlow trotted over to the extra animals and cut two mules loose. Holding the rope to them, he rode up beside Muldoon. "I took two mules for packin'. Might's well get on with my duties. I'll meet you somewhere up the trail when I've made some meat."

Muldoon nodded. "Sounds good to me, Mr. Barlow."

"Name's Will." He turned and galloped southeast, Buffalo 2 running alongside. They soon slowed, once they were away from the wagons. Out here, they could not be heard now, which Barlow thought was just fine. If he couldn't be riding with White Bear, or spending his time with Natividad, he would just as soon be alone as be with a bunch of men he neither knew nor had reason to trust. Of course, he had no reason to distrust them either, but a few of them, at least, had an avaricious look about them. He would be mighty wary around them for some time—until he learned that he could trust them. Or until he knew he couldn't.

A few hours' ride brought him into range of a small cluster of buffalo grazing placidly on what was left of the sparse brown grass. Their overpowering odor wafted over him, so he knew he was where he needed to be. The buffalo would not catch his scent. He dismounted. With the reins in one hand and his rifle in the other, he walked toward the buffalo. He kept his movements slow and steady, not wanting to do anything to spook the big, shaggy animals.

When he was about seventy-five yards away, he stopped. He ground-staked Beelzebub. It wasn't really necessary, since the mule, despite his occasional stubbornness, was loyal. But he couldn't be sure about the two he had brought along as pack animals. With them tied to Beelzebub, who was bigger than both the others, they would not go anywhere.

He walked a few yards farther, then stopped and knelt, Buffalo 2 next to him. The dog seemed eager, as if he knew he would be having some good eating soon without having to work for it. Barlow checked his rifle, then brought it up to his shoulder, sighted for a moment, and pulled the trigger.

A buffalo jerked and dropped onto its side, kicking its spindly legs and raising puffs of dust. None of the other buffalo seemed to notice or mind. They just continued grazing placidly.

Barlow took his time reloading, the movements practiced and smooth. Ready, he fired again, and another cow went down in a quivering, dust-raising heap. Barlow stood and reloaded once again. Then he looked at Buffalo 2. "All right, boy," he said, humor in his voice, "go chase them buffler away so's we can get to butcherin'."

The Newfoundland looked at him, head cocked, then turned his short snout in the direction of the buffalo. Suddenly he bolted forward. When he was within twenty-five yards of the big animals, he began barking furiously.

The animals looked dumbly around. They knew something was not right, but they couldn't figure it out.

Buffalo 2 kept charging, settling on one target. He skidded to a stop right behind the big beast and, still yapping, began nipping at the buffalo's heels.

The bison snuffled, kicked out a few times, but hit nothing. Buffalo 2 was too quick for her and darted out of the way, then shot back in and started nipping at the buffalo again.

The beast grunted in annoyance, then started running. The others, startled, shuffled off after her, picking up speed quickly, until they were galloping wildly away across the windblown prairie. Buffalo 2 chased after them for a bit, then stopped and trotted back toward Barlow, his tongue lolling sloppily.

Barlow shook his head at the stupidity of the great beasts. They made good eating, but they were as dumb as tree stumps. Rifle reloaded, he stood and looked around, checking to make sure there were no unwelcome guests lurking about. There were none that he could see, or hear, once the sound of the rumbling buffalo had faded.

He climbed into the saddle and kicked the mule into motion, towing the two pack mules behind. He stopped by the first buffalo he had killed, dismounted and ground-staked Beelzebub again. Leaning his rifle on the still quivering bison, he pulled his knife and set to work butchering. It had been a long time since he had done this, and he had almost forgotten how tough—and messy—it was. He sighed. It was to be his lot for the next month or so, until they reached Missouri.

He wasted no time in his butchering, though he was in no particular hurry. Buffalo 2 had come up and plunked his behind down on the ground a few feet away, waiting expectantly.

Barlow grinned and made the dog wait a little longer. Then he suddenly tossed a small chunk of meat to him. The dog's power jaws snatched it out of the air, and he gulped it down without actually masticating it.

"Damn, boy," Barlow said with a short laugh, "you're supposed to chew it some first."

The Newfoundland paid him no attention, just sat and waited for another hunk of meat to come flying his way.

Barlow resumed his butchering, every couple of minutes tossing a piece of meat to the dog, who continued to swallow them practically whole, as if he had not eaten in weeks.

Barlow was judicious in the meat he took from the two buffalo he had killed—the hump meat, tongues, livers, kidneys and some of the more choice cuts of rump meat. He considered taking the hides, since they were nicely thick with early prime winter fur, but he decided that would be too much trouble, though he could manage if he wanted to. But even if he did, he had no time nor place to tan the hides.

He did, however, cut some pieces of hide off and wrapped the meat in them. He tied the bundles to the two pack mules, and then mounted Beelzebub. "C'mon, Buffler," he said, grinning a little as he watched the dog steadfastly gnawing away at the innards of one of the buffalo.

"I said, c'mon, boy," Barlow said more sharply.

The Newfoundland looked up at him, his muzzle covered with blood, and seemed to be trying to decide whether he should disobey his master to continue feeding on this succulent meat. He took one more bite, tearing out a large hunk of buffalo flesh, and then trotted toward Barlow.

"It's about time, you damn fool mutt," Barlow muttered, but he was still grinning—at least as much as he ever grinned these days. What with Anna's loss still powerful in him, plus all his recent troubles, and the absence of White Bear, he had little to smile about.

He cut the Santa Fe Trail two hours later. He stopped and squatted, examining the ground for a few minutes. He determined that the wagons had already been by here, but he figured they couldn't have gotten too far ahead, as slow as they had to move.

He mounted Beelzebub again started trotting alongside the ruts, which, while not very deep, were certainly quite visible and easy to follow.

Barlow caught up with the wagons in midafternoon. Muldoon was glad to see him, thinking that since he had been gone so long something must have happened to him.

"Just took my time, Mr. Muldoon," Barlow said. "Couldn't see any need to rush."

"None at all," Muldoon agreed. "Not with as slow as we're travelin'. I wish we could pick up the pace some. At this rate, winter's gonna catch us a long way from the Settlements."

"Them mules look pretty sturdy," Barlow said. "I reckon they could move some faster without bein' hurt none."

"You think so?" Muldoon asked hopefully.

"Yep. Not that you want to run 'em into the ground, but you should be able to make twenty, twenty-five miles a day."

Muldoon rode away without saying farewell, his brows knitted in thought.

12

THE CARAVAN MADE slow but steady progress. Seamus Muldoon pushed the men and animals harder, confident in Barlow's assessment of how well they would do and wanting to beat the winter back to the States. It was obvious to Barlow that Muldoon had never done this before, at least not as the head of such a wagon train, but he listened and learned quickly. Only one day in the first week were they slowed considerably, when a gully washer of an icy rainstorm swept over them, turning the prairie to mud, hindering their progress. But the next day, the sky was blue, with just a few lingering clouds, which soon drifted away. The sun dried out the ground by midday, and they picked up the pace again.

During the first week, Barlow spent much of his time out away from the wagons, hunting. After a couple of days, he overheard some of the men grousing about being tired of eating buffalo meat. He couldn't understand that—as far as he was concerned, there was no better eating than fresh buffalo. But he wasn't the only one to be fed, so every other day or so, he brought in deer or antelope meat. One day he brought some bear for the men, who decided right off that they didn't like the greasy, fat-filled meat of the winter-ready grizzly. Not that any of the men complained to his face—they were all afraid to. But word quickly passed around and reached his ears.

In that first week or so, Barlow also learned that he could
not trust any of the men, except perhaps Carlos Camacho
and Tom Kilkenny. The others were standoffish, wary and,
while not showing any outright hostility, quite unfriendly
toward Barlow. He ignored it for the most part, but wondered about it. At times, while everyone else was sitting
around the nightly fire, he would drift out onto the prairie
in the darkness and circle around to where he was within
hearing distance of the men. Most times he heard nothing
of any importance, but as time passed, the men seemed to
grow a little looser in their talk.

As often as not, Enos Priddle, Ignacio Sanchez, Robert
Dunsmore, Jorge Gutierrez, José Abrego, Normand Daigineault and Lachlan O'Hagin stuck together, ignoring Barlow, Muldoon, Kilkenny and Camacho. They often built
their own small fire—made of buffalo chips like the fire the
others had—got their ration of meat from Barlow and beans
from Muldoon, and ate off on their own, keeping away from
the four other men.

Barlow considered that mighty suspicious. Seamus Muldoon was a good boss, one who treated his men fairly and
with respect. Why the majority of them shunned their leader
was something that baffled Barlow. He did not say anything
about it, however, not wanting to alarm Muldoon unneces-
sarily. But it did make him extra wary when he was around
the wagons, and filled him with worry when he was out
hunting.

That concern drove him to spend less time away from the
wagons, so he wasted no time when he was hunting and
butchering. He didn't want to leave Muldoon, Camacho and
Kilkenny for too long, lest the seven other men try something deadly. He didn't think that likely, but he had seen
enough men who would do such things, and he intended to
be as suspicious as possible just in case.

Barlow's concern grew with each passing day, but he was
still reluctant to say anything to Muldoon, especially since
he had no proof of anything. It was more a hunch he had
that Priddle—the leader of the group of standoffs it quickly
became apparent—was going to do something. And do it
before too much longer.

One afternoon, as he and Muldoon rode alongside each

other a short distance ahead of the wagons, Barlow casually asked, "How well do you know these boys?"

"Not real well," Muldoon said, glancing over at Barlow, wondering what he was getting at. "I hired most of 'em just before we pulled out. I was havin' trouble findin' men. Seems that most of the ones who have experience on this trail were long gone already."

"So I heard," Barlow noted casually.

"Why do you ask?"

"No reason. Just curious," Barlow said easily.

But Muldoon was not fooled, and Barlow realized that the man was too astute not to know something was bothering Barlow or he would not have asked such a question.

"Hogwash, Will." Muldoon smiled a little to let Barlow know he was not really upset, but that he didn't believe that statement.

Barlow cursed under his breath at having been found out. He should have known better. "I ain't sure why I'm asking, Seamus," he said truthfully. "I just got me a hunch that them boys're gonna try makin' some mischief before we get to the States."

"Like what?" Muldoon didn't seem too concerned.

Barlow shrugged. "Ain't sure. I just don't trust them boys one little bit."

"I'll be on my watch, Will. But I think you have it all wrong. They're just used to each other's company, and maybe it don't shine with them to sit jawin' with the boosh-way."

"Maybe you're right, Seamus. I hope so." He paused, then asked, "Were you ever a mountaineer?"

"For a short time." He grinned. "What gave me away?"

"Some of the expressions you use, ol' hoss." He offered a little grin. "It's somethin' of a wonder that we never met up at a rendezvous somewhere."

"Truth to tell, Will, by the time I hitched on with a trap-pin' brigade, the beaver trade was damn near dead. I went to two rendezvous, both of 'em the damnedest dead affairs you ever saw. I was some disappointed, I tell you. After the stories I'd heard of rendezvous, I was expectin' a time of frolickin', drinkin', gamblin' and fornicatin'." He chuckled ruefully. "I still ain't sure whether all those stories were lies, or if I was just too late gettin' out to the mountains."

"Oh, they was wild, shinin' doin's, all right," Barlow said,
remembering those days with fondness. "I mind the time I
was at one of them doin's up on the Green—near Horse
Creek, I reckon it was. Some boys was deep in their cups
after two days of doin' nothin' but swillin' down that pan-
ther piss the traders called whiskey. Seems a few of 'em
took it to mind to set one of their amigos alight. They
doused him with some of that whiskey and tossed a torch
at him. That ol' hoss went up like a Roman candle." He
shook his head at the memory. "He was so drunk, it took
him a bit to realize he was on fire. Then he started hollerin'
like the devil was chewin' on his ass. His friends knocked
him down and whapped the fire out with blankets and such."
He scratched the rough new beard that had sprung up in the
past week or so. "I never did hear what happened to that
ol' hoss."

"I don't expect he came to a good end," Muldoon mused
aloud.

"I reckon you're right on that."

They rode along in silence for some time, before Barlow
said, "You best keep a watch out on them boys, just in case
they are plannin' somethin'. I'd sure hate to see you get
made wolf bait out of by such riffraff as them."

"I'll be alert," Muldoon said. "And I appreciate your concern."

Barlow shrugged. "You're a good man, Seamus. Don't
know as I can say the same for Priddle and his *compañeros*."

Muldoon turned in the saddle and looked behind. Seeing
nothing untoward at the moment, he turned back.

"I'd also advise you to quit ridin' out in front like this.
If they do plan somethin' wicked, you ridin' with your back
to 'em all the time is just like an invite to 'em."

Muldoon sighed. "I still think you're making too much
of this hunch of yours, Will, but I'll keep what you've said
to mind. I'd rather be a little extra cautious than be put
under."

Muldoon did take Barlow's advice, and began riding off to
the side—changing sides every so often—of the caravan.

He even occasionally dropped back to where he was following the wagons for a while.

Barlow was pleased to see it. He just had a plain bad feeling about some of the men Muldoon had hired. And since he had come to like the wagon master, he did not want to see anything bad happen to him. So it was with a slightly better frame of mind that he rode out for the day's hunting. When he returned to the wagons that afternoon with a load of antelope meat, he could sense a tension in the air. Something wasn't right, though he couldn't really say what it was. Priddle and his friends seemed to be more furtive in the camp that night, constantly glancing around to make sure that no one else was within earshot. And they spoke in whispers. It did not bode well, but Barlow was reluctant once again to say anything to Muldoon. He had warned the man once. To do so again would make him out to be a worrier and possibly even faint of heart.

The next morning, he delayed as long as he could without raising suspicions before he rode out for the day's hunt. But everything seemed normal to him, so he tried to put his concern out of his mind. He managed somewhat, but not enough, so he moved faster than normal, wanting to get the hunting and butchering done as quickly as possible and get back to the wagons.

But, as often happened, when he wanted things to go swiftly, everything conspired to slow him down. He found no game within a few miles of the wagons. He had to ride on farther and farther before he encountered a small group of buffalo. As they grazed, the great, brown animals paid little heed to the light dusting of snow on the ground. Barlow ignored the snow, too, but the wind made the low temperature seem even colder. Whether he liked it or not, winter was here, and would only get worse. He just hoped that they got a break and had some Indian summer for a few weeks, so they could continue to make good time on the Trail.

He wasted no time in dropping two cows and then having Buffalo 2 chase off the others. His butchering was perfunctory, as he hacked and whittled with haste and abandon. Buffalo 2 was disappointed that Barlow was not tossing him as many delicious morsels as usual. The dog whined occa-

sionally, knowing something was wrong with his master but
not knowing how to fix it.

As Barlow worked, a premonition swept over him and
lingered. At first he figured it was just his imagination con-
juring up trouble where there was none. But the longer the
portent lasted, the more he began to consider it something
real. His thoughts flashed to White Bear and he shook his
head. He was beginning to believe that, like his friend, his
own medicine had gone bad. He tried to shake that feeling
off, but was only partially successful.

Working faster now, Barlow finished the butchering and
tossed the skin-wrapped bundles of meat on the two pack
mules. With only a cursory cleanup, he mounted Beelzebub
and cantered off, a confused Buffalo 2 trotting alongside,
casting frequent glances up at his master.

When he came to the ruts indicating the Trail, Barlow
stopped, dismounted and squatted close to the ground examining it. He nodded and patted Buffalo 2 on the head.
"They been by here already, boy," he said to the dog. He
felt some relief. They were not too far ahead, he deduced,
and he had seen no sign of trouble. He petted the Newfoundland's head again and ruffled the dog's neck fur.
"Maybe I'm just gettin' old and worrisome," he muttered.
The dog lapped at his hand.

He mounted up again and trotted off up the trail. Half a
mile on, Buffalo 2 suddenly darted ahead, barking wildly.
"C'mon, Beelzebub," Barlow snapped, kicking the mule in
the ribs. The animal bolted forward, the two pack mules
galloping in an effort to keep up.

Buffalo 2 stopped once and looked back for Barlow. Once
certain the man was coming, he raced ahead again.

The feeling of dread swept over Barlow again as he rode
hard, quickly catching up with the dog. They tore ahead—
Beelzebub, with Barlow on his broad back, and the big
Newfoundland, side by side.

Suddenly Barlow jerked Beelzebub to a stop—though
Buffalo 2 still raced forward—when he saw two of the wagons. Barlow proceeded more slowly then, eyes avoiding
what he expected to see ahead, not because he was afraid
to view it, but because he wanted to make sure the perpe-
trators were not still around lying in wait for him. Of course,

out here in the openness, there was no place for anyone to hide from him, really, though he supposed one or two could be lying on the ground a hundred yards or so farther on, and not be seen. He doubted that, though.

He finally stopped, slid out of the saddle and ground-staked the mules. Buffalo 2 had plopped down ahead of him, but not too far. Rifle in hand, Barlow moved forward, dreading what he knew he was about to see. He found Carlos Camacho's body first. He had been shot twice in the chest and once in the head. In the coldness, the blood had coagulated fairly quickly, a dirty red puddle amid the patchy snow.

Tom Kilkenny's corpse was not far away. He had an old single-shot, muzzle-loading pistol clutched in his cold, dead hand. Without pulling it out of the young man's hand, Barlow checked it. It had been fired. Barlow only hoped that Kilkenny had hit someone who was now in terrible pain. Kilkenny had been shot twice, once in the stomach, and once in his left bicep. He also had been battered pretty well by a gun butt or ax handle.

"Shit," Barlow muttered as he pushed himself to his feet. He looked up and saw Buffalo 2 sitting again several yards ahead. The dog barked. "I'm comin', boy," Barlow said dully. He moved forward, moccasins crunching on the frosty grass.

As he knew he would, he found Seamus Muldoon's body. He had been shot in a leg, an arm and in the chest. He also had had his throat slit, and someone had gutted the wagon master.

"Fuck," Barlow shouted, rising again. He stood looking around. The men who did this had abandoned three of the wagons, not having enough manpower to drive them. Barlow walked slowly around. The killers had dumped a bunch of the goods they had no use for. From the looks of it, they had also taken some of the booty and put it on other wagons.

"These here are some bad goddamn doin's, Buffler," Barlow said. He was torn. He wanted to go charging after the men who had caused so much carnage, but at the same time, he knew he should give the three dead men as decent a burial as he could manage. He decided that the latter would have to be his first concern. For one thing, he could not leave the bodies of good men out here to be ravaged by animals or, worse, Comanches. Plus he figured that the wagons couldn't get all that far ahead of him at the pace they traveled. Even if Priddle and his men had whipped the mules mercilessly—which Barlow would not put past them—he should still be able to catch them sometime tomorrow. He leaned his rifle against one of the wagons and then set to work at his grisly task.

13

BY THE TIME Barlow had scraped out a shallow hole big enough to fit all three bodies into, carried the corpses there, laid them gently down, and then covered them up, it was close to dark. The temperature had fallen, and a light snow was falling.

Angry, irritated and frustrated at having to wait to chase down the men who had killed Muldoon, Camacho and Kilkenny, Barlow smashed some chunks of wood from one of the wagons, brought out his fire-making kit and got a blaze going. He carved off some hunks of buffalo meat and hung them over the fire to cook. Then he put a pot of coffee on to boil. That done, he cut more meat off and fed Buffalo 2, who hungrily gulped down the pieces. Barlow was too annoyed to even chide the dog for swallowing the meat first without chewing.

After he ate and had one cup of coffee, he pulled the rest of the meat off the two pack mules, tossed it in one of the wagons and rubbed the two beasts down. Then he unsaddled Beelzebub and tended to the big animal, too. He went back to the fire and had another small piece of half-raw buffalo meat, then another cup of coffee while he smoked his pipe.

Finally, he knocked the ashes from the pipe into the fire, set out his bedroll and crawled in. Despite his anger and concerns, he was asleep almost instantly.

Barlow woke once during the night, when Buffalo 2

started growling deep in his throat—a warning. Barlow looked around and saw the glowing eyes of a number of wolves. They had smelled the fresh meat, he figured. He grabbed a burning stick and tossed it at the animals. They backed off, snarling viciously, but then began easing forward again.

"Goddamn fractious beasts," he mumbled. "You don't know who you're goin' up against, you ignorant critters."

He pulled himself most of the way out of his warm robes into the cold night air. He pulled his rifle up, checked it, then took aim at what seemed to be the leader of this particular pack of wolves. He fired, and the wolf yipped and tried to turn to run away, but fell before he got halfway around.

The other wolves stood there for a few minutes snarling and growling. Then the head female edged up onto the still-quivering carcass of the dead male. She nipped at the corpse, then darted away, several times. She finally went to the carcass and took a tentative bite. Then a bigger one. The other wolves slowly came around, one of them a young, vigorous looking wolf who was almost all black and nipped at several of the lesser companions, until he and the main female were tearing apart the remains of the dead leader.

"That ought to keep those goddamn beasties occupied for a spell," Barlow said softly as he reloaded his rifle. He slid back into his sleeping robe and closed his eyes. If the wolves decided to come for him again—or the meat he had stored in the wagon—Buffalo 2 would warn him. He glanced over at the big Newfoundland. The dog was tense, legs bunched up beneath him, ready to charge if that became necessary. Barlow closed his eyes again, and to the sound of the wolves ripping apart their former companion, he fell back to sleep.

Barlow did not wake again that night. When he did awaken, to the cold, crisp dawn, he concluded that the wolves had left because of the campfire, the gunshot, Buffalo 2's presence, and because they were at least partially sated by having feasted on their dead leader. It didn't matter much, Barlow thought as he climbed out of his sleeping robes and put coffee on the fire. As long as they were gone, he didn't really care why they had left.

He had two cups of coffee and a sizeable portion of buf-

falo meat well sizzled over the fire. He fed Buffalo 2 pieces
of the meat—one raw, one cooked. Fortunately, the mules
had been able to find enough forage despite the light coating
of snow, which they used for water. But Barlow was glad
that the snow had stopped falling.

Normally Barlow would have preferred the snow, since it
would be much easier to track someone in it. But with the
Trail's ruts so obvious, he was just as glad that the snow
stopped.

"Well, Buffler," Barlow said as he stood and tossed the
dregs from his coffee cup onto the fire, "it's time we went
and paid those sons a bitches a little visit, don't you think?"

The dog's tail wagged wildly and he offered up a small
growl, as if he understood perfectly what Barlow had said.
Every movement showed his eagerness to be on the way.

With economical movements, Barlow saddled Beelzebub
and loaded the still large assortment of buffalo meat he had
left onto the two pack mules, distributing it evenly so neither
would be too burdened. With the weather as cold as it was,
the meat would stay fresh for a long time, saving Barlow
from having to hunt while trailing his quarry.

Barlow pulled himself into the saddle. As he did, his determination for vengeance grew. He slid his rifle through a
loop on the front of his saddle just behind the horn. Taking
the rope to the pack mules in one hand and the reins in the
other, he clucked, putting Beelzebub into motion. Buffalo 2
barked a couple of times and then trotted out ahead of Barlow, his whole body a picture of excitement.

As darkness began to approach, Barlow realized with annoyance and anger that either Priddle's men had killed Muldoon and the others a lot earlier than he had figured, or else
Priddle was moving the wagons a lot faster than Barlow
would have thought wise.

He growled and stopped just before night fell completely.
He had brought some of the wood from the one wagon with
him, and he used it to build a fire before he tended to the
animals. Finally he sat and ate morosely, trying not to let
his gloominess spill over onto Buffalo 2. Still fuming, he
turned in shortly after eating. To his relief, he slept the night
through without interruption.

He was awake before daybreak, pleased to note that the temperature was a bit higher than it had been the past few mornings. Not that it was much warmer than freezing, but at least it had edged above it. He went about his breakfast and other tasks with practiced haste, and just as dawn's pinkish-gold light was creeping up over the horizon, he climbed into the saddle and took his leave, moving at a good clip. He was determined not to lose another day in his search for the killers.

He heard the wagons at midmorning. Judging by the noise, he figured that Priddle was not nearly as dutiful as Muldoon had been about greasing the axles. It was just as well, Barlow thought, as it gave him a chance to know where they were long before he got there, and it would let him get right on top of them before they knew he was there.

He rode on steadily, eyes flitting from the horizon to Buffalo 2 to the sides, alert to anything that might be out there. He most often kept his glance on the dog, who was trotting several yards ahead of him, knowing that the Newfoundland would discover before he would when they were getting close to the wagon train.

The dog did not fail him. Buffalo 2's ears suddenly perked up and he slowed down. He emitted deep, low growls.

"That's a good boy, Buffler," Barlow said. "Now you hold back here by me until we get up close enough to do them ol' boys some harm."

With small snarls still emanating steadily up from his powerful chest, Buffalo 2 waited until Beelzebub was next to him, then moved forward again, keeping pace with the mule carrying his master.

Barlow rode forward slowly, quickly growing annoyed at the noise of the wagons. While the grating sound would cover his approach, listening to it was irritating almost to the point of madness.

Within half an hour, Barlow could see the rear of the last wagon in the distance. He stopped and looked around. Much to his chagrin, there was nowhere he could hide to sneak up on the wagon train. There was no cover at all. He would just have to ride up on them and hope for the best.

"These here goddamn doin's don't shine with this ol' hoss

no way," he said into the wind, the words torn from his mouth and scattered across the prairie. He sighed. "Well, Buffler, looks like we got no choice. So let's just go do it."

The dog's tail wagged furiously and his eyes gleamed in readiness.

"C'mon, boy," Barlow said as he got the mules moving again. When he was about a hundred yards from the last wagon, he stopped and quickly dismounted. He walked forward, tugging the three animals behind him. An eager Buffalo 2 padded next to him.

Barlow hated giving up what little advantage he had—being able to see much farther while on the mule. On the other hand, it was also a great disadvantage, because any one of the men with the wagons could more easily spot him if they happened to look behind.

Every few yards, he would stop, step into one stirrup and pull himself up for a quick look before moving on again. On one of those times, he saw someone riding a horse alongside the wagons. He assumed it was Enos Priddle. It also explained why three wagons had been left behind instead of two. There had been enough men to drive seven wagons, but only if each of the bandits took the reins of one. With Priddle riding Muldoon's chestnut horse, only six men were left to handle wagons.

Less than fifty yards away, Barlow stopped. He dropped to one knee and brought the rifle to bear on the driver of the last wagon. He neither knew who it was nor cared. He fired, and when the powder smoke cleared, he could see that there was no longer anyone on the seat of the cart.

He swiftly reloaded, then swung up onto Beelzebub's back. He ignored the rope to the two pack mules and heeled the big mule into a run. Far ahead, he could see Priddle turning his horse and stopping, trying to figure out what was going on. He spotted Barlow and started racing toward him.

The others snapped the reins on their mules, and the wagons lurched forward and into a sluggish run. The last one, now driverless, followed the others, but with no one to control the mules, the animals soon veered off to the left, and moments later the wagon hit a series of bumps and flipped over, rolling and shattering, scattering goods across the prai-

rie. The mules, freed of the weight, picked up speed and
soon disappeared in the distance.

Barlow swiftly closed the distance to the wagons, but
Priddle was equally fast heading toward him, though he was
on the other side of the wagons. Barlow whipped his rifle
up and fired at Priddle. He cursed loudly when he missed.
He shoved the rifle through the loop on the saddle, and then
flattened out on the mule's neck when he saw Priddle ready
to fire. The ball whizzed over his head, close enough for
him to hear its buzz.

He straightened and pulled his single-shot pistol. He raced
up alongside the wagon that was now last, stuck his pistol
out and fired at Normand Daigineault.

Just as he did, the wagon bumped over some ruts, bouncing wildly, and the shot plowed into the wood on its side.

"Shit," Barlow roared. Beelzebub was still thundering
along, closing in on the next wagon. Barlow shoved the
pistol away and pulled out the small Colt Paterson revolver.
He drew alongside the next wagon, driven, he now saw, by
Jorge Gutierrez. He fired all five shots, and Gutierrez
slumped sideways, then rolled off the far side of the wagon,
where he was run over by the wagon behind him. Gutierrez's wagon, like the first one, soon veered off the track
now that it had no one to guide it. It crashed, too, and the
mules raced off.

Barlow nodded. He had done some damage without being
harmed. Still, the odds were not good. Five of them remained, and only one of him, and all his guns were empty.
He shoved the small Colt into his belt and grabbed his rifle,
reloading as he galloped, though he had swung off to his
right, away from the wagons.

Barlow glanced back. Buffalo 2 had leaped onto the back
of Daigineault's wagon, scrambled up to the front, and
latched his teeth into Daigineault's shoulder. A jolt of the
wagon knocked the dog's muzzle away from the man, and
before the Newfoundland could sink his fangs in again, Priddle pulled up short and fired. Buffalo 2 yelped and tumbled
off the side of the wagon, landing hard and bouncing a few
times before coming to a halt, where he lay still.

Barlow's heart froze when he saw his faithful dog go
down. It was the second time he had lost a dog to an enemy.

And, like the last time, he was determined to get revenge on the ones who had killed him.

With a howl of rage and anguish, Barlow yanked Beelzebub's head around and once more raced toward the wagons. As soon as he had a good view of a driver—in this case, Ignacio Sanchez—he raised the rifle and fired again. He knew he hit Sanchez, but the man stayed upright. "Shit and damnation," Barlow barked. He continued racing forward until he was near Sanchez. He turned the mule so he was racing alongside the fast-moving wagon.

Suddenly he jumped from the mule, landing in the back of the wagon. The uneven pile of goods did not allow very good footing for some moments, but he finally steadied himself, though on hands and knees. He crawled toward Sanchez, who looked back in fear.

The Mexican driver grabbed his single-shot pistol. He stuck it over his shoulder with one hand while he fought to control the reins with the other. Without sighting, he fired.

But the harsh jolting of the wagon, combined with Sanchez's awkward position and fear, made the shot go well wide.

"Shoot at me, will you, you piece of shit?" Barlow bellowed. He scrabbled forward. Just behind Sanchez, he reared up as tall as he could on his knees and clamped his big, strong hands around the driver's neck. He squeezed, but not enough to kill Sanchez. Not yet. He jerked the man's head up until his bottom left the seat, then slammed him back down again. He repeated the maneuver. The activity caused Sanchez to pull in the reins, and the wagon slowed a little, then a little more, though it was still hurtling along at a great clip.

Barlow pushed to his feet, hauling Sanchez up as he did, and started to increase the pressure on the driver's neck. Sanchez dropped the reins and clawed at Barlow's hands, frantically trying to get free.

Then Barlow felt a searing pain in his head, and then nothing. He did not know he fell off the side of the wagon, landing hard on one shoulder and flopping to a stop.

14

WILL BARLOW AWOKE in a dim place. It was somewhat familiar yet entirely unknown at the same time. He knew he was inside, that much was certain, since there was little wind, at least compared with what he could hear blowing outside.

He rolled over onto his back and looked up. When he saw the hole and an odd assortment of what seemed to be poles, it slowly came to him that he was in an Indian lodge, which was disconcerting. As far as he knew, the only Indians out this way were Comanches. Or maybe Kiowas. Either way, it was not a comforting thought. From all that he had heard, either tribe was poor doin's for any white man who wound up in their hands.

His head throbbed fiercely, but he battled to ignore it as he tried to think. He needed to find out exactly where he was, how he got here and what was going to happen to him. Once he did that, he could make whatever plan he could come up with. He only hoped that these Indians were not as bloodthirsty as he had heard they were.

He was surprised to realize that his hands were not bound, and he considered that a good sign. He reached a hand up and touched his head, where his fingers encountered a swath of crusted-over dried blood along his left temple.

He remembered then the searing pain as the bullet grazed his head. He could not recall falling. He did, however, remember with a stab of agony in his heart that Buffalo 2 had gone under. He had seen the dog go down and not get up again. The pain of losing the faithful Newfoundland made the pain in his head seem inconsequential.

Barlow rolled over onto his stomach and started to push himself up. He quickly decided that was a foolish idea, and he flopped back down. He was sweating despite the fact that it was quite cool in the tepee, since there was no fire. His head pounded, and he felt sick to his stomach. He fought to keep from vomiting, though he supposed that even if he did, there wasn't much in his stomach to come out. Still, he did not want to go through it anyway.

As he rested there, the pain in his head lessened a little, and he got to wondering how long he had been unconscious, both out on the trail, and here in this lodge. Not that it really mattered, or would change anything; he just wanted to know.

He began drawing in long, slow, deep breaths, easing them out, hoping it would calm both his stomach and his head. It worked to some degree, though the pain remained intense. Then he made an effort to concentrate on relaxing and ignoring the pain. That did not work as well, and as the agony rose anew, the world went black on him again.

Once more he had no idea of how long he had been out. It was pretty much pitch black in the tepee, and up through the smoke hole he could see a few stars. "Night," he whispered. "Of the same day?" Knowing was not important, but not knowing was troublesome.

He tried again to get up, and this time succeeded, though he was quite unsteady once he got to his feet. He stood there, his head reeling, until the lodge, lit only by those stars above, stopped spinning around so wildly.

Gathering his strength and resolve, he shuffled to the flap that covered the opening. He pushed the buckskin aside and peered out. He saw few people around, and those were hurrying from one place to the next in the chill of the night. Plumes of vapor escaped Barlow's nose and mouth as he breathed steadily.

Deciding he had nothing to lose, he stepped outside. The cold night air was refreshing, and helped clear his head con-

siderably. He wondered if he should just walk off, find Beelzebub and then ride out. It seemed no one was paying any
attention to him.

Then he decided against it. He had no proof that these
Indians meant him any harm. After all, he was not bound
and there were no guards watching over him. Perhaps they
had brought him here to recover. With some tribes he had
met, that would not be unthought of; but with the stories of
the Comanches and their allies, the Kiowas, still in his mind,
he had a hard time believing that was the case.

Besides, it was cold and likely to get even colder before
dawn, and he had no blankets, food, weapons or sleeping
robe. It would be almost certain death to just head out now.
But if not tonight, then certainly in the next several days.

Shivering a little, he went back inside and sat. His stomach growled with hunger, but despite a search of the lodge—
moving slowly on his knees and simply feeling every inch
of the place—he found nothing at all to eat. Nor was there
anything else useful to him—no weapons, no blankets, no
old buffalo robes.

With a sigh, Barlow lay down, curling himself up as
tightly as he could to conserve his heat, and let himself drift
off to sleep.

He awoke stiffly in the morning. Sunlight poured through
the smoke hole. The pain in his head was almost gone,
which was a relief. All in all, he was in good spirits. Or at
least he was until he remembered Buffalo 2, which soured
him on life again. And he pledged then and there that he
would get out of this village—if they tried to keep him here
against his will—and track down Enos Priddle and his four
remaining cronies and kill them, not only for slaughtering
Muldoon, Kilkenny and Camacho, but also for the slaying
of Buffalo 2.

Barlow stood and walked to the entrance, shoved aside
the flap and looked out. There was a fair amount of activity,
about what one would expect in any Indian village when
the weather was like this. He stepped out into the bright but
hardly warming sunlight. Several of the tribespeople looked
at him, but he could not read their faces. They could have
hated him or had pity for him, or just thought of him as a
potential friend. He had no idea of what to think.

He glanced around, wondering if he should just approach someone and ask for something to eat. Then three warriors strode toward him. Their hair was loose, their faces, thankfully, unpainted. All wore moccasins, buckskin leggings and blankets held around their shoulders to ward off the cold. The three were fairly short, somewhat bowlegged, flat-nosed and dark-skinned. They looked mean to Barlow, though that did not really frighten him.

The warriors stopped in front of Barlow. The one smallest of height, a man several inches shorter than Barlow, spoke. "You come with me," he said forcefully, his accent thick and almost unintelligible. "We talk." He turned, ready to walk away.

"Hey, hold on there, hoss," Barlow said. "I need to fill my meatbag somethin' awful."

The warrior turned back to face him. "We talk. Then food."

"Nope. Food first. Then talk." Barlow was tired of all this already. His head still hurt—though not badly—he was tired, hungry, frustrated, angry. He figured that if they were going to kill him, they might as well try to do so now. If they weren't planning on killing him, they could surely wait a few minutes before questioning him for whatever reasons they might have or think they had.

The warrior stared at him for more than a minute. Then he nodded once, curtly. "We eat," he announced. "Then talk. Come." This time he did not turn until he was sure Barlow was going to follow him.

"Lead on, hoss," Barlow said with a gracious sweep of his arm.

He followed the short warrior, while the other two fell in behind him. He didn't like that, but there was nothing he could do about it, so he said nothing and just walked.

The four entered a large, colorfully painted tepee. Barlow was impressed. Judging by the pictures on the lodge, this warrior was one to be reckoned with. His exploits were imposing, and Barlow figured him to be a chief, though perhaps only a war chief. To look at him, one would never have come to that conclusion.

Inside, the three Indians and Barlow sat around a decent-sized central fire. There were no social amenities, which

surprised Barlow. Any tribe he had met before would have
had a pipe and offered the smoke to the Four Directions,
before having any kind of important parley.

Instead, two women—one old, wrinkled and looking frail,
the other young and almost attractive—served food to the
men after a command by the leader. They ate mostly in
silence, only the slurping, gobbling and swallowing breaking
the quiet. Barlow was powerful hungry and scoffed down
four bowls of buffalo stew and three cups of coffee. He
pulled out his pipe. "You boys mind?" he asked.

The chief shook his head. Realizing that Barlow had no
tobacco, he took some of his own and tossed it to the white
man.

Barlow nodded. "Obliged," he said as he stuffed the bowl
of the pipe with tobacco. He grabbed a small burning stick
from the fire and used it to get the tobacco going. He sighed
as the smoke hit his lungs. "Now, hoss," he said, "I reckon
it's time we had us our talk."

"I am Slow Eagle," the chief said.

Barlow nodded. "I am Will Barlow. What tribe are you?"

"We are Nermernuh—The People. Others call us Comanches."

Barlow nodded again. It was a common thing among Indian people. All of those he had encountered had a name
for themselves that meant that or something similar.

"How long have I been here?" he asked.

"We found you yesterday," Slow Eagle said slowly, struggling with his English. "We bring you here."

Barlow was still having trouble understanding the middle-
aged warrior, but he was getting the gist of it.

"Why did you bring me here?" Barlow figured there was
no reason to delay in asking his questions.

The three Comanches talked for a bit among themselves,
in their own language. Finally Slow Eagle looked at Barlow
and said flatly, "We will make you die. Slowly. You'll have
much pain."

Barlow repressed an involuntary shiver. That meant they
planned to torture him, not a very settling thought. "Why?"
he asked, glaring across the fire at Slow Eagle.

"You our enemy." It was said simply, as if that explained
everything.

"Me?" Barlow said in surprise. "Your enemy? How the hell do you figure that, hoss? I ain't even seen you—or your people—before this."

"You and friends, you attack our village."

"Like hell I did, hoss," Barlow snapped, irritation growing. He had no idea where these Comanches had gotten such a notion. "Like I said, I ain't ever seen none of you before you come for me just a little bit ago. Hell, I ain't ever even been in this land before."

"You lie," Slow Eagle snarled. "You and the others killed four of my people."

"When was I supposed to have done this?" Barlow asked, growing angrier by the second.

"Three moons ago," Slow Eagle said after taking a few moments to figure out the timing.

Barlow shook his head. "Look, hoss, three months ago, I was way to the west, out by the big water. A place called Californy. Me and my amigo, White Bear. He's a Shoshoni." He threw that in because he vaguely recalled White Bear once telling him that the Comanches and Shoshonis were distant relatives. Barlow now hoped it was true and that it might help convince these warriors that he had had nothing to do with an attack on their village.

The three Comanches talked among themselves again for a minute or two, then Slow Eagle shook his head. "Not believe," he said harshly.

"Then you're a goddamn moron," Barlow snarled, letting some of his temper emerge.

Slow Eagle started, and his eyes narrowed angrily. No one had ever spoken to him in such a way, and he vowed that when the time came to torture this bulky, loudmouthed white man, he would make sure the pain lasted a long, long time.

Barlow ignored the dangerous look the chief gave him. "If the ones who did that to you are the ones I think they are, then they're my enemies, too." He was a bit more calm, though it was not easy to maintain that fragile serenity. "Them skunks kilt three good men yesterday. Or, I reckon, it was the day before now. Kilt them, then stole all the goods on the one man's wagons. When I chased 'em down, I kilt two of them before one of 'em give me this." He touched the crusted blood on his head. "Even worse, they kilt my dog. He was worth more'n all them scabrous bastards put together." The remembrance brought another wave of heartache to Barlow, and he struggled to choke it back, with only partial success.

Slow Eagle grunted in annoyance. "You probably shot by one of the men you and the others robbed," he said tightly.

"Listen, you dopey sack of sh—"

"Enough!" Slow Eagle roared. "Like all white men, you speak with the tongue of a snake." He held out his hand with the first two fingers separated a bit, indicating a reptile's forked tongue. "You will die for what you—and those others of you—did to The People. The more you deny, the longer your death takes."

Barlow tensed. He knew he could easily take these three men, no matter how good they were as warriors. But what would that get him? Such a fight would stir up a lot of noise, and that, in turn, would bring the rest of the warriors running, and while he knew he was good and a hell of a fighter, he could not take on ten, twelve, maybe fifteen warriors all at once. Especially not when he was unarmed. He sat, seething but breathing deeply to keep himself from doing something rash.

"You go now," Slow Eagle said with finality. "We will come for you when the time right. Tomorrow maybe. Or the day after." He shrugged. "Maybe longer. Who knows?" He looked from one of his fellow warriors to the other and spoke in his own language.

The two jumped up and grabbed Barlow. While one wrestled Barlow to the ground facedown—he didn't know it, but Barlow allowed it—the other quickly bound Barlow's hands behind his back with some braided rawhide rope. They hauled him up and marched him out of the lodge, through the village and to the tepee in which he had awakened. On the short trip, he was subjected to a heap of abuse—virtually all of it in Comanche, so he couldn't understand it. He could, however, see how the people looked at him. And it took no genius to know that he was hated when old women spit at him and threw small rocks or sticks at him. He kept his face stolid throughout, but he cursed when he was shoved into the lodge and landed hard on the same shoulder he had hurt when falling off the wagon.

15

SINCE HE WASN'T going anywhere for a while, Barlow lay there for a long time, assessing his condition. His head still hurt but it was not much more than a minor distraction. His shoulder was painful, but when he was able to move it a little—which wasn't much because of his bonds—it didn't seem to be broken. It would not hamper him too much in a fight, which was looking more and more likely if he were to get out of here.

As for his situation—it didn't look good at all, and he knew it. Still, he was determined to get out of this village before the Comanches could begin torturing him. Just how he was going to do that was yet to be seen. He had no weapons; didn't even know where they were. Same with Beelzebub, though if it came down to it, he could as easily ride a Comanche pony if he had to. He'd miss the mule, of course, but that would be the least of his concerns. Without weapons, he was in serious trouble. That was the main problem, since he probably would have to fight his way out of here. For that he would need weapons to have any chance at all of success. And even if he didn't have to battle his way out of the village, without weapons he would be in serious trouble out on the prairie. He would be unable to hunt, unable to defend himself if the Comanches came after him.

Then there was also the matter of his possibles. Most he

could probably live without—even a few smaller necessities such as his folding knife and tobacco—though he did not relish the thought. But without his sleeping robe—or some stolen blankets—he would most likely freeze to death before he got more than twenty miles from here.

Barlow fell asleep after a while, worn out from his working over his situation in his mind, as well as from the residual pain from his head wound. When he awoke, his mind was clear, but his way out of here still was not.

He was hungry again, and he wondered if the Comanches were planning to starve him to death. That would be a hell of a way to die, he thought. But a couple of hours later, they brought in a bowl of the same type of buffalo stew as he had that morning, though he quickly found out this was considerably less tasty and mighty spare on the meat. He guessed that since the Comanches were going to kill him, they didn't have to worry about feeding him.

When the boy of about twelve warily entered the lodge with the bowl of food, Barlow asked, "You speak English, boy?"

The boy gave him a quizzical look, which Barlow took to be a negative. The youth—who would, Barlow presumed, go on his first hunt and maybe even his first war party in the spring—set the bowl down a few feet from Barlow.

The white man jerked his arms to his side as far as he could and with his chin sort of pointed to the rope binding him. "Ain't you gonna take these off me, boy?" he asked, knowing the youth wouldn't understand the words, but would, with hope, understand through the gestures.

The youngster shook his head vigorously, backed up until he was almost at the flap leading out, then spun and slipped outside.

"Goddamn heathen bastards," Barlow muttered, his temper flaring. He stewed for a few minutes, then shrugged and sighed. If he was going to eat—and he would have to if he was to keep his strength up—he would have to make do. He fell to the side, then managed to roll himself until he was on his stomach. He crawled like a snake until his face was above the bowl. Feeling the anger surge inside him again, he lowered his head until his mouth was touching the meal.

Eating in such a way wasn't easy, and the food was poor, but he managed to get most of it down. He rolled onto his back and belched, wincing at the reminder of the foul meal. He sighed. Being humiliated by being forced to eat in that manner was far from his most important worry—which remained finding a way out of here.

No plan presented itself over the next several hours, and Barlow began to worry that he might not be able to accomplish what he had promised himself he would do. He struggled to sit up, then looked around the lodge. He had done so before, several times, and had found nothing he could use. But he wanted to give the tepee another survey, this one more slowly, eyes looking for anything, no matter how small, that might help.

His eyes flicked over the dirt an inch at a time, but the biggest thing he saw was a pebble, and that was far too small and too round to do him any good. He fell back, hitting the back of his head on the dirt, though not hard enough to hurt. He lay there uncomfortably on his bound hands, staring up at the smoke hole, hoping for inspiration, but none was forthcoming.

He dozed off again, and when he awoke, it was dusk. Once more he struggled until he was in a sitting position, in anticipation that he would be brought more food. He didn't think they would feed him out of the goodness of their hearts. He figured they would simply feed him enough of whatever dregs they had to keep him alive and relatively healthy so that he would last longer while being tortured.

He didn't have to wait long before another warrior-to-be brought in another bowl of the same watery slop. The youth put the bowl down next to the empty one, before picking that one up.

As he turned to leave, Barlow asked, without any real hope, "You speak any English, boy?"

He turned back and said, "Some."

Barlow's eyes widened. "What's your name, hoss?"

"Lame Dog."

"I was wonderin', Lame Dog," Barlow said slowly so the youth would understand, and carefully so it sounded like an innocent question, "who was it among your people who got my mule and weapons?"

The youth did not seem upset at the inquiry. "Slow Eagle take guns. One big, two little. Running Bull take mule. Put it with his horses. Many ponies."

"Is Running Bull a great warrior?"

Lame Dog nodded. "Great. Very. Almost like Slow Eagle."

"Then it looks like those most deserving got my plunder," Barlow said quietly, as if musing.

Lame Dog nodded. "I go now," he announced, and without saying anything else, he spun and left.

As Barlow maneuvered clumsily into position to slurp down his meal like a dog, he was pleased with himself. He had learned where his mule and weapons were. If—no, he corrected himself in his head, when—he got out of here, he would know where to go for them. And he *would* get them. He was as sure of that as he was of escaping.

He finished his meager meal and rolled onto his back, then up until he was sitting again. He wiped his chin and mouth off as best he could on the shoulders of his shirt, craning his neck as far as he could to do so. As with everything else since he had been bound, it was an uncomfortable action, but as with all the rest, he ignored it as best he could.

It was fully dark now, though a good-sized moon provided a bit of light. Barlow looked up at the smoke hole and once more tried to figure out a way to escape. But still nothing came to him. In annoyance and anger, he began flexing his arms, straining to either break the rawhide bonds or at least loosen them enough to where he might be able to wriggle free of them.

But he made no progress that he could feel, and after what he estimated as half an hour, he gave up. He was breathing heavily from the exertion, and from anger. He waited awhile, then began striving at his binds again, getting nowhere, resting, trying again.

Finally he could struggle no more, and he fell back, chest heavy, to rest. Moments after he did that, he could hear a terrible chorus of growling and snarling dogs. While it was not unusual for the many dogs running rampant in an Indian village to fight for dominance, this sounded far more serious. It went on for what seemed like a long time, and then slowly wound down until it finally stopped.

Barlow groaned. The canine battle had brought back vivid memories of Buffalo 2, and the loss once more weighed heavily on his heart. "Goddammmit, dog," he muttered, "why'd you have to go and get yourself put under?"

He sighed, trying hard to put the gloomy thoughts out of his mind. He did not really succeed, though he did manage to lessen them somewhat.

He rolled over on his side, planning to get some sleep. Maybe he could think more clearly in the morning, and maybe even find some way to help himself. Maybe when they fed him in the morning—if they fed him—whoever brought it might have a knife on him. Barlow was pretty confident that even with his hands bound behind his back, he could take most any man, or at least knock him down and then jump on him or something. He realized it was a foolish idea, but he was beginning to think that something such as that would be the only way he could get out of this lodge, and this village.

As he tried to shut down his whirling mind so he could fall asleep, he suddenly heard something outside the lodge. That was not all that unusual, except that this sound came from the rear of the tepee. "What the hell?" he mumbled. He pushed himself up and listened intently. The sound came again, familiar enough to tug at his mind. He scooted on his behind toward the back of the lodge, stopped and then listened again.

Suddenly there was a great rending sound, and something big and dark burst through the fresh opening that appeared in the skin of the lodge.

"Sweet jumpin' Jesus!" Barlow muttered urgently, taken aback by the sudden apparition. He rocked backward, hoping to get out of the way of whatever ravaging beast was attacking him. As he landed, he accidentally rolled onto one side, taking his sight away from the creature. Before he could do anything to flee or protect himself, the beast was on him.

What poor doin's this is, Barlow thought. *All those years in the mountains facing Indians and grizzly bears and wolves and bitter cold and snow taller than any building I ever saw, here I'm goin' under in a Comanche lodge, tied up like a chicken for some beast's dinner.*

Barlow braced himself, as he expected large chunks of his flesh to be torn out any second now. He felt the creature's hot breath on his face and then . . .

He jerked his head around, and his eyes widened until they were the size of a warrior's war shield. "Buffler?" he gasped as the big Newfoundland laved Barlow's face with his tongue. "Goddamn, boy, where'd you come from?" he whispered.

The dog stopped licking and pawed at Barlow's shoulder. "Leave off doin' that, Buffler," Barlow hissed. "I'm all tied up here, and can't pet you."

Buffalo 2 went back to licking his face, and Barlow suddenly laughed, realizing that the dog was lapping his face as much for the residue of Barlow's supper as for his joy in being reunited with his master.

"Dammit, now, Buffler," Barlow said sternly, though still quietly. "leave off doin' that, I said."

The dog backed up a little, and Barlow strained to roll over on his stomach. When he did, he rested his right cheek in the dirt. "Chew off them ropes, Buffler," he said, jerking his hands as much as he could, to get the Newfoundland to look at them.

Buffalo 2 was puzzled for a bit, and Barlow continued to coax him into doing what he wanted. The dog finally caught on and gingerly began gnawing at the rawhide rope.

Barlow was glad Buffalo 2 was a Newfoundland, with his fairly short snout. It made it a lot easier for the dog to get his teeth working on the bindings.

It seemed like hours before the bindings were gnawed through enough for Barlow to snap them the rest of the way, but he knew it was probably less than thirty minutes. Barlow pushed himself up, easily now, until he was sitting. He rubbed each wrist for a few minutes, trying to get the circulation going again. Then he grinned a bit and grabbed Buffalo 2 gently behind the ears and massaged the spots vigorously. The Newfoundland whined quietly in happiness.

"Damn, boy, if you ain't some now," Barlow said eagerly but also softly. He did not want to alert any Comanches who might be walking by the lodge. "How'd you get away, Buffler?" He rose up to his knees and started stroking the dog's neck and shoulders. He immediately encountered a patch of dried blood across the back of his neck. "So that's what happened," he muttered. "Winged you just like they did me," he said. "Damn, I thought you was gone under for certain."

He continued to pet the dog for some more minutes, trying to allow his relief and joy to calm down some. He wanted to get out of here immediately, but he was so excited that roaming through the village in his state might be suicidal.

Finally, though, he decided he was ready. "It's time to get ourselves out of here, boy." He stood up, brushing dirt off his clothes. He stretched, feeling some of the effects of the gunshot, the injury to his shoulder and of being tied up for so long. He was stiff and sore, but feeling rather good otherwise, now that he was about to be free.

"Let's go, Buffler," Barlow said, pushing past the dog, heading for the hole that Buffalo 2 had torn in the back of the lodge. "But you got to be quiet, boy. You know that, don't you?"

Buffalo 2 snuffled and butted the palm of Barlow's hand with his nose, as if to say, *Of course, I know that, you fool.*

Barlow stopped at the opening, pulled it apart a little and stuck his head out just far enough to be able to look both ways. He did not expect to see anyone back there, but he had to be sure. When he was certain, he slipped out of the tepee and turned left. Buffalo 2 was right behind him, a black shadow amid the black shadows.

There was enough moonlight out in the open to be able to see pretty well, so it was relatively easy for man and dog to meander toward Slow Eagle's lodge. At one point, a warrior came out of a lodge and went behind it to relieve himself, Barlow and Buffalo 2 froze, crouching in shadows, until the Comanche went back inside.

Several dogs wandered a bit closer, taking an interest, but a low growl from Buffalo 2 sent them packing. Barlow realized that the dogfight he had heard must have been when Buffalo 2 entered the village and was challenged by the ragtag curs that lived there. Since the Newfoundland looked none the worse for wear, and judging by the village canines' reaction to Buffalo 2's growl, the big Newfoundland must have been the victor in that little brawl.

Minutes later, they stopped outside the rear of Slow Eagle's lodge.

16

BARLOW SQUATTED OUTSIDE Slow Eagle's lodge for some time, wondering how he should go about getting his weapons, saddle and possibles back. No matter how much he hated the Comanches for what they had done—and planned to do—to him, he had no real desire to sneak into the lodge and kill everyone in there so he had the time to leisurely find his belongings. On the other hand, he could not sit out here all night, waiting for the daylight, when the people would all leave the tepee. Avoiding detection would be impossible then.

The chill wind began to seep into him, and he knew he had to do something soon. Staying here much longer would be unhealthy for him, and as he grew colder and colder, his job would become that much more difficult.

He sighed, his breath creating a large, fast-fading cloud in front of his face. He had no real choice; he could not try running with no weapons, coat, sleeping robe or fire-making gear. He simply had to go in there and try to get his things without hurting anyone. And if someone did discover him, he would do whatever was required.

Barlow patted Buffalo 2's head for a few moments, then said, "You stay out here, boy. Keep watch in case anyone comes around." He pushed up to his feet as the dog licked his hand.

Barlow stooped in front of the flap and eased it open, just

enough for him to slip through. He stopped where he was, squatting, listening intently and letting his eyes adjust to the darkness. Once they did, he could see pretty well with the brightly glowing embers of the fire in the center of the lodge. He carefully looked around. Slow Eagle was asleep, snoring softly, a woman next to him, at the rear of the lodge. A younger couple slept to his left. Three children were off to his right, and near them was an old woman, who muttered and snorted in sleep.

His saddle, sleeping robe and possibles sack were along the buffalo-skin wall of the tepee between Slow Eagle and the young couple. His rifle and pistols dangled from a weapons rack, which surprised him. He had thought the weapons would be hidden, though when he thought about it now, there was no reason Slow Eagle would have hidden them. The warrior had nothing to be afraid of where they were concerned.

He did not see his tomahawk or knife, but he could take one of those belonging to one of the Comanches if need be.

He crept forward on hands and knees, moving slowly, trying to make no sound. Twice he froze, his breathing shallow, as one of the people shifted in sleep. Once the Comanche was settled again, Barlow moved on, edging ever closer to the weapons rack, which was between the fire and where Slow Eagle and the woman slept.

When he reached it, he rose, and then stood silently, making sure he was still unnoticed. Satisfied, he eased the pistols off the rack and stuffed them into his belt. He slid the powder horn and shooting bag over his shoulder, then took the rifle in his left hand.

He walked now, rather than crawled, with the rifle in hand, toward the saddle. He took a step, stopped, waiting a second or two, then repeated the process. At last he reached the saddle and knelt. The sleeping robe was tied to the back of the saddle, and the drawstring on the possibles bag was looped over the saddle horn, as were the bridle, bit and reins. Taking a few deep, quiet breaths, Barlow reached down with his right hand, grasped the saddle horn and smoothly hoisted it up, swinging it slightly so that the saddle rested down his back, his hand holding the saddle horn on his shoulder.

Once more he waited to make sure his movements had

not wakened anyone. The younger warrior stirred, but settled right back down. Barlow turned and began heading toward the flap and freedom, again moving one step, stopping, waiting, then proceeding.

He had almost completed his short, tense journey when a stirring behind him made him stop and look back over his shoulder. The young Comanche woman had risen and was stumbling toward him. She did not appear to have seen him, and he assumed she had simply gotten up and was heading outside to relieve herself. Trouble was, he was right in her path, and he could not let her give the alarm. He spun as quickly but as quietly as he could to face her.

She stopped, her eyes widening in surprise and fear as she noticed him for the first time. As she opened her mouth to scream an alarm, Barlow jerked the rifle up over his shoulder, took a step forward and slammed the woman in the head with the rifle butt. She went down like a sack of salt with the bottom ripped out.

Barlow stood, waiting to see if the action had roused anyone else. He didn't think so, since the woman had fallen without a sound. The only noise was the thunk of the rifle hitting her head. He was just thankful that she had not landed in the fire. She didn't miss it by much. He shrugged. It didn't matter how far she had missed it by, just that she had.

Barlow gave it a few more seconds, standing absolutely still, listening. But except for the usual sounds of people sleeping, there was nothing to indicate that anyone was the wiser about his presence. He turned slowly, took two silent steps, bent and slid out the entryway, shutting the flap as quickly as he dared so he would not let any cold air in and wake the people up.

Barlow breathed deep of the cold air. After the hot interior of the lodge, it was refreshing, and it cleared his head. Suddenly he was eager to be on the move. Everything seemed possible now in the crisp chill of the starlit night.

"C'mon, Buffler," he said quietly, "time we was shed of this here place." He stepped off, heading toward the horse herd not far away. He marched around and behind lodges, keeping out of the open as much as possible. He walked fast, Buffalo 2 at his side, their breathing making plumes in the frosty air.

As he neared the horses, he slowed, then stopped, looking around. Since he knew nothing of the Comanches' habits, he didn't know if they would have young men and older boys watching the herd at this time of year. Moments after he spotted one man—or boy, he wasn't certain—a cloud slid across the moon, darkening the area. But it did not last long, and when he could see fairly well again, he noticed a second horse herder. He spent a little longer watching, but saw no one else around the horses.

"Looks like we still got us a little work to do before we get out of here, Buffler," he muttered as he set down the saddle. Then he strode off, heading toward the first horse guard he had seen, keeping to the shadows whenever he could.

As he neared the man, he slowed, inching forward, coming up behind the guard—a boy who might have gone on his first hunting party this past summer. Barlow paused. Once more he had no desire to kill this youth. He crept forward, as silent as a ghost. He gave the youth the same treatment he had given the woman in Slow Eagle's lodge, only this time he slammed the Comanche in the back of the neck instead of the forehead. The Comanche slumped to the side with the barest of groans.

"One down, boy, one to go," Barlow said to the dog as he started moving again, heading for the other guard. This one, he found, was still young, though in his late teens, and therefore probably a seasoned warrior. As such, Barlow had a lot less compunction about killing him, seeing that he was a grown man. He slipped up behind the Comanche and snaked a thick left arm around the young man's neck, jerked him up and squeezed his throat before the warrior could cry out. In moments, he let the body fall.

"Well, that takes care of . . . ," he started. Then Buffalo 2 growled. Barlow frowned. "What is it, boy?" he asked, turning to look around. Before he had gotten all the way around, someone tackled him. As he and his assailant rolled on the frosty ground, Barlow realized he was in the grasp of a full-fledged warrior. Like many Comanches, this one was rather short, though he had a broad chest and powerful arms and legs.

They scrambled and scrabbled, each using fingers, feet, knees, fists trying to find a vulnerable spot in his opponent's defenses. Barlow was not afraid of this warrior, and was certain he could take him. His only concern was that the man might shout an alarm before he could be silenced.

Buffalo 2 bounded around frantically, hoping to be able to attack the man wrestling with his master. He wanted to bark, but understood somehow that such a thing would not be good.

The Comanche, half on top of Barlow, kneed him in the thigh, missing his groin by mere inches. The pain was quite bearable for Barlow, but it sent a surge of anger rushing through him. He had had his fill of these Comanches. He managed to grab a fistful of the Comanche's long hair and jerked the warrior's head back a little. He snapped his right hand up, the heel of it smashing into the underside of the warrior's jaw.

The Comanche grunted and shifted a little to the side as much of the fight went out of him. Barlow slammed the heel of his hand into the warrior's underjaw again, and the Indian slumped. Barlow shoved him off and to the side. He rose, then stomped on the Comanche's stomach, chest, face and neck. Finally the warrior lay still.

Barlow stood there, chest heaving, letting the anger in him simmer down some. Then he knelt and tugged the Comanche's tomahawk out and shoved it in his own belt. Then he pulled out the Indian's knife, slit the rawhide thong holding it on the young man's belt, tied it onto his own and slid the knife away.

Barlow ruffled the thick hair on Buffalo 2's head and neck. "You done good, boy," he said quietly. "Now, let's fine Beelzebub and get the hell out of this goddamn pit."

They walked off, wandering through the horses, looking for the big mule. It took a while, but Barlow finally found him. He grabbed the mule's mane and tugged him along. "C'mon, Beelzebub, you fractious ol' critter," he said. But his voice was soft, soothing. The black mule resisted only a moment, then allowed himself to be directed toward the side of the herd.

Barlow wasted no time saddling and bridling the mule, then mounting up. He sat there. "Well, dammit, Buffler," he said quietly, looking around, "which way should we go?"

He gave that some thought, then decided to head pretty much due north. He would cut the Santa Fe Trail, he assumed, not too far away. But then, he decided, he would continue heading north. He figured the Comanches would assume he began following the Santa Fe Trail as soon as he found it. But he couldn't travel fast enough to outrun the Comanches, unless he exhausted himself and Beelzebub.

He slipped on his blanket coat against the still dropping temperatures, then rode on. He skirted the village, moving slowly, not wanting to alert the villagers or their dogs, who might set up a cacophony of barking.

Then he was clear of the village and moving a little faster. He wanted to put as much distance between himself and the Comanche town as he could as fast as he could. Yet he was not about to run Beelzebub into the ground. He just set a decent pace and let the mule go. Buffalo 2 had no trouble keeping up.

As he rode across the lightly rolling barrenness, he loaded his rifle, then his pistols. As soon as he started to do so, he realized that he had very little in the way of powder and ball left. With such a long way to go to get to Missouri, he was going to have to carefully husband the powder and shot he had. That would make hunting a little tough. Even worse, if the Comanches caught up with him and a battle ensued, he could be in deep trouble.

He rummaged around in his possibles sack and came up with a few strips of jerky. He had nothing else to eat, so it would have to do. He was hungry, having eaten very little in almost two full days. He gnawed at the jerky, hating it, but needing the sustenance it would provide.

It began to snow, though it was not coming down hard. At first, Barlow was annoyed by it. Then he realized that if it kept up, it would cover any tracks he might make, thereby making it more difficult for the Comanches to track him.

By morning, he had reached what he thought was the Arkansas River, some miles north of the Trail, which he had cut across a couple of hours earlier. It was still snowing, though it was rather fitful. He took the risk of firing a shot and downed a lone buffalo he spotted. He butchered out as much meat as he thought he could safely carry—he wasn't worried about it going bad in these temperatures, but Beelzebub could carry only so much. Barlow walked, then, having loaded the mule as much as he dared. He had considered staying there for a day or two and just feeding off the buffalo carcass, but decided that might be dangerous. The Comanches—or the Kiowas or perhaps even warriors from some other tribe—might find him there. So he walked two miles, roughly following the river east.

Tired, hungry and still irritated at all that had happened to him, Barlow finally called it a day. He pulled into a thick stand of trees and brush abutting the river. He unloaded the meat from Beelzebub, then unsaddled the mule and tended him perfunctorily, but good enough for the time being. He gathered wood, built a small fire and set some meat on to cook. He searched his possibles sack again and found enough coffee for perhaps a cup or two, and his small, battered coffeepot. He put the coffee on, needing its heat and energy. He would worry about being without tomorrow. Or the next day.

He ate heartily, grateful for the rich, red, life- and energy-giving meat. He regularly tossed chunks of it to Buffalo 2, almost grinning as he watched the dog gobble them down.

Barlow drank the coffee slowly, however, savoring it. He drank about half of one cup while he ate, saving another half mug or so for afterward, when he dug out his pipe, packed it with tobacco and lit it. There was enough for one last, not-quite-full mug of coffee, which he saved for the morning.

He leaned back against an old log and relaxed, puffing. Had he been elsewhere—and had his old companion White Bear been with him—he would have been close to contented.

Finally he knocked the ashes from the pipe into the fire, slipped out of his capote and slid into his sleeping robe. It took only a few minutes for him to warm up, and not much more than that to fall asleep near the fire, Buffalo 2 stretched out alongside him.

17

IT WAS NOT the easiest journey he'd ever had, but he had faced far worse. He had spent all that day and the next in the spot where he had stopped. He needed the rest, as did the mule, and he figured that the Comanches would be looking for him well to the east.

Finally, however, he headed off again. He hunted only every third or fourth day, trying to stretch out the ammunition he had. He would take out enough meat to last for a few days, but he ate sparingly of that, too, because he was limited in how much could be carried.

He followed the basic course of the Arkansas River, heading east and northeast. It kept him on a steady path, as well as providing an unlimited supply of fresh water. The heavy stands of trees along the banks, only a couple of hundred yards from the barren prairie, offered fuel for fires.

It snowed off and on, never accumulating much, but it was enough to be aggravating. After a few days, he didn't care much that it would cover his tracks. He was just sick of the snow, how it blurred the horizon, how it melted and seeped down his neck, how it made finding dry wood difficult at times.

With some frequency, he had to cache in the wooded spots along the river to avoid small parties of warriors—most likely hunters—of one kind or another. He was not familiar with the tribes down this way, but from what talk he had heard from fellow mountaineers back in his mountain days, he figured there had to be Kiowas, Cheyennes and Pawnees, at least. It was irritating to have to hide like that, and bruising to his ego. He knew he could kill the two, three, maybe four men who were in these small hunting parties. But he could not afford to waste the powder and ball on taking them out. He had to conserve it in case he was attacked. That did not mean he liked it, though, so he did only what was necessary.

He crossed the Arkansas River a couple days after leaving his camping spot, seeming to recall that Seamus Muldoon had said the river headed too far east and not nearly north enough for him. He picked up the Santa Fe Trail on the north side of the river. Over the next couple of weeks, he crossed seven creeks or so, none of which he was familiar with. This was, for him, all uncharted country. A few weeks after that, he came to a spot that looked like a staging area for wagons heading to Santa Fe. He remembered that Muldoon had told him about this place, calling it Council Grove.

Barlow decided to spend a couple of days there. He was in no hurry, really, and wanted to rest himself, Buffalo 2 and Beelzebub. Plus he knew that he must be getting fairly close to the Settlements, though he still couldn't afford to waste ammunition. He was almost out, and if he stayed here a couple of days, he could eat his fill of fresh meat—he was sure he could find some—without having to overburden himself or the mule. It would give him the rest and strength he would need for the last leg of the journey.

As he had all along, while he stayed at Council Grove, he wished he had coffee. Fresh water and melted snow were all right now and again, but a man needed coffee to live as much as he needed meat, which he ate plenty of during this short hiatus. But he had no coffee, and he tried to push the desire for it out of his mind and just relax. Almost as bad as not having coffee was not having any tobacco. He had finished the last of it more than three weeks ago.

But the worst was being without female companionship. He could not help but recall the times he had spent with Rosaria and Natividad—especially the latter. He could easily see her lush body, the smoky look of lust in her eyes. It was near to almost driving him mad at times.

Despite the lack of these much-desired items, the time spent at Council Grove was generally restful. When he finally resumed his trek, he was in a better frame of mind.

He was a little surprised as he traveled that he had not seen any sign of Muldoon's stolen wagons and cargo. He had thought he would, and that Slow Eagle's Comanches—or another band—would have encountered them while looking for him. Unless, he thought, they had found the bandits before he had gotten back on the Trail again.

He more than half hoped that he would come across the wreckage of the wagons on his travels—and the killers' bodies carved up by the Comanches. On the other hand, the longer he rode, the more he became determined that the men who had done this to him and the others had to be brought to account for their heinous misdeeds, and he planned to be the one to visit that vengeance on them. He did not want the Comanches to have that honor.

Since he had not seen them—or their remains—on the Trail, he would have to try to track them down once he was in the Settlements, and that would be no easy task, he figured. He was certain that Enos Priddle and his men would be long gone from anywhere near Independence or Westport, the cities that were the terminus for the Santa Fe Trail. There was a good chance that they had moved on to St. Louis, which had a bustling and diverse population, a city where men like Ignacio Sanchez and José Abrego would not seem any more out of place than Enos Priddle or Robert Dunsmore.

He finally made it to Westport, and he spent several days there, looking for the men who had killed Muldoon, Carlos Camacho and Tom Kilkenney and left him and Buffalo 2 on the prairie to die. He had some money left, so he bought some powder and ball first off. He had no luck finding any of Priddle's men, so after a few days, he bought enough supplies for a couple of days and headed to Independence, less than a day's ride east.

Barlow spent some time there, too, once more looking for the bandits. As in Westport, there was no sign of them. Using most of his rapidly dwindling funds, he bought more supplies and headed for St. Louis. In two weeks of leisurely riding—taking his time as much to give Beelzebub a break

as because of the periodic snow, sleet and hail—he reached
the outskirts of St. Charles. He stopped there and sat to think
for a spell. While he wanted to go the short distance to St.
Louis and hunt for Priddle and the others, for some reason
he felt pulled toward visiting St. Charles. That was quite
strange. He had not been back there—his hometown area—
since he had left more than a dozen years ago. It was in-
explicable that he would suddenly feel a compulsion to return.

He had nothing there, really—his parents had wanted
nothing more to do with him when he left, and he had no
reason to think they would feel differently now. Nor had he
and his brothers ever gotten along. And, after all this time,
what few friends he had would probably not even recognize
him. He expected that they would all be married, settled
down on farms or in town jobs and not have time for the
likes of him—a half-savage former mountain man. A man
with plenty of blood on his hands. A man with a long string
of romances behind him with women of various Indian
nations as well as Mexicans. A man who had married an
Indian woman and had two children by her. A man whose
best friend now was a Shoshoni warrior with a British accent. A man whose wife and infant son had been slaughtered
and his young daughter kidnapped. A man who had spent
years searching for that daughter, only to leave her in the
care of a Mexican family when he finally tracked her down.

Any of it would shock the good people of St. Charles,
even his old friends.

He shook his head in annoyance. Maybe that was why he
was being pulled toward the area—to shock the people
there. To show them that a man could have a passel of
adventures the likes of which they could not even dream of.
He suspected that he just wanted to show off, to rub the
noses of his family and old friends in the fact that he had
done so much, while they sat there and rotted on their farms,
likely as not with a nagging wife and a brood of howling
children. They would be old before their time. And worn
out, exhausted by the daily fight for survival, by the strain
of trying to bring in enough money to feed their children;
by the constant pressure of having to pray for rain, or an
end to the rain; for sunshine, or for floods to bypass them;

for no late freeze in the spring, or early ones in the fall.

Suddenly Barlow's life, even with all its faults, flaws, trauma and heartache, seemed pretty damn good. A lot better, he believed, than the lives of anyone he had known before he had left here for the mountains.

Not arguing with himself any more, he simply clucked to Beelzebub and headed toward St. Charles. He looked fondly at Buffalo 2, trotting a few yards to his left and ahead of the mule. The people of the St. Charles area would be impressed with the Newfoundland, too, he was sure.

The town had grown considerably since he had last been there. It was a thriving place, the Missouri River waterfront bustling with activity. Steamboats were tied up at several docks and goods of all kinds were being loaded and unloaded. He clacked down a cobblestone street a block from the waterfront, taking in the new shops and such. He stopped in front of a tavern and shook his head. What had been the Pig Iron Tavern—his favorite watering hole when he was younger—was now the Bull's Horn Tavern. He shrugged, dismounted, tied Beelzebub to a hitching post and headed inside, rifle in hand, Buffalo 2 at his side.

He stopped just inside and took a quick survey. He recognized no one. Not even the bartender, though when he thought of it, he couldn't figure why he would have believed the same bartender would be here after all these years. Smiley Watkins had been no youngster back then; if he was still alive—which Barlow doubted—he would be well up in years.

Barlow walked to the bar and set his rifle on it. As the bartender sidled over, Barlow laid down one of his few remaining coins. "A bottle of your best," he said.

The bartender scooped up the coin, got a bottle and a glass, and set them down on the bar in front of Barlow. "Enjoy, mister," he said with absolutely no hint of respect in his voice.

Barlow shrugged, pulled the cork from the bottle and poured some into the glass. He gulped the whole thing down in one swallow, then smacked his lips in pleasure. "Ah, that's some now," he said, half grinning down at the dog.

He refilled the glass, turned and leaned back against the

bar so he could watch the people in the saloon. He pushed his floppy old hat back and took a sip. Two young men at one table were glaring at him and talking silently between themselves. Barlow held his glass out to them in a mock salute.

Face suffused with anger, one of the men jerked to his feet and stomped toward Barlow. Buffalo 2 growled low and bared his fangs a little. The man hesitated. Barlow looked down at the Newfoundland and said quietly, "Relax, boy." He looked at the man approaching him. "You don't need to be afeared of this dog, hoss," he said evenly.

The man's face burnt even hotter, and he marched forward again. He tried to look fierce, but he kept flicking his eyes at the Newfoundland, who maintained a wary eye on him. The man stopped a foot or so in front of Barlow, who had not really moved. He still stood, resting on one elbow on the bar, a drink in his hand.

"Somethin' I can do for you, hoss?" Barlow asked casually, but with a hint of iron in his words.

"Seems you been starin' at me and my pal over there. You got a problem with us?"

"Not a'tall, hoss."

"Then why was you starin' at us and mockin' us?" the young man demanded. He was angry and cocky, and had forgotten all about the dog.

"I didn't do no such thing, hoss," Barlow said a little more harshly. "Now, go set your ass back down over there before I'm forced to raise hair on you."

"You sure talk funny, mister," the man said with a hollow laugh.

Barlow shrugged. "What's your name, hoss?" he asked, voice polite again for the time being.

"Luke Fitzhugh," he spat out, "not that it's any of your account."

"Well, Mr. Fitzhugh," Barlow said quietly, though his eyes pierced his pest's, "my name is Will Barlow. Now, I expect that don't mean much to you, but you might want to listen to me. I got the hair of the bear on me, boy, and I ain't ever took shit from a skunk like you. Now, if you got any sense a'tall in that thick goddamn head of yours, you'll go on back to your table, set your ass down and leave me the hell alone."

"Or what?"

"You really don't want to know that, hoss." Barlow's voice was calm, but there was no denying its strength and warning.

"Go to hell, you dumb ol' fart," Fitzhugh snapped. "I ain't afraid of no ancient feller like you. Hell, you put on that funny—and high goddamn smellin'—outfit and expect us all to tremble? Shee-et, you must be dumber'n I thought."

"You sure you don't want to just go on back there and set down? Hell, I'll even buy you and your amigo there a drink."

"I don't want no drink from you, dammit. I just—"

Still holding his drink in his right hand, Barlow pushed off the bar with his left elbow and then launched a short, powerful fist that nearly broke several of Fitzhugh's ribs.

Fitzhugh's air whooshed out, and he doubled over. "Damn," he managed to gasp.

Barlow slammed the side of his fist down on the back of Fitzhugh's neck.

The young man fell flat on his face at Barlow's feet and lay there moaning.

Barlow leaned back against the bar, watching Fitzhugh's friend. As that man started to rise, Buffalo 2 walked toward him, growling, his fangs bared. "It's all right, Buffler," Barlow said.

The Newfoundland stopped and looked at his master. Then he suddenly bolted toward Barlow. In a second he had leaped onto the top of the bar, his snarling face inches away from the bartender's face. The barman swiftly dropped his shillelagh and backed away fast, slamming into the back bar.

"Call him off, mister," he squeaked.

Barlow looked over his shoulder, grinned malevolently at the bartender, then said, "C'mon on down off there, Buffler."

The dog growled a few more times, then gingerly turned and jumped down from the bar.

Barlow turned toward Fitzhugh's friend. "Best come and pick up your amigo here, hoss, and git him home. And maybe you'll learn to watch who you sass next time."

When Fitzhugh had been helped out, Barlow turned and faced the bar. He refilled his glass, wondering why Fitzhugh had tried to challenge him like that. Then he almost grinned as he came to the realization that he had been the same way when he was that age. All piss and vinegar—and no sense. He downed the drink.

18

BARLOW DISMOUNTED IN front of the house, which looked considerably more weather-beaten than when he had left. Hand resting on the saddle horn, Barlow turned, taking it all in. The chicken coop was still there, and the hog pen. A few more trees had been cut down, their stumps left, though, looking like short sentinels watching over the farm fields, which were fallow now, with patches of snow scattered about. The trees were bare, their branches starkly jabbing the partly cloudy sky.

All in all, the place seemed almost deserted. Only the smoke coming from the old stone chimney gave any sign that there was life inside the log structure.

Barlow wrapped the reins loosely around the saddle horn, which would allow Beelzebub to graze on whatever grass or forage he could find. Barlow wasn't really worried about the mule running off. He shook his head, knowing that he was stalling, and irritated at himself for it. He had come all this way; he could not refuse to go the last few steps.

With a sigh, he moved. Still feeling odd about all this, he hesitated a few seconds before raising his right hand—his rifle was in the other—and knocking on the door. He was gentle at first, then realized that anyone inside likely could not hear him, so he pounded a bit harder. Then he stood and waited.

After an eternity, a time in which he more than once

considered just turning around and leaving, the door creaked open. An old woman looked up at him. "Yes?" she asked, her creased face scrunched up a bit in question.

"Ma?" Barlow said tentatively. He wasn't sure it was her. It had been so long, and she had aged considerably. Still, some instinct told him this was, indeed, his mother.

She stepped closer to get a better look at him. Then her rheumy eyes widened. "Will?" she questioned, not quite trusting her old eyes.

"Yep, Ma, it's me." He smiled hesitantly.

"Oh, my Lord," Mary Barlow breathed. Tears welled and then dribbled down her age-crinkled cheeks. "Come in, son. Come in." She stepped back, allowing him to enter. As he did, she noticed the dog for the first time as Buffalo 2 walked into the house with his master. She gasped.

Barlow glanced at her and noticed where she was looking. "It's all right, Ma," he said softly. "He ain't gonna hurt you none." He patted the big dog's head. "Are you, boy?"

The Newfoundland let loose a happy little whine, and his tail whipped back and forth.

"What's his name?" Mary asked, closing the door.

"Buffler 2."

"Buffalo 2? That seems a strange name."

"Had another dog a long time ago named Buffler," Barlow said with a shrug. "He was kilt by some Injins. This'un come along not too long after."

"Well, I'm sorry about that other dog of yours, son." She stopped in the kitchen and indicated with a hand that he should sit. When he did, she asked, "Coffee?"

"Reckon that'd sit well with this ol' hoss," he said, not even thinking about how he was speaking. He was so used to using the mountain man vernacular that he rarely realized when he was speaking it.

"What's that?" Mary asked, turning to look quizzically at him.

"Yes, Ma, I'd like some coffee." He had to make an effort to speak plainly.

"Are you hungry?" she asked as she poured thick black coffee into a large pewter mug.

"Reckon I could fill my meatbag ... Um, I mean, yeah, Ma, I could do with something to eat."

Mary Barlow fussed about preparing food, grateful at being occupied. She needed a little time to accept that fact that her youngest son—the wildest one, who had left home so long ago under cloudy circumstances—was sitting at her table. She kept taking surreptitious glances at him, and her pride in him grew. He had turned out handsome, big, and he certainly looked mighty strong. He seemed self-assured, but wary, as if expecting trouble. She wondered what kind of adventures he had gotten himself into over the years. She quickly cut off that line of thinking. Whatever things he had done since he had been gone would most likely horrify her, as she suspected that he had done a lot of terrible—and sinful—things.

Soon she placed a knife, fork and full plate in front of him. She refilled his coffee cup, then poured some for herself and sat across from him.

"You're not eatin'?" he asked.

"I ain't hungry, son. I ate before. You fill yourself. There's plenty where that come from."

Barlow nodded and dug in. It had been a long time since he had had good bacon, eggs, hog sausage and real bread. So long that the foods seemed a bit foreign to him. But enjoyable, and more so the more he ate. He finished that plateful, and his mother replenished it, as well as the coffee mug.

When Barlow finished that plate, he considered asking for more, but then glanced over at the stove and realized there was precious little left. It suddenly dawned on him that she had not eaten because she didn't want to deprive him. He also wondered if she had only a little to start with. The possibility bothered him.

Instead of having more to eat, he filled his pipe and lit it. He rested his forearms on the table and sipped coffee as he puffed away at his pipe, acrid smoke curling up around his head.

The two sat there silent, awkward, not sure what to say to each other. It had been so long, and their parting so unpleasant, that they were left speechless. Barlow began to wonder why he had come back here. There was nothing here for him anymore. He decided after some time that one of them needed to break the silence, and it might as well be him. "Where's Pa?" he asked.

"Dead and gone these past two years now," Mary answered quietly. She had long since gotten over her mourning for her husband, William. While she had cared for him—maybe even loved him—his harsh Presbyterian temperament and his strict religious bent had been difficult to live with, and in some ways it was a relief that he was gone, though it left her bereft, lonely and in hard financial straits.

"I'm sorry, Ma," Barlow said cautiously, not sure how she really felt about it. "I didn't know." He didn't much care about his father. They had parted on bad terms, and he knew they would never have been able to reconcile. His father was just too overly pious and set in his self-righteous ways.

"Of course you didn't know," Mary said, a little angry. "You haven't been home since . . . since . . ." She stopped and was able to compose herself. "What are you doing back here now, son, after all this time?" she asked calmly.

Barlow wondered what and how much to tell his mother. He did not want to shock or upset her, and the truth would likely do both. His pipe had gone out, so he set it down on the table. He rubbed the short, ragged beard he had grown since leaving Santa Fe. "I was with a wagon train of goods comin' back here from the Mexican lands, Ma," he started. "The trail ends in Independence or thereabouts. Once we got there, I figured I was so close to here, I'd come by."

"You was gone a long time, son. Why didn't you ever come home before this?"

"Never been this close before, Ma. Not since I left here."

"Where've you been all this time, then?" Mary was interested, despite herself.

"Most every place there is to be out in the West, Ma," Barlow said proudly. Thinking about it, he knew that what he had said was true. He had never realized that before. "Spent a heap of time in the Stony Mountains. Took some missionaries to the Oregon land. Fought me some fierce goddamn Injins . . ."

"Watch your tongue, boy," Mary warned as if by rote. Her aged, arthritic fingers, twisted and thick-knuckled, toyed with each other on the table.

"Yes'm." He was abashed, but got over it in a hurry. "I've been all over the Mexican lands—lands that now belong to America after the war we had with the Mexicans. I been in high mountains and deep valleys, crossed ragin' rivers and mountain passes filled with snow deeper'n a horse. I've survived deserts and the howlin' winds of the vast, empty prairie. I've fought Injins and been friends with some; same with Mexican people. I've had me more'n my share of Injin wom—" He slammed to a stop.

"I've had more'n my share of dealin's with all kinds of Injins," he added lamely after catching himself. "I've trapped freezin' streams and traded with folks from Santa Fe to the Oregon country. I've hunted down the festerin' maggots who kidnap—" Once more he slapped his mouth shut lest he say too much.

But it was too late this time. "Somebody you know was kidnapped?" Mary asked, surprise and even some anger flickering across her worn features.

Barlow sighed, then nodded. "My daughter," he said quietly.

"You had a daughter?" Mary asked, wonder, pride and a bit of disappointment in her voice and eyes.

He nodded again, then added, voice almost breaking, "And a son."

"Lord, Almighty," Mary breathed. "I wish we'd known about them, son. We could've had them here for some proper schoolin' and such, instead of them livin' out there in the wilds with you."

Barlow shrugged.

"Where's your wife now?" Mary asked sternly. "You haven't left her out there on her own, have you? Alone to face perils the kind of which no woman should be subjected to. The kind—"

"Whoa, Ma," Barlow said, holding up a hand to cut her off. "She ain't out there alone. She's . . . She's . . ." He choked back the sudden surge of loss and anger that rose up and almost overwhelmed him. "She's gone under, Ma. Dead."

"Oh, my Lord," Mary gasped. "What happened?"

"She was kilt by some Injins who attacked our little homestead up in the Oregon country. Near the Willamette

River. They kilt my infant son, Little Will, too, and stole my daughter, Anna."

"I'm so sorry, son." Mary reached out a gnarled hand and patted one of his huge, powerful, callused ones.

"It's all right, Ma," Barlow said, regaining his composure. "It's been some years now."

"What was her name?"

"Sarah Stewart."

"A good Scots name," Mary offered with a nod.

"It was." He hesitated, wondering if he should mention Sarah's mother's parentage, then decided against it.

"Where was this?" Mary asked suspiciously. "I ain't ever heard of white women out in those places you spoke of."

"Plenty of white folks in the Oregon country," Barlow said soothingly. "Mostly Britishers and Scots. They work for the Hudson's Bay Company." He paused, then added, lying, "A lot of them boys brung their women out there with 'em. Sarah was the daughter of one of 'em."

"Sounds mighty dangerous, bringin' white women out to such a place." Mary disapproved of the whole notion.

Barlow shrugged. "Most of them live in or right around a tradin' post called Fort Vancouver. Since I didn't work for the Hudson's Bay folks, I wasn't livin' near the fort. Wasn't too far away, but, well, it weren't that close either. The two missionaries I led out there came with their wives, and they were nearby. The Injins didn't bother them none."

"I didn't know the savages believed in Christ, our Lord."

"Some do. That's what the missionaries was doin' out there. But them ones who attacked weren't Christian Injins. I reckon they didn't molest the missionaries because they thought they were mad as hatters. Most Injins I've met are right scared of people who're mad, and usually give 'em a wide berth."

There was silence for a while, before Mary asked, "Whatever happened to your daughter, Will?"

Barlow said nothing for some time, long enough that his mother began to wonder if he would answer at all. But finally he said, "I looked for her for a number of years, but . . ." His great shoulders rose and fell.

"I'm so sorry, son," Mary said, trying to keep back the tears that threatened to begin flowing.

"It don't matter none now, Ma," Barlow lied. He was upset enough that he could not see that his mother knew he was not telling the truth. "She's gone—been gone a spell—and there ain't no gettin' her back. A man's got to go on."

"Have you found another woman? A man your age should have a wife. And kids. And settle down somewhere." She paused. "There's a might good many places around here that could provide a good home and farm for a hardworkin' young man. And you're still plenty young enough to start another family."

Barlow fretted, trying to ease his buttocks on the hard seat. He was embarrassed some, especially since he could not tell his mother the truth—that if he was going to marry again anytime soon, it would be to a Mexican woman named Natividad Santiago. Nor did he want to tell her that he had absolutely no desire—or intention—of staying here and settling down. He had long ago realized that he was no farmer, and never would be.

"Well, Ma, I ain't give it much thought, really," he finally said. "To tell true, I been doin' a mite too much travelin' the past few years to consider settlin' down. But I'll cogitate on it some whilst I'm here." He hoped that would satisfy her, at least for a while.

Mary nodded. "What're your plans, son?"

"Don't rightly know, Ma." He was uncomfortable again, and was beginning to wish he had resisted the urge to come see the old homestead.

"You'll see your brothers?" It was more of an order than a question.

"Sure, Ma. Soon's I can."

Mary smiled. "It's good to have you home, Will. You'll spend the night here?"

"If it won't put you out none."

"It won't."

19

BARLOW SPENT SEVERAL days with his mother. Pleasant days, they were, for the most part, even if they remained awkward for both of them.

Unfortunately, he couldn't say the same for the visit with his two brothers, Finlay and Clyde. Neither had been very jovial, especially around Will, and they had grown into bitter, sour men, ones who gave every appearance of hating their lives as husbands, fathers and farmers. They were penurious, often overly pious and utterly devoid of any humor or lightheartedness. Barlow had hoped they had changed over the years he had been gone, but it was evident from the moment he entered Finlay's house that such was not the case.

Barlow had thought it only proper that he visit Finlay, as the oldest of the brothers, first. It was an uncomfortable time. Finlay, shorter than Will, stocky, though turning paunchy, was ill at ease. Despite the season, he thought he should be out in the fields doing something useful instead of sitting here with his slothful youngest brother. Finlay soon sent Derek, the oldest of his seven children, to fetch the middle Barlow brother, Clyde. Derek quickly returned with news that Uncle Clyde would be there before long.

True to his word, Clyde arrived soon after with his wife, Sophie, and three of their five children—the two oldest, introduced as Clyde the Younger and Boyd, and the youngest, Donald, a babe in arms.

The two older boys burst into the room like wild men, howling and shouting, as boys were wont to do. Then they stopped cold when they caught their first glimpse of Buffalo 2. "Lawd a'mighty," Clyde the Younger whispered, fear tingeing his voice. He looked a lot like his father—taller than either Finlay or Will, but not nearly as blocky as either. He was rather tall for his age, but still mighty skinny.

Boyd was speechless as he stared at the big Newfoundland, who had risen when the boys entered and now stood next to Barlow with a puzzled look on his snort-muzzled face.

Derek, sitting at the table, was grinning hugely. He favored Will more than his own father. At not quite thirteen, he was bullish of build and appeared to be older until one saw his boyish eyes and face. He had also been impressed with Buffalo 2, but had hid it well.

"He ain't gonna hurt you, boys," Barlow said. "Are you, Buffler?"

The dog looked up at him, head cocked as if trying to figure out whether there was any danger here. His master did not seem concerned, so the dog looked back at the youngsters.

"Come on over and greet ol' Buffler, boys."

The two tentatively eased up on the Newfoundland. They were scared but trying hard not to show it. Finally they were close enough to begin petting Buffalo 2, running their skinny, dirty fingers through the thick fur along the dogs neck and sides. When the Newfoundland lapped each boy on the cheek in turn, they giggled and petted him more vigorously. In moments they were great friends.

Everyone sat, and the talk was mostly general, and totally strained. For a time, though he was the biggest of the three Barlows overall, Will felt intimidated by his brothers, as if they were all still children and he, as the youngest, had to defer to them. His feeling began to ebb, however, as he watched his dour siblings grumble and clump around Finlay's cabin.

Finally Sophie and her sister-in-law, Beatrice, served the meat, beans and potatoes that the latter, as mistress of the cabin, had cooked up. The two women joined the others at the table, and they ate with an uncomfortable silence enveloping them. No one was sure what to say. Finlay and Clyde were only mildly interested in what their brother had been up to in all these years, and they realized that, surprisingly enough, Will had little curiosity about their lives beyond the obvious asking about nieces and nephews he had never met. The women cared not a whit either way.

As the meal ended, however, and the men leaned back with pipes and whiskey-laced coffee, twelve-year-old Derek asked, "Where've you been all these years, Uncle Will?"

"Here and about, boy," Barlow said tightly. He swiftly realized, however, that the boy was interested, and he reined in his annoyance. It didn't hurt that the boy favored him so much in looks and build. "Been over a mite of country, hoss," he added, even offering a small smile. "From the Settlements hereabouts to the great water at the end of the Oregon country. From Blackfoot country in the Stony Mountains, to the deserts of the Mexican lands."

"What'd you do out there?" Clyde the Younger tossed in.

Barlow glanced from one boy to the next. Both were wide-eyed, eager to hear more. He took a few puffs, spewing smoke around the room. "Well, I'll tell you, boys," he continued, jabbing the smoke between himself and the boys with the stem of his pipe a few times for emphasis, "I done about everything an ol' hoss can do out there. Faced starvin' times as well as shinin' times. Had me a heap of shinin' doin's at the rendezvous with other mountain men. Trapped me a heap of beaver, and even done some tradin'. Hunted buffler from the back of my ol' mule and feasted on buffler entrails and beaver tail and a heap of other shinin' vittles. Had more'n my share of ruckuses, too."

"You ever meet any Injins?" Derek asked, his eyes looking like dinner plates, they were so wide.

"Well, sure, I did, hoss. You cain't travel nowhere in them Stony Mountains or across the Great Plains without runnin' into a heap of Injins of all tribes."

"You ever fight any of 'em?" Clyde Junior's jaw was slack with wonderment.

Barlow let go a few more clouds of bluish pipe smoke, glancing at his brothers through the screen. Both were glaring at Barlow, and he grinned lightly, knowing they could not really see it behind the smoke. He began to feel better about himself. He looked at his nephews. The two, and the younger Boyd, sat with mouths agape, waiting with barely contained eagerness for him to continue. It gave him the impetus to set his brothers' teeth on edge even more.

"Of course, I have, boys," Barlow said with an indulgent grin. "More times than I can count. Fought all kinds of 'em, too. Hell," he went on, ignoring the grunt of irritation that Finlay tossed at him, "jist before I come here I was being held by Comanches in a village of theirs somewhere down off the Santa Fe Trail. Them red devils was fixin' to do me some terrible harm before liftin' my hair."

"How'd you get away?" an awestruck Derek asked.

"Ol' Buffler here, he come and got me loose from my bindin's. Then we snuck into the chief's lodge, stole back my weapons and possibles, then got ol' Beelzebub—that's my mule—and lit out."

"Did you kill any of them savages?" Derek asked, as impressed as ever.

"That'll be enough of such talk, son," Derek's mother, Beatrice, said sharply.

"But, Ma, they're just savages," Derek pouted.

"Don't sass your ma, boy," Finlay snapped. He looked at his wife. "The boy's right, Bea," he said more calmly. "They ain't but savages and don't deserve our concern."

Beatrice clapped her mouth shut, knowing better than to argue with her husband, especially in front of others, even if they were family. She rose from the table and began fussing around the stove. Sophie joined her.

Barlow almost smiled at the altercation. "All Injins ain't savages, Fin," he said quietly but firmly. "Some're plumb bad all right, like the Blackfeet. Them boys're the meanest goddamn buggers," he added, eliciting a gasp of horror from the two women at the blasphemy, "this ol' hoss ever come across. I ain't had much dealin's with the Comanches till just recent, but I hear tell they're as bad as the Blackfeet. What's a mite odd about it all is that the Shoshonis are distant cousins of the Comanches, but are right friendly and helpful to white folks. My closest friend these days is a Shoshoni named White Bear. Hell of a feller he is."

"You're friends with a red savage?" Finlay asked, shocked and angered. "After you went to war with Injins back in the Black Hawk War in these parts?"

"Like I said, hoss, not all Injins is the same. You ain't too fond of Otto Schmidt and his clan are you?"

"That's different," Finlay said stiffly.

"Like hell it is," Barlow snapped, his temper flaring.

"Yes, it is," Finally insisted. "They're—"

"That's enough, Fin," Clyde said mordantly. "Will's just baitin' you is all."

Barlow grinned, but covered it by stuffing the stem of his pipe in his mouth. He glanced at his three nephews, his eyes sparkling. "Of course," he said evenly, "even amongst the tribes there're some better Injins than others."

The three boys—twelve-year-old Derek, eleven-year-old Clyde the younger and nine-year-old Boyd—looked at him with a mixture of confusion and wonder, waiting.

Barlow rested his forearms on the table and leaned forward. In conspiratorial tones, he said, "Them Injin women are mighty special, boys. Mighty special." Out of the corner of his eye, he could see anger and dismay coloring the cheeks of both of his brothers. "Lord a'mighty, they plumb know how to treat a man. Lordy, Lordy, when they fetch off all their clothes and—"

"Enough!" Beatrice shrieked, startling everyone but Barlow. Beatrice moved closer, stopping to stand between Derek and Boyd, directly across from Barlow. Her face was flushed with anger. "How dare you come into my home and spread such shameful filth. I'm appalled that you would fill the ears of our children with such . . . such indecent—and sinful—thoughts."

She paused, but she was not through; only gaining steam. "If I remember it right, you left here under a cloud of indecency. As I recall, you put a young girl in . . . ," her voice dropped to barely a whisper, ". . . the family way, and then fled your responsibilities to her." Her voice soared again. "You are a despicable man, a wicked, revolting libertine. You will leave this house now, you reprobate. And you are not expected back. Ever."

"Beatrice," Finlay warned, "that's not—"

"I don't care if he is your brother, Fin," Beatrice said,

turning her baleful glare on her husband. "I will not have him here filling our children's heads with such immodest and sinful ideas."

Finlay needed no convincing. He had been about to throw his brother out anyway. The only reason he had tried to stop his wife was to prevent her from saying something blasphemous inadvertently. He nodded and looked at Will. "Beatrice is right, Will. It's time you were gone. You've been fed, which is the least a family can do for a wayward relative. But now you must be leaving. I'd be obliged if you were not to stop here again, brother. There is only so far family members can go with such an outcast as you." He rose, glowering at his brother. Clyde did the same.

Barlow pushed himself to his feet and slid his pipe into the leather holder he wore around his neck. He glanced at his nephews, who sat, frightened, worried. He winked surreptitiously at them. "C'mon, Buffler," he said, "time for us to be gone. Seems these ol' critters don't like hearin' of our shinin' adventures."

He grabbed his hat from the table and slapped it on, then lifted his rifle from where it rested against the table. "I'm obliged for your kindness, brothers," he said, only a hint of sarcasm coating the words. "If there's any way I can return such benevolence, I insist that you not hesitate to call on me."

He winked at the boys, turned and sauntered, unashamed, toward the door, with Buffalo 2 in tow. Outside, Barlow climbed into the saddle on Beelzebub. "Where away, Buffler?" he asked, looking down at the dog. He gently kicked the mule with the heels of his moccasins and moved off, not certain of where he was going. Until he realized that he had unconsciously started heading toward St. Charles—and the Bull's Head Tavern.

As he tied Beelzebub up outside the saloon, he hoped he would find someone he knew inside, unlike the day he had first returned. He entered with Buffalo 2 and stopped to look around a moment. Then he grinned. He strode toward a big, bulky man sitting at a table playing cards. There was a mug of beer on the table in front of him, and his back was toward the door—and the direction from which Barlow was coming.

Barlow stopped behind the man and slapped a thick hand on his big shoulder. "Folks round these parts don't take kindly to card cheats, hoss," he growled.

The man half spun in his chair, angry face thrust out, looking up at his accuser. "Who the hell're you callin'—" He stopped, and a smile swiftly spread across his face. He jumped up and clamped burly arms around Barlow, who returned the gesture. "Will!" he bellowed, clapping Barlow hard on the back. "Will Barlow! What the hell're you doin' here?"

Barlow grinned. "Come back for a small visit, Tom," Barlow said happily. "I was hopin' to see you."

Tom Wallenbach turned and tossed his cards facedown on the table. "I'm out, boys," he said, not thinking an explanation was needed. He grabbed his mug of beer and with Barlow and Buffalo 2 walked to an empty table, where both men sat. The dog flopped heavily down on the floor next to Barlow's chair.

Wallenbach called for a beer for Barlow and a refill for himself. When the drinks were delivered, the two men made a silent salute to each other with their glasses and took a gulp.

"So, old friend, where the hell've you been all these years?" Wallenbach asked. "Out in the mountains?"

Barlow nodded. "For the most part. Been all over, though. Since the beaver trade died off some years ago, I've been roamin'."

"Just roamin'?"

Barlow wondered how much he should tell about his life, but then decided that he might as well tell Wallenbach. "Spent the past several years chasin' after my chil'," he said simply, not revealing the sudden pain that had stabbed his heart.

Wallenbach's eyes widened in question, so Barlow explained Sarah and Little Will's deaths, Anna's abduction and the search for his young daughter. He left out a lot of the particulars, but gave a decent accounting of the tale.

"Damn, Will, that's a shame about your daughter and all," Wallenbach said. He sipped some beer, not sure what else he could say to his old friend. He could do no more than offer condolences, which he figured Barlow neither wanted nor needed.

"It purely was," Barlow agreed sadly. He paused for some sips of the amber liquid, then went on to briefly explain the past few months: the run from Taos and then Santa Fe, his capture by the Comanches, his escape—and the visit with his mother and then two brothers.

"Sounds like you should've stayed out there in the mountains," Wallenbach said with a sour chuckle.

"Might've been better." A gulp, and a reorder of beer, then Barlow added, "So what about you, hoss? What's gone on in your life?"

"Got married," Wallenbach said with a shrug. It was to be expected, and so not worthy of much more than a simple statement.

"To Molly Rose Maguire, I assume?" Barlow questioned, smiling a little.

Wallenbach laughed. "Yep. We got us six kids, and another on the way." He paused, then grew serious. "It's been a good life, Will," he added. "My farm's doin' pretty well, the kids're healthy and I still got a hankerin' for Molly Rose."

Barlow nodded. While he had no desire to be a farmer, he did have a certain amount of jealousy about the comfortable, loving life Wallenbach and Molly Rose had found. Many was the time he wished he could have the same thing.

20

"SO, WHAT'S NEXT, Will?" Wallenbach asked.

"I aim to go get the bastards who kilt Muldoon and the others and left me out there to the tender mercies of the desert or the damn Comanches."

"I wouldn't expect no less of you." Wallenbach drank for a few seconds, then set his mug gently down. "When you leavin' on this mission?"

Barlow shrugged. "Ain't thought about it much. But since I've seen Ma and my brothers, and there ain't no more reason to stay longer, reckon I'll head on out soon."

"You're welcome to come stay with me and Molly Rose for a spell," Wallenbach offered.

Barlow pondered that for a few moments, then said, "That'd shine with me, hoss. You sure it won't put Molly Rose out none?"

"Nah. She'll be glad for it."

Barlow wasn't sure his friend was speaking the truth, but it didn't matter much right now. If Molly Rose objected to his staying there, he'd just leave the area sooner rather than later.

Wallenbach suddenly glanced askance at him. "You aimin' to see Emma Sue, Will?" he asked, not trying hard to hide his grin.

"Emma Sue Longstreath?" Barlow asked, surprised. He had not really thought of her in years, except for briefly the

other day at his mother's, even though she was the main
reason he had left the area, at first to fight Black Hawk's
Sauk and Fox Indians in the short-lived war, and then for
the mountains. Not that he really blamed her for chasing
him away from the St. Charles area. That was the best thing
that had ever happened to him. However, the scandal that
had been attached to his leaving had not set well with him—
or his family—and he was ashamed and bothered by that.

Wallenbach grinned widely. "Well, she's Emma Sue Concannon now, but, yep, that Emma Sue."

"Concannon?" Barlow questioned.

Wallenbach nodded. "She married Elmer Concannon not
long after you left here. Been married to him ever since.
They got four kids last I heard."

Barlow shook his head. "I don't reckon I'll go and see
her," he said seriously. "I got no reason to do so, hoss."

"She still looks good, four kids or no," Wallenbach said
with a laugh.

"That gal caused me more'n enough problems years ago,
hoss. I don't need to go lookin' for no more of that kind of
trouble."

"Don't look like all those hard adventures you had out
there did much to give you courage," Wallenbach said,
laughing some more.

Barlow grinned. "Not the kind of courage needed for
them doin's, hoss," he agreed. "Stake me out in front of a
passel of Blackfeet and I'll show you some courage, hoss.
But facin' some *loco* wench who sent me packin' years ago
with lies and deceit, and . . . Well, it ain't the kind of courage this ol' chil' has an abundance of."

They chatted idly while they finished off the beers they
had and another round. Then Wallenbach said, "Well, Will,
I best get on home or Molly Rose'll have my hide. If you're
comin', now's the time for it. Or," he added after a moment's thought, "if you'd rather stay here a spell, I can draw
you out the way to get to my place."

Barlow paused. "I got no reason to stick round here, hoss.
Let's get on to your place." He smiled slyly. "I expect Molly
Rose'll have got us somethin' to sup on, eh?"

Wallenbach laughed and patted his broad stomach. "You
bet she will. This didn't come from havin' a wife who don't

know how to feed her man, you know, Will."

"Didn't think she was starvin' you." He smiled. "C'mon, Buffler. Time for some fine vittles." He glanced at Wallenbach. "As I remember it, Molly Rose had more than a fair hand around the cookstove."

"She did, and she still does."

Half an hour of slow riding brought them to Wallenbach's small but growing spread. "I started out with forty acres my pa give me," he said proudly as they approached the trim little cabin. "Since then, I've gotten three more parcels."

"Hundred and sixty acres?" Barlow said. "That's not so bad, hoss. You've done well."

"I think so. I've been lucky, though, too. My crops've been substantial each year. It was close a couple of times, I guess, but things always worked out. It's good land," he said, stopping his mule to look with satisfaction across his acreage. "Good for wheat and corn, and a heap of other crops."

He moved on, Barlow alongside him, smiling slightly.

A woman appeared at the door of the cabin. She stood there looking out at them, wiping her hands on her apron, then shading her eyes with one hand. She could tell that one of the riders was her husband, but she had no clue as to the other man or the big dog with him.

The men and dog finally stopped right in front of the cabin. "Molly Rose," Wallenbach said as he and Barlow dismounted, "you remember Will Barlow, don't you?"

"Will," Molly Rose said, eyes brightening as recognition dawned. She stepped forward to hug her guest. "My, it's been a time, Will," she added, stepping back.

"You're lookin' mighty fine, Molly Rose," Barlow said. She had thickened considerably around the waist and breasts, but she still had a young woman's face. Her eyes were still sparkling, her hair barely touched with gray.

"Well, thank you, Will," she said, almost curtseying. "How kind of you to say so." She suspected he was lying, but she also figured it was because he was being gallant, and she appreciated that. "And who's this?" she asked, kneeling in front of the dog.

"That's Buffler, ma'am," Barlow said.

The woman patted the dog's great head, and he licked at her hands and chin, taking to her right away. Molly Rose stood and glanced from Barlow to her husband. "You boys hungry?" she asked.

"Yes, ma'am," Barlow said. "I'm so hungry I could eat the tail off ol' Beelzebub here." He patted the mule's neck a couple of times.

"Well, come on in, then, I've got a mess of beans and fresh ham, and the last of the peas."

Barlow stayed with his friend's family for two days, spending a few hours each evening in the Bull's Head with Wallenbach, playing poker, drinking and reminiscing. On the third morning, he began thinking of leaving. He had seen everyone he wanted to—or thought he should—see, and the drive to find Enos Priddle and his men and make them pay for their treachery was growing in him. Still, he was not yet tired of the Wallenbachs' hospitality, so he delayed leaving for a few more days. The trip to St. Louis would take him less than a day, so he really needed nothing in the way of supplies. Which was a good thing, considering that he had only a few small coins left.

Having made the decision to postpone his trip, he and Buffalo 2 headed into St. Charles in plenty of time to meet Wallenbach, who had had a number of errands to run in the town that day.

He was almost to the Bull's Head, where he figured he would use the last of his money for a drink or two, when he spotted someone who looked familiar. He stopped Beelzebub and sat for a minute staring. "Damn," he suddenly muttered as he realized it was Emma Sue Longstreath—or, rather, Emma Sue Concannon. He kicked the mule lightly to get him going.

But it was too late. Emma Sue had seen him. Her eyes grew wide and she stopped, staring at him. Then she smiled widely and tentatively headed toward him.

"Dammit all," Barlow muttered. He stopped the mule and dismounted as she approached.

"Will?" she asked hesitantly as she stopped right in front of him, looking up into his face.

"Emma Sue," he said, pulling off his hat.

"It's been a long time," she said, voice torn between joy, regret and fear.

"Not long enough," Barlow replied honestly.

"What?" Emma Sue snapped, taking a step back, shocked.

"If you'll recall, ma'am, you was the reason I been gone so long. You and your treachery."

"My what?" she was shaken, even more fearful than she had been moments ago.

"You know damn well what I mean, Emma Sue," Barlow snapped. As he had given her little thought over the years, he also had not given much consideration to the anger he had felt toward her. At least not after the first year or so he had been gone. There was too much new and exciting since then to waste time and energy on an old matter he could not change and which was unlikely to ever enter his life again. But now the anger was surfacing hot and fresh.

"But . . . I . . . I never meant to chase you away, Will," Emma Sue said, eyelashes fluttering, tears beginning to form. "I just wanted to marry you and settle down with you, raise a family."

"Well, gal, you sure as hell picked the wrong way to go about it. Do you really think I'd want to marry you after the story you spread?"

"Well, I . . ."

"What would have happened if we married and then people found out you weren't pregnant?" He was no more sure now than he had been then whether she had really been pregnant. This, he figured, might be a good way to find out.

She shrugged, but then said, "I would've just told folks I miscarried—lost the baby—is all."

Barlow still wasn't sure she was confessing to an out and out lie, and there'd been even less he could do about it at the time. "I reckon that might've worked," Barlow said, still fighting back his anger. "But do you think I'm the kind of feller who'd stick around after being tricked into marriage? Or baited into it? Especially if you'd lost the baby?"

"I don't . . ."

"If you was pregnant at the time, and you did have a miscarriage, do you think I would've stayed here?"

"Maybe not, but . . ."

"Maybe not, hell, woman. I would've been gone first

chance I could get. Then where would you have been? Answer me that. You'd have been a married woman with no husband around—which means you'd have no one to give you a home and sustenance. You'd have to turn to whorin' to make your way in the world." He paused, then added viciously, "Though I reckon that might not've been such a hardship for you, Emma Sue, considerin' your proclivities for the bed."

Emma Sue's face burned red with anger and shame. "You're a disgustin' man, Will Barlow," she snapped, not really caring if anyone heard her. "How I could have ever thought I loved you and wanted you for a husband is beyond me. I must have been crazed."

"Most likely you were, woman. Crazed with lust, if not with general madness." There was no pity, no forgiveness in Barlow's voice.

"Well, then, sir, I think we have no more to discuss," Emma Sue said stiffly, drawing her plumpness up to her full height. "I was wrong in what I did, I reckon, but I can see now that I was even more wrong in thinking that I ever wanted anything to do with you." She turned on her heel and stalked away, back straight, held high.

Barlow watched her for a few moments, his emotions roiling inside of him. She had put on some weight since he had last seen her, but she was still a fine-looking woman. A little fullness to her figure only made her more pleasing to the eye, he thought. And he could not help but remember the times they had spent together, the feel of her, the softness of her skin, the warm wetness of her womanhood, her insistent tongue, her hot, raging lust.

On the other hand, his renewed fury at her duplicity, and her apparent disregard for him, left him hard-pressed to talk nicely to her, let alone forgive her.

With a sigh, he tried to calm himself. He knelt and petted Buffalo 2's head for a minute, letting the Newfoundland know he was not angry at him, that his rage was directed elsewhere, so the dog did not have to concern himself over it.

Barlow climbed onto Beelzebub and completed the short trip to the Bull's Head. He used almost all the few coins he had left to buy two beers and headed for a table to wait for Wallenbach.

His farmer friend was not long in arriving, and he gratefully downed in one swift gulp half the mug of beer Barlow had for him. He leaned back in his chair with a contented sigh and swiped beer foam from his face with a sleeve.

"You get all yours errands done, hoss?" Barlow asked.

"Most all," Wallenbach replied. He drained his beer mug and called for another for him and his friend. When they were on the table, he looked at Barlow. "Something botherin' you, Will?" he asked quietly.

Barlow tried to grin but couldn't quite manage it. "Guess who I run into on the way here just a bit ago?"

Wallenbach shrugged. He was cold and tired and had too many chores facing him, as always, to want to play guessing games.

"The dear Emma Sue Concannon," Barlow said flatly.

"That a fact?" Wallenbach said unemotionally. He drank more beer.

"It is." Barlow filled his pipe and lit it with a Lucifer, one of the sulfur-head matches he had come to rely on.

"I thought you wasn't of a mind to track her down."

"I wasn't. And I didn't track. I was just ridin' down the street there, headin' for here, when I spotted her. I tried to turn off and git away, but she'd already seen me. I didn't figure I should run at that point. So I alit and waited for her to sashay up."

"From the look on your face, old friend, I'd reckon the meetin' didn't go all that well."

"Not in the least bit," Barlow admitted. He puffed his pipe a few times, guzzled some beer, and then explained the encounter to Wallenbach.

"You ain't aimin' to see her again, are you?" Wallenbach asked when Barlow had finished.

"I'd as soon have Satan hisself come against me face to face than meet up with that goddamn harpy again," Barlow said firmly.

21

SEVERAL MUGS OF beer managed to calm Barlow considerably. Several more, interspersed with a few healthy gulps of rancid whiskey, had him feeling damn near good. He and Wallenbach and Buffalo 2 finally left the saloon and headed to Boudreau's Mercantile Store not far down the street, where Wallenbach needed to pick up a few things.

While his friend conducted his business, Barlow wandered around the spacious store. He had absolutely no use for most of the things he saw, but occasionally something caught his eye and he would momentarily wish he had money enough to buy it. One such item was a big, heavy six-shot Colt pistol. He asked a clerk to show him the revolver, which weighed almost five pounds when it was loaded, he was told. He liked the feel of the heavy weapon and could sense that it would be a worthy purchase. With a sigh of regret, he handed it back to the clerk, who put it away. With the few pennies he had left in his possibles bag, he couldn't even afford enough powder and shot to load the revolver once, let alone buy the weapon itself.

He turned away from the glass-enclosed case of various pistols and almost stepped on Emma Sue Concannon, of all people. Still feeling the warming glow of the alcohol surging through his veins, Barlow offered her a small, but genuine smile. He did not catch the brief shrewd look in her eye before it slid away and she returned his grin.

"You're not mad at me no more?" Emma Sue asked, trying to keep the deceptiveness out of her voice. She had decided a moment after spotting him in the store a few seconds ago that she would do whatever it took to seduce him. She was sure she could do it if she could get close to him at all. She was rather amazed that he had been so friendly so soon after being so angry at her. But she planned to use it to her full advantage if she could. When she suddenly set her mind moments ago on seducing him, the whole plot had sprung into her mind full blown: Once she had enjoyed the pleasures his body could give her, as she knew she would, she would file a complaint with the law, charging him with rape. In doing so, she thought, she would get back at him both for having left her all those years ago, humiliating her, and for his insufferable behavior toward her earlier in the day. He would be in prison for a long, long time, or perhaps even be hanged, and she would be vindicated; have her shame wiped away in the blood and anguish of the man who had wronged her so long ago.

"Nah, I ain't mad at you, Emma Sue," Barlow said somewhat uncomfortably. He regretted having been so harsh to her earlier, though he knew that he had reason for it. Still, such was not his way, especially when it came to women.

Emma Sue turned on the charm. Her smile was warm and inviting, her eyes full of lust. "I'm sorry I said those things to you, too, Will," she said, voice catching with manufactured sobs. Her bright brown eyes clouded over with tears. "I don't want to fight with you."

"Well, I reckon I don't want to fight with you neither, Emma Sue," he said, even more uncomfortable. He wondered where this was going.

"Well, Will, that's a start." Emma Sue moved a little closer to him. Her sobs had stopped, as had the tears, but the latter had left her eyes glistening in an enticing way. "I . . . I . . . Well, Will, I'd kind of like to make it up to you." Her smile at him sizzled.

"Make what up to me?" Barlow was beginning to wilt under the assault of her shining eyes, wet, parted lips, the sudden touch of a finger on his cheek, the lusty aura emanating from her.

"What I done to you all those years ago." She inched

closer to him, the front of her thick coat nearly brushing his. "I never really was with child back then," she admitted, tears forming again, and a few leaked out to streak down her soft, cold-flushed cheeks. "I jist . . . Well, I just wanted you to be my husband, Will." She put on a look of shame mixed with loss, and a touch of defiance.

Barlow's resistance and anger were just about gone. He wondered how he could have ever thought she was evil, or even just plain mean. How could someone with such soft, gentle eyes, such a warm, inviting mouth, such easy tears, such obvious love and caring in her heart be a bad person?

Emma Sue could see that she was getting through to Barlow, and she moved in to finish him off. "I can make you feel wonderful, Will," she said, her voice husky, full of lust. "And I'd sure love to do that for you."

"You would?" Barlow gulped.

"Yep." She paused. "And you won't regret it neither."

"I don't know, Emma Sue," Barlow said, uncertain, but losing his resolve.

"It'll be fun, Will," Emma Sue cooed.

"What about your husband?"

"He won't ever have to know," she said unconcernedly. "And I do feel I owe it to you, Will," she added hastily, not wanting to lose him now that he was just about eating out of the palm of her hand.

Barlow wasn't all that concerned with Elmer Concannon. He didn't know the man, and owed him nothing. He had just wanted her to remember that she was married before she continued on with this. Now that it seemed she had no qualms about such a thing, the last of his resolve fled. "Reckon that wouldn't put me out none," he said.

"Good," Emma Sue said brightly. "Come to my house tomorrow morning, a couple of hours after daylight. Elmer'll be gone for the day, and I'll send the young'uns off to my mother's on some pretext. We'll have the place to ourselves." She quickly ran a soft finger along his cheek again. "Like last time," she added. Then she turned and hurried off before he could change his mind or start asking questions.

Barlow was still mulling over the extraordinary occurrence several minutes later when Wallenbach strolled up and said, "Let's go, Will."

Barlow followed his friend out, realizing that Wallenbach must have missed the entire episode. Had he seen it, Barlow was sure, he would have had something to say about it. Barlow was relieved.

The next morning, as Barlow headed toward Emma Sue Longstreath Concannon's place—he had casually asked Molly Rose about where Emma Sue lived last night, so he knew where he was going—Barlow wondered about what he was letting himself in for. He clearly remembered the trouble she had caused all those years ago. And he knew damn well that spending the day with Emma Sue would do nothing but lead to more trouble. Still, he could not turn down the woman's offer. He wasn't sure why; he only knew that it was true.

By the time he reached the dilapidated farmhouse, his questions had fled. He was not one to overly worry about such things. If there was trouble from this tryst, he would worry about it when it arrived.

Barlow pulled to a stop, and Emma Sue poked her head out of the rickety door. "Put your mule around back, Will."

His eyebrows rose, but then he realized she was just being cautious, which made sense. He rode slowly around the back, dismounted and tied Beelzebub to a post between two troughs. He made sure there was hay in one and water in the other, and that the animal had enough rope to reach both. Satisfied, Barlow hefted his rifle and, with Buffalo 2 at his side, headed around the building and in through the door.

Emma Sue was waiting just inside. She stepped up and enthusiastically kissed him hard on the mouth, her tongue searching wildly for his, then connecting.

He reciprocated with equal zeal, sucking her tongue into his mouth and toying with it.

Breathing heavily, Emma Sue finally pulled back and looked up at him. Her face had plumped up some, but still retained considerable handsomeness. She had never been a true beauty, but she had always been pleasant of face, and the years had diminished that only a little.

"Come," Emma Sue said, taking Barlow's hand and turning. She led him across the kitchen/eating area, toward a door at the rear of the main room. The main room was shabby and not very clean, but Barlow didn't much care. In fact, he didn't notice.

They entered the room at the back, which contained a rickety bed, a small cradle in one corner and a stiff wood chair with a quilt resting across the back and on the seat. A table with pitcher and basin, candle and a hairbrush stood next to the bed. A small window looked out over the farm's fields. Next to it was a bureau that listed seriously to one side, and on the top of which rested a large Bible, the kind all families had.

Before she shut the door, Emma Sue looked at Buffalo 2. "Can't he stay outside?" she asked, pointing at the dog.

"Buffler goes where I go," Barlow said flatly.

"But he'll—"

"He won't take no mind of what we're doin', Emma Sue," Barlow said. Then he grinned. "He's used to such doin's," he added. "Go lay down, boy," he ordered. The big dog seemed to shrug, then circled a spot in one corner several times before sprawling out. Barlow took a step forward, grabbed Emma Sue and pulled her into a vigorous embrace. He kicked the door closed behind him, bent, scooped Emma Sue up into his powerful arms and strode to the bed.

She shrieked a bit when he lifted her. She knew that after four children, she had gained some weight, but he had picked her up as if she were still a child. It was a wonderful feeling.

Barlow dropped Emma Sue lightly on the bed. He swiftly pulled off his belt and other accoutrements and tossed them aside, then climbed onto the bed, straddling Emma Sue's ankles. He leaned forward, resting his bulk on his arms and kissed her full lips hard, then trailed smaller, light kisses across her forehead, closed eyelids, too-small nose and round chin.

When he reached her bodice—like the last time he had been with her, she was wearing just a simple cotton dress, one that covered everything but concealed very little—he grabbed the thin material and tore it easily off of her, baring her heaving tits.

Even as a girl, Emma Sue's breasts had been large and

very round, and they had grown over the years with the birth
and feeding of four children. They sagged some, but what
they had lost in firmness, they had gained in fullness, nipple
size and sensitivity.

Emma Sue moaned softly as Barlow's tongue and lips
glided tantalizingly across her coral-colored nipples, which
had stiffened to the size of Emma Sue's thumbs, and traced
rings around the areolae, which darkened considerably
against her pale breast flesh.

Barlow continued exploring southward on Emma Sue's
plump torso, eliciting a steady stream of moans and sighs.
He straightened, grabbed the ragged edges of Emma Sue's
dress and tore the rest of it apart, exposing all of her to his
hungry eyes. He ran his hands along her wide, voluptuous
hips and down onto her deliciously thick thighs.

Barlow yanked the shredded dress from underneath
Emma Sue and tossed it to the floor alongside the bed.
"Damn, if you still ain't a fine-lookin' woman, Emma Sue,"
he said throatily.

"I ain't too weighty for you?" she asked. She had worried
a little about that, but had decided shortly before Barlow
arrived that her body had attained a woman's fullness, not
grown fat. But it would still be nice, she thought, to hear it
voiced.

"Not a'tall, woman," Barlow said. He rose and climbed
off the bed to stand next to it. As he began tugging off his
shirt, Emma Sue got up on her knees, facing him, and began
undoing the buttons on his buckskin pants. She had them
undone and let them slip to the floor before Barlow had
gotten the cloth shirt up over his head and dropped it.

Emma Sue was so short that Barlow's rigid manhood was
level with her face, and she stared at it in delight. She had
wondered if the many years that had passed since their last
encounter had exaggerated her remembrance of his size and
thickness. She knew now that they had not. Barlow was far
larger than her husband Elmer was, and now she knew why
she often sought out other men, hoping to find someone
large enough, eager enough and with enough stamina to
please her. She had the sudden sinking feeling that perhaps
Barlow was the only man with those qualifications. Not that
she regretted that at all; just that she was having second

thoughts about seeking revenge against him. She wondered now whether she should just try to please him better than any woman ever had—or ever would—and try to keep him here, even if only as an illicit lover.

She leaned her head forward, mouth parting in delicious anticipation, until her lips engulfed the head of his thick, hard lance, making him groan now. She slid her mouth forward, inching down his shaft. She grabbed the root of his manhood in her hands and helped steady it as she kept trying to stuff more of him into her willing mouth and less-accommodating throat.

Barlow groaned again, and gasped as pleasure raced through his staff. He reached out and took a handful of her shiny, curled, long, slightly graying sandy-colored hair and held tight. He wanted to shove her face forward, but was afraid she would choke, so he forced himself to hold back.

Finally he pushed her head back. "Enough," he croaked. "At least for now." He got into the bed and lay on his back. "Come," he said. "Let me pay attention to that sweet cunny of yours."

Emma Sue did not hesitate. She simply climbed atop him, sliding up until her dripping, dark-haired triangle was directly above his waiting mouth. She lowered herself, and shuddered as his tongue slid along the inner folds of her womanhood and then flicked across her love bud. She grabbed hold of his hair this time, and held on with one hand, while the other hand gripped the iron bedstead to balance her.

Barlow continued laving Emma Sue's sweetness, listening to her climax starting to build, slowing, then rising with blinding swiftness, until she was overcome with shuddering so violent that he thought she would fling herself to the floor in the throes of her passion.

She hung on, though, and when she had settled down again, Barlow renewed his ministrations to her most private parts, until she was racked by another explosive orgasm.

As Barlow took up his delightful task one more time, Emma Sue panted, "No, Will, no more. Not now. I can't hardly catch up my breath."

With his face still buried in her crotch, he grinned. He pulled his head back a little and smiled up at her, his mouth wet. "Then move on down, woman," he ordered gently. "There's more shinin' doin's to be had here."

Emma Sue squiggled downward, lifted her fleshy hips and then eased herself down onto Barlow's thick, muscular shaft. She whimpered as her bottom landed on his thighs. But she waited only a second before she began rising and falling on his now slippery lance.

Only moments later, both howled their release as their pent-up passions burst forth in a body-jarring eruption of ecstasy.

Finally they slumped together, breathing heavily, sated. It took just a short nap before they were ready for another round, one that lasted much longer as they slowly explored each other's body, teasing, tempting, encouraging the most pleasure that they could. They took turns playing with each other, stroking, kissing, licking, sucking, touching. Emma Sue experienced numerous blasts of elation as she spiraled toward a big climax, with Barlow's persistent encouragement.

Then they once more reached the peak together in a roaring thunderclap of euphoria.

Soon after it was time for a meal, which did wonders to restore their energies.

Two more times that afternoon they melted together in concupiscent bliss, wearing themselves to a frazzle with their delightful exertions. In between, they ate again, building up their strength for the next delirious bout of lovemaking.

Finally, though, it was time for Barlow to leave. He rose and dressed slowly, partly from tiredness, partly from a reluctance to depart such a warm, lust-filled bed.

"You'll come back tomorrow?" Emma Sue asked. She still lay on the bed, naked, unashamed at being so exposed. Indeed, she enjoyed enticing Barlow as she stretched out her pudgy, yet still well-formed legs.

"Reckon that'd suit this ol' hoss just fine," Barlow responded. He wasn't sure he would be able to perform after today's long round of sexual antics, but he wasn't about to admit that. At least not to her. But he had confidence in himself, and he was pretty certain that with a good night's sleep and a couple of good meals in him he would be up to a repeat performance of equal proficiency.

22

DESPITE THE PLEASURES of Emma Sue's plush body and wanton ways, after two days, Barlow had about had his fill of her. Plus the itch was growing more powerful to be on the move, hunting down the men who had killed Seamus Muldoon and left him and Buffalo 2 to die.

The issue was settled late that afternoon as he was sitting in the Bull's Head with Tom Wallenbach drinking beer. Buffalo 2 growled softly and got up from where he had been lying next to Barlow's chair. His hackles rose and he stared warily at a determined-looking man who was approaching the table.

Barlow turned his chair, bracing for trouble. After all their years together, he knew well the meanings of Buffalo 2's different growls. Barlow calmly watched the big, burly man heading toward him.

The man stopped next to Barlow. But he bobbed his head curtly at Wallenbach, muttering, "Tom," as a way of greeting.

Wallenbach simply nodded in response.

The man looked back at Barlow. "You the son of a bitch been keepin' company with my wife?" he asked harshly.

Barlow glared balefully up at him. The man was taller than Barlow and almost as broad of shoulder. He had a large, square face dappled with freckles and a shock of strawberry hair. "Depends, I reckon," Barlow finally drawled. "Who might you be?"

"Name's Elmer Concannon. Emma Sue's my wife."

Barlow scrunched up his chin and nodded. "Then I reckon I have been keepin' company—as you so quaintly call it—with your wife." He ignored the shocked look on Wallenbach's face.

"Then, sir," Concannon said forcefully, "we got some business together. I don't take kindly to such actions."

Barlow's face hardened as he rose. "You challengin' me, hoss?" he asked, voice flat and steely.

"I am," Concannon responded just as firmly.

"Don't be a fool, hoss. That strumpet ain't worth the ass whuppin' you're gonna git."

"Enough jabberin', boy," Concannon snapped, his face flushed with anger. He reared back and let fly with a punch from a fist as wide as a mule's shoe, and with the same power, Barlow thought as he easily dodged it.

Barlow slid one step to the side, half spun, grabbed Concannon's shirt with both hands and slammed him back down onto the table top. Keeping his grip, he leaned over the man. "This is foolishment, boy," he snarled. "You might be some bigger'n me, hoss, but you ain't used to fightin' for your life the way I am. Goin' agin' someone ain't no game to me, hoss."

He let go of Concannon's shirt and stepped back, not lessening his vigilance any.

Concannon rose slowly, eyes ablaze with anger. Once on his feet, he launched himself at Barlow, shoving off one huge foot and plowing into his buckskin-clad adversary. He swept beefy arms around Barlow, pinning his foe's arms to his side, and drove him backward, until Barlow's back smashed up against a wall, rattling the building. His head bounced off the wood, dazing him momentarily.

As the shouts and catcalls of the bar's patrons rang in his ears, Barlow shook his head to clear it. He was having trouble breathing as Concannon squeezed his chest.

"Ain't so tough now, are you, boy?" Concannon gasped, as he struggled to increase the pressure around Barlow's torso.

Barlow didn't waste his breath on answering. He sucked

in as much air as he could manage with his chest being constricted as it was, then leaned forward and latched his teeth into Concannon's red-veined nose. He bit down hard.

Concannon bellowed in pain. He drew his arms away from Barlow's torso and swiftly pounded him in the ribs several times.

Barlow grunted as the blows landed, but did not release his foe's nose until the fourth shot had landed. He suddenly unclamped his teeth, then brought up a knee with a jerk. He missed Concannon's groin, but did manage to connect with the farmer's thigh.

Concannon yelped and stumbled back a few steps. Barlow pushed off the wall and swarmed over his opponent like a spring-hungry bear on a honey-rich beehive. His fists flashed, muscles bunched and exploded, knuckles cracked against bone.

Concannon was driven back and back. The suddenness and fury of the onslaught did not allow him to find a moment to brace himself to retaliate. All he could do was retreat and try to fend off the majority of the blows that rained on him, something at which he had only mediocre success.

Finally Barlow had the bloody, battered Elmer Concannon backed up against the bar, where the farmer hung on, weaving, groggy.

"You had enough now, hoss?" Barlow asked, voice ragged with exertion and fury.

Concannon managed a small nod, as he hung on the bar with his elbows, his chest heaving.

Barlow stood for some moments, allowing the rage in him to settle down into something manageable. Then he stepped forward, pleased to note that Concannon did not flinch or cower even though it was obvious he thought Barlow was about to resume pummeling him. But Barlow simply took one of the man's big arms in his and tugged him gently forward. "Come on, hoss," he said quietly, "let's go set and have us a mug." He just hoped Wallenbach would be willing to pay for a round or two for Concannon. Barlow had but a few cents on him and would not be able to afford it.

Concannon allowed himself to be led back to the table where Wallenbach and Buffalo 2 waited. He sank wearily into a chair that Barlow provided for him. He was beginning to hurt all over, and knew the next day would be hell. He sighed, knowing he had asked for it.

With the three men seated, the dog once again lying placidly next to the table and fresh mugs of foamy beer setting before them, they drank quietly for a few moments. Then Barlow asked, "You willin' to listen for a spell, hoss?"

Elmer glanced at him, still fighting to regain his focus. Then he nodded. He figured that listening to this man berate him and insult him was still a lot better than being hammered by him.

"Me 'n' Emma Sue had us some intimate doin's way back," Barlow said after a few seconds. "We was hardly more'n children ourselves then, though we thought we was better'n we was. Anyways, after them doin's, she tried to force me to wed her. I wasn't of a mind to at the time."

"Why not?" Concannon had perked up a bit with the beer and the beginning of Barlow's tale. "She's a good woman, my Emma Sue."

"She's a goddamn harlot, hoss," Barlow said, a bit of his anger resurfacing. "That was a big part of why I wasn't aimin' to let myself be pushed into marryin' her. I weren't the only young man she'd lain with back then, and I was certain I weren't gonna be the last neither, weddin' or no weddin'."

Concannon started growing contentious again, and looked as if he was going to protest, but Barlow cut him off.

"It's true, hoss," Barlow said flatly, back under control. "I know it ain't somethin' you want to hear, but it's time you did. For your own damn good." He paused for a swig of beer. "Soon after I turned her down, she went around the area tellin' everyone in these parts that she was with chil', and I was the pa."

Concannon looked closely at Barlow, then shook his head. "Cain't say as any of our young'uns favor you in looks," he mumbled.

"Didn't reckon they would, hoss. I didn't think she really was carryin' a chil' a'tall, let alone mine. But ever'body got their drawers in an uproar over it and tried to force me into makin' a 'good woman' outta her. Such doin's didn't shine with this chil', so I went off to fight Black Hawk's people.

Hell, Tom here was there with me. Even took him a Sauk and Fox arrow."

Concannon glanced at Wallenbach, who nodded. "It's all true, Mr. Concannon."

As Barlow continued, Concannon turned toward him again. "I figured them doin's would last a spell, and when they was over, I could come back here and live in peace. But damn if those Injins didn't up and quit fightin' barely a couple months into it. Instead of comin' back here and havin' to face Emma Sue and all them folks who was angry as hornets—includin' my dear ol' pa—I figured it was best to just mosey on. I ain't been back since, till I rode in here just a few days ago."

"And headed straight for my Emma Sue," Concannon said bitterly, gulping down a fair swallow of beer.

"Hell, hoss, I was tryin' to avoid her. I didn't hold no good feelin's for her after what she did that sent me packin'. We ran into each other right on the street the other day, and we had us some row." Barlow almost grinned. "I was even more determined not to have anything to do with her after that, hoss. But," he added with a rueful shake of the head, "later that afternoon we run into each other again. And . . . well, I'm plumb ashamed to admit it, but she won me over."

Concannon's faced reddened even beyond its natural ruddiness, but he said nothing.

"I decided yesterday when I left her that it was time for me to move on. I can't help but thinkin' that after what she done so long ago, she just might have some more tricks in store for me." He paused, sipping beer and surreptitiously watching Concannon. Finally he said, "It ain't really none of my concern what you do, but was I in your place, hoss, I'd divorce Emma Sue soon's I could. Like I said, I weren't the only young man back in the old days to lay with her, and I expect you ain't the only one she's been with in the time since. I'd also wager she'll continue to fornicate with other men long's they find her attractive and willin'."

"I'm not sure I can do that, Mr. Barlow," Concannon said seriously. "She's a good woman in many ways."

"She might be, hoss. But she ain't ever gonna be faithful to you nor to nobody else. If you can live with that, then so be it. That's your concern, not mine." He paused. "But if

that's where your sticks floats, hoss, you best either get some
blinders or be ready to go agin' any number of fellers on a
regular basis."

A few minutes later, Barlow, Wallenbach and Buffalo 2
left Concannon sitting at the table. Outside, Wallenbach
said, "You *are* a goddamn fool, ain't you, Will?" He smiled
a little as he said it, figuring to take some of the sting out
of the words.

Barlow chuckled. "Reckon I am." He paused, then grew
somber. "But it don't really shine with me to cavort with
another man's wife. I don't know what the hell I was
thinkin'." He sighed. "But I ain't aimin' to cause no more
trouble here," he added decisively, breath smoky in the cold
air. "I'll be headin' out tomorrow, first thing."

The next morning Barlow left Tom and Molly Rose Wallenbach's farm and headed into St. Charles, where he caught
a ferry across the Missouri River. It was an interesting ride,
with the water carrying old logs, debris and even chunks of
ice rapidly downriver. Back on land, Barlow settled himself
into the saddle on Beelzebub and turned east and a little
south, riding steadily under a ponderous gray sky that occasionally spit rain, snow flurries or sleet.

Shortly before nightfall, he entered St. Louis. The first
thing he did was find himself a place to spend the night. He
was glad that Wallenbach had lent him a few dollars to tide
him over, but he wanted to be frugal with it, since he was
not sure how long it would have to last. He took refuge in
a boardinghouse that was more like a barracks, with a dozen
small beds crammed into one stifling, foul-smelling room.
Rather than leave his possibles there unguarded, he carried
them with him as he went in search of sustenance. After
eating, he went back to the boardinghouse, glared at the men
who were there, in warning that he did not want to be disturbed, and stretched himself out on the straw mattress. Just
before falling into a deep sleep, he offered up a hope that
he would not be burdened with lice when he awoke.

When morning rolled around, he filled his stomach well
and then set out on his hunt. He went from saloon to saloon,
from one foul eatery to another. He prowled the docks and
the nearby streets. He sauntered down alleyways and dirty

side streets. He checked boardinghouses and fetid wharfside inns.

Two days of fruitless searching left him angry, frustrated and irritated. He was low on money again, disgusted with the rooming house in which he was staying and repulsed by the meals he had been eating. The only way things would improve, he finally admitted to himself, was if he found work.

So on the third day in St. Louis, he changed the focus of his hunt. It didn't take him long to find work. With winter settling in for the long term, he took a job as a dock worker. He toted cargo, loaded and unloaded ships, and where there was no work of that form, he learned how to caulk boats. The work was hard, but for a strong man like him, it offered no trouble. It was boring work, and the pay was not great, but it would allow him to soon lease more suitable housing, and right away it meant he could afford a slightly better round of eateries.

More importantly, the job gave him a good opportunity to nose around. He was certain that if Enos Priddle and his men were in St. Louis, which he still thought likely, they would spend a fair amount of their time near the docks. Such men, Barlow figured, would not be comfortable in the city's more high-class establishments, no matter how much they had made with the goods and money they had stolen from Seamus Muldoon.

Barlow was sure he would find the five men he sought, that he would find them in St. Louis—a wide-open city in many ways, one that encompassed a diverse bunch of people without raising too many questions—and that he would learn of their whereabouts on or near the docks.

Despite his desire to find and punish Priddle and his co-horts, he missed the closeness of a woman. More than once he thought about making a quick trip back to St. Charles for a tryst with Emma Sue Concannon. He did not, though, because traveling was arduous at this time of year. But more importantly, he knew that seeing her again would bring nothing but more trouble. She was a strumpet, that was all there was to it. Besides, he had come to like Elmer Con-cannon some and did not want to cause the man any more pain. So he stayed put, hoping he would soon find a willing woman to share his bed.

He did, though it was not in the way he had expected. A week or so after taking the job, while strolling home from a saloon in the late afternoon, he and Buffalo 2 saw three men accosting a woman in the dark, cold streets.

He began running toward the small group, but Buffalo 2, knowing what he was supposed to do, was well ahead of his master. The big dog got within ten feet of the men and leaped just as one of them turned at the sound of the dog's growls. Buffalo 2 slammed into the man's chest, knocking him down. Before the man could pull a gun, or any other weapon, the Newfoundland was tearing at his throat, ripping out chunks of flesh—and eliciting screams of pain and fear.

Barlow charged up, coming to a stop near another of the men. His feet slipped a little on the rain-slick cobblestones, but he managed to stay upright. The man snarled and raised a fist—which contained a large knife he was ready to plunge into Barlow. But the former mountain man blocked the blow with his rifle, which he held crossways in his hands. Then he swung the rifle butt around, smashing the man across the bridge of the nose with it.

The man screamed. Barlow dropped his rifle, grabbed the man's knife hand and twisted the assailant's arm until several bones cracked. He let go of the man, who slumped to the ground, crying with agony.

The third assailant turned and fled as fast as he could on the slippery stone street. Barlow spotted him and grinned evilly. "Go get him, Buffler," he commanded. The dog bolted.

Barlow turned to the woman. She stood there trembling, both from cold and fear. Fright lingered in her grayish eyes, as she waited for this new monster to attack her. "You all right, ma'am?" Barlow asked quietly, soothingly.

"Ye-Yes," she said tentatively. "I'm afr . . ."

"I ain't gonna hurt you, ma'am," Barlow said, still comfortingly. "I just want to make sure you're all right. Then me 'n' Buffler will escort you to your home. If you want us to, though I'd think that would be the safest for you."

Some of the fear left her at his words, his tone and his open, honest look. She almost managed a smile. "Thank you, sir. It was a most frightful experience. I . . . Who am I thanking?"

"Name's Will Barlow, ma'am. And you?"

"Dulcy Polzin. I'm . . . Well, I'm a charwoman." She was embarrassed at the revelation.

He could see it in her eyes. "Ain't nothin' to be ashamed of in that, Miz Polzin," he said softly.

Buffalo 2 trotted up, black muzzle darkened even more by blood. Barlow patted the great head. "Well, Miz Polzin, where to?"

Dulcy hesitated. She didn't really know what to say. To describe her accommodations as shabby would be an extreme case of putting the best view on things.

Barlow smiled. "My quarters ain't nothin to speak of, Miz Polzin," he offered. "I cain't even say truthfully that I've ever had worse lodgin's. So if that's what's botherin' you, don't concern yourself over it."

She wondered if he were lying to make her feel good. But that didn't make any sense, once she thought about it. He had no reason to lift her spirits, not after having saved her from those men.

Then she thought that perhaps he was trying to get her to agree to go to his place on the pretense of showing her how shabby it was. Once there, he might force himself on her. She immediately realized how foolish that idea was. If that's all he wanted, he would have taken her right here and now, especially after having risked his life—and his dog's life—in saving her. He was certainly big enough and powerful enough to have his way with her without expending much effort. Perhaps he was a bad man, she thought, but now that her fear was almost gone and her brain was beginning to work again, she didn't really think so. She decided she would trust in her instinct.

Dulcy nodded. "It's two blocks over," she said, concluding that she really had nothing to lose in having this big, though somewhat brutal man escort her. And she told him so.

He smiled once more, making the last of her fear beat a hasty retreat, as he offered her his arm.

23

BARLOW SPENT WHAT time he could with Dulcy Polzin over the next several days, and they soon decided that as much as they wanted to make love with each other, doing so in either's lodgings was impossible. So, as soon as he got his next pay, Barlow found a place, which he bought. It wasn't much—a single-room cabin on a marshy stretch of riverbank just south of the docks. It was old and dilapidated, sagging heavily in back, which was why he could afford it. It had no windows, but the roof was solid and had only one hole. The fireplace and chimney were in reasonably good shape and there was even a cookstove that worked. Barlow managed to finagle a heavily scarred, whiskey-stained table and two chairs from one saloon for just pennies. Dulcy had a few pots, pans and dishes they could use, and Barlow laid his sleeping robe on the floor in one corner. It was as comfortable as they could make it.

Just after having sex for the first time, Dulcy made it clear that she would have no objections to sharing these new quarters with Barlow.

Barlow thought about it for a few minutes. He thought the idea was marvelous, but he wondered what would happen to his hunt for Priddle and his men. He was not about to abandon that search for Dulcy Polzin or any woman. Finally he explained it to her, from his signing up with Seamus Muldoon's wagon train, to the attack and the deaths of Muldoon and his two loyal employees, Carlos Camacho and Tom Kilkenny, to his being left to die only to be found by the Comanches, to his escape and long trek back to the Settlements.

"I aim to get the bastards who done it," he concluded. "I figure they're in St. Louis, or leastways somewhere nearby."

Dulcy's clear gray eyes clouded over with worry. "I understand you got to do that," she said quietly. "I even think that it's the right thing to do."

"But . . . ?" Barlow questioned, knowing it was coming.

"But I'm worried about you, Will. I know we ain't known each other long, but I got a hankerin' for you. I don't expect we'll be man and wife anytime soon—if ever. But I'd hate to let my heart go out to you even a little bit only to see you get yourself killed in the next few days or weeks, leavin' me to fend for myself again."

Barlow scratched his chin as he thought of how to respond. Then he said, "Even if I was to go under soon—which ain't likely, mind you—you wouldn't really be no worse off'n you were when we met. You'd even be maybe a bit better off. I'll draw up papers first thing that'll let you keep this place. It ain't much, but it's better'n those lodgin's you had before, and it'd be all yours."

"You'd do that?" Dulcy asked in wonder. No man had ever treated her with such respect.

Barlow shrugged. "Why, sure. Can't see why not."

"Don't you have family or such?"

"Some, sure. But none who'd want this place, and none I'd want to give anything to in any case."

Dulcy pondered that for a few moments, then said, "But I'd still miss you if you was gone."

Barlow sucked in a big breath, then let it out slowly. "You'd miss me if you wasn't livin' here, Dulcy," he reasoned.

That made sense, Dulcy thought. She smiled. "Come here," she said quietly.

He rolled toward her on their makeshift bed, and she offered herself to him with a fierce passion.

Afterward they lay quietly, Dulcy encased in the fold of Barlow's big shoulder. He smiled into the growing darkness, thinking of how Dulcy compared with Emma Sue Concannon. They were complete opposites. Where Emma Sue's body was pleasing in its roundness, Dulcy Polzin was thin to almost boniness. Her breasts were thin though perky, with small, light-colored nipples and areolae. Her stomach was so slim that her pelvis bones were pronounced. Her arms and legs were thin as sticks. But she was every bit as passionate as Emma Sue ever was.

Not that he planned to stay with Dulcy. He wasn't sure what he would do after he had taken care of Muldoon's killers, though he had no plans to stay here. But that was for later. Even if he found his quarry soon, he did not think he would leave St. Louis before spring.

He was interested to see, however, that Dulcy fleshed out a little bit over the next several days with regular and filling meals. It gave her more energy, too, which led to even more lustful lovemaking.

Settled in, Barlow began in earnest his hunt for Priddle and his men. He kept his eyes and ears open as he worked, and spent several hours a day in saloons talking to people, looking, always looking.

Dulcy was not happy with all the time he was spending away from home. She knew, of course, what he was doing, and she still thought it right, but she missed him. She was savvy enough, however, to hold her tongue.

Weeks passed, with little success in his quest, but after his experience in trying to track Anna for all those years, Barlow was used to it and had developed at least a veneer of patience. Frustration did arise, however, and grew as the days passed. After a time he began to believe he was wrong in thinking that Priddle and his men were in St. Louis. It had seemed a likely place for them to be, but it was beginning to seem like a foolish notion. He considered moving on to Independence or Westport to see if he could track them down there, but he was reluctant to make the trip with winter hard on the region. He also was reluctant to give up Dulcy's charms, such as they were. She was no Natividad Santiago by any stretch of the imagination, but she was warm and caring, and that went a long way with him.

Then he spotted what he thought was one of Priddle's

men leaving a saloon. He picked up speed, hustling through the throng of people in the gathering dusk, dancing around slow movers, shoving past those who needed shoving.

The man turned a corner, and Barlow caught enough of a look at his face to know it was Lachlin O'Hagin. Barlow almost broke into a run. He considered sending Buffalo 2 chasing after the man, but there were too many people about, and the dog would not know which one to chase. All Barlow could hope for was that they got close enough on a mostly empty street and then he'd sic the Newfoundland on him.

When Barlow skidded around the corner, he slipped on the thin coat of ice on the foul street, banging into the wall of the building across the narrow alley. There was no one in sight. "C'mon, Buffler," he snapped as his irritation grew. They hurried down the short lane, and gingerly stopped at the end. Barlow looked left down the street, then right. There was still no one to be seen.

"Dammit!" he snapped quietly, the word filled with anger and irritation. He sighed deeply, exhaling a cloud of vapor that drifted up into the deepening darkness. "Well, boy, we best get on home," he finally said. He and the dog turned and headed back up the alley as a gloom descended on Barlow's shoulders.

He was not about to give up, though. For the next several days, he spent whatever time he could manage either in the Long Rifle Saloon or standing in the cold across the street from the bar to watch the comings and goings of the patrons. He figured it made more sense to keep an eye on the one place, assuming that O'Hagin would return, than to keep searching the scores of saloons scattered throughout the city in hopes he might spot O'Hagin or another of the men he was hunting.

Days passed, and once more discouragement rose up in him. He had to fight back the urge to run around smashing things in his frustration.

But he stuck it out, day after day for more than a week. Finally, though, as he was leaving the Long Rifle one night, he almost bumped into O'Hagin.

The Irishman's eyes rose wide in fright and surprise. There was no mistaking the massive blanket-coat-clad man

with the enormous black dog. O'Hagin spun and raced off,
knocking people down in his haste to get away. He was
slowed only a bit by the bulky coat he wore against the
coldness and the ice-dotted ground.

But Barlow was not to be denied after all this time. He
charged out of the saloon, his thick legs churning powerfully
in the tall, thin Irishman's wake. He easily leaped over people O'Hagin had knocked down in his flight. Others frantically dodged the large man and his dog.

Barlow was catching up quickly, but when O'Hagin slid
around a corner, Barlow bellowed, "Buffler, go get him.
Hold him for me! Go on!"

The dog put on a burst of speed and tore off around the
corner. A few seconds later, before Barlow reached the corner and could see for himself, he could hear O'Hagin
screaming, and Buffalo 2's powerful growls.

Barlow raced around the corner and fell after slipping on
some ice. It did nothing to improve his disposition. He
scrambled up, giving his rifle a quick look to make sure it
had not broken, then moved ahead. He stopped where Buffalo 2 had O'Hagin pinned to the ground. The big Newfoundland had his front paws planted on the Irishman's
chest, his slavering fangs barely two inches from the man's
florid face.

"Let him up, Buffler," Barlow said softly.

The dog backed up slowly, fangs still bared, throaty
growls boiling up and out. A clearly frightened Lachlan
O'Hagin scooched himself backward until his head was
against the wall, then shoved with his feet until his back was
partially up the wall. He rested there, chest heaving in fear
and anger. "What you want with me, mate?" he asked. Both
hands dropped into his lap.

"You know goddamn well what I want with you, hoss,"
Barlow said flatly. "You got to pay for what you done to
Seamus, Carlos and Tom Kilkenny. And for what you and
the others done to me, leavin' me out there to die from
Nature's doin's or at the hands of the goddamn Coman-
ches."

"You have the wrong man, lad," O'Hagin insisted, staring
up at Barlow's angry face. He began edging his right hand
toward his belt—and the single-shot pistol there.

"I reckon not, hoss," Barlow said flatly. "You don't think I'd forget you or any of them others, do you, boy?" He took a step closer, smirking. "Next time you aim to kill a man, you best make sure you finish the job and not leave it for others. Even the Comanches ain't no match for the likes of this ol' chil, boy."

"I don't know what in bloody goddamn hell you're talking about, bucko," O'Hagin said, trying to keep Barlow talking and occupied.

"You realize," Barlow said, ignoring the man's last statement, "that if you do manage to reach that pistol in your belt that I'm gonna have Buffler here chew your hand off before you can fire it. You ain't gonna be such a big man with the ladies—either hereabouts or back in Santa Fe—with only one hand, hoss. Most expect a heap more of their men."

O'Hagin froze, his fear doubling. He had thought he could easily catch Barlow unawares, draw his pistol and gun down the large, thick-chested man without problems. He was worried about the dog, but he figured he could take care of the animal somehow. After all, besides the pistol, he still had one large knife in a sheath on his belt and another tucked into the top of one boot. But Barlow had been more alert than he had expected, and that did not bode well for him.

"Now, ease that pistol out of your belt with your left hand, hoss, and you just might make it out of this alive." Barlow had no intention of letting this man live, but he concluded it would keep O'Hagin calmer for a while if he thought he could survive the confrontation.

O'Hagin gingerly, slowly, did as he was told, his eyes flicking nervously between the big man armed with a rifle, and the large dog who still looked like he wanted to make a meal out of O'Hagin. The Irishman tossed the weapon gently to his left. It landed a few feet away with a clatter on the icy ground.

Barlow moved up and kicked the muzzle-loading pistol even farther out of the way, then said, "Now the knife."

Without revealing anything on his face, O'Hagin slid the knife out of the belt sheath and pitched it after the pistol. "All right, bucko?" he asked tensely.

"You want to take that pig sticker out of your boot, hoss?" Barlow asked nastily, "or should I just put a lead pill through that leg to make sure you don't do somethin' really foolish?"

O'Hagin let loose a low-voiced chain of Gaelic that Barlow could not understand but knew was insults and regrets. With sinking heart, the Irishman reached down, gently tugged up his pant leg, slipped the knife out of the boot and threw it into the faltering light.

"That's a heap better, hoss," Barlow said. He squatted next to O'Hagin's left lower leg.

Buffalo 2 took up a post between the Irishman's legs, sitting, tail wagging gently, tongue lolling, eyes wary.

"Now, hoss," Barlow said, resting his rifle butt on the ground in front of him, "I'd be obliged if you was to tell me just where I can find your cronies."

"What friends?" O'Hagin was thinking furiously, desperately trying to come up with some way out of this. He was not stupid enough to think that Barlow was going to let him walk away from here, whether he told him anything or not. So he wanted to stall for time, hoping that some solution would present itself.

"You know who I'm talkin' about, hoss," Barlow said patiently. "But just in case fear—or contrariness—has made you forgetful, I'm lookin' for Enos Priddle, Ignacio Sanchez, Bob Dunsmore, and José Abrego."

"I never heard of any of those buckos, mate," O'Hagin said, his brogue thick.

"Then, hoss," Barlow said in a voice as cold as the swiftly approaching night, "you're gonna experience a heap of pain for nothin'."

O'Hagin sighed as he looked into Barlow's flint-hard eyes, and he felt hopelessness crawl all over him. He had to try once more, though, at least. "I don't know where they are, bucko," he said, voice beginning to quiver. "They were here for a time, but then they left. I was having a good time here, so I stayed."

"And they didn't tell you where they were going?" Barlow found that hard to believe. He figured the others would at least have told O'Hagin that they were heading toward some specific place, not just that they were leaving St. Louis.

"Maybe they did, bucko," O'Hagin said, trying to put on a brave face. "But I don't remember. Honest, bucko. I had me a heap of whiskey when they told me, so I don't recall too well just what they said."

That was possible, Barlow thought, perhaps even plausible. But he still did not believe it. He squatted there for some moments, eyes never leaving O'Hagin's. Darkness crept up, and with it a serious drop in the temperature. The cold was pushed by a brittle wind blowing off the river and weaving in between the buildings. Barlow didn't much feel it, though.

He slowly pushed himself to his feet. Standing, resting his hands on the muzzle of his rifle, the butt of which sat on the cold, icy ground, he stared down at O'Hagin. He was sure now that O'Hagin was not going to tell him anything—unless he was encouraged. He had had to persuade others in the past, but he never did get any joy in it. Had he been looking for news of his daughter Anna, he would not have hesitated for even a second in inflicting whatever torture was needed to extract the information he was seeking.

Still, there was no other way to find out what he needed to know, he decided. He had spent far more time searching for the men than he had wanted, and the only luck he had had was accidentally running into Lachlan O'Hagin. There was no alternative but to convince the Irishman to talk to him.

He squatted again, laying his rifle carefully alongside him. "One more chance to save yourself a heap of painin', hoss," he said tightly. "Where's Priddle and the others?"

O'Hagin shrugged. He tried to prepare himself for what Barlow was going to do to him.

24

BARLOW PULLED HIS knife, reached out and sliced the small possibles sack off O'Hagin's belt. Sliding the knife away, Barlow pulled open the leather bag and began extracting items, tossing them aside after a cursory examination.

There was the usual flotsam many a man carried with him on a daily basis—folding knife, pair of dice made from old lead rifle balls, a couple of loose fulminate of mercury caps, a small metal container of Lucifers, some scraps of rawhide thongs, a chunk of hardened tobacco twist along with a plethora of tobacco scraps, a small horn spoon, a few tiny items that Barlow assumed had some personal meaning for O'Hagin, and a small buckskin pouch.

Barlow took the last and opened it. As he had hoped, it was full of coins. A pretty nice amount, too, as far as he was concerned, though he had, in truth, expected a lot more. He held out the money. "Where's the rest, hoss?" he asked.

"Ain't no more," O'Hagin growled.

Barlow thought that over. There were three possibilities: O'Hagin was lying; he had spent a lot more than Barlow might have thought he would; or Enos Priddle had not given O'Hagin a very large share of the booty. Each was as probable as the other. Barlow gave O'Hagin's person a cursory patting down but discovered no more coins. It was also possible, he decided, that O'Hagin had left the lion's share of his loot in his rooms, wherever they were, but Barlow tended to doubt that. Lachlan O'Hagin was not a very subtle man, and he'd be paranoid enough to carry all his money on him, lest someone sneak into his quarters and steal it.

Barlow sighed. It didn't matter, he decided. With what he had just taken from O'Hagin, he would have more than enough to buy some supplies to travel anywhere he might need to track down Priddle and the rest of his men. And if he didn't have to travel—if the killers were all in St. Louis—this would be enough to live comfortably through the winter on, even if he gave up his job on the docks.

The coins clinked loudly in the silence as he dropped them back into the pouch and then stuffed the pouch into his own possibles bag. He picked up his rifle and rose. "All right, hoss," he said, "let's take us a little *paseo* over yonder."

"Where are we going?" O'Hagin asked nervously as he pushed himself up, using the wall behind him as a brace.

"Someplace where we won't be disturbed," Barlow said flatly.

O'Hagin did not like the sound of that, but there was nothing he could do. At least not right now. He resolved to keep alert to any possibility either to escape or to kill Barlow. "Which way?"

Barlow pointed with his rifle, and O'Hagin shuffled, toward the Mississippi River, which roared in majesty not far away. Barlow rested his rifle in the crook of his left arm, not feeling the need to keep it pointed at O'Hagin's back.

As they crossed a fairly well-traveled street, O'Hagin decided it was time to act. He suddenly bolted, sprinting past a knot of several people and dodging a number of others, some individuals, some in pairs or trios. He darted toward the corner, hoping that once around it, he could lose himself in the human traffic there.

He didn't make it. As soon as O'Hagin took off, Barlow shook his head in annoyance and said quietly, "Go get him, Buffler. Hold him for me."

The dog bolted off, easily avoiding the humans who froze, unable to move out of the big dog's way. Before O'Hagin reached the corner, the Newfoundland was on him, pouncing on the Irishman's back, knocking him facedown into the slushy dirt. Growling, Buffalo 2 stood with front paws on O'Hagin's upper back, holding him where he lay.

Barlow strolled up. "Back off, Buffler," he said quietly, ignoring the strange looks the passers-by cast their way.

The dog did as he was told, and Barlow said, "Get up, hoss."

O'Hagin rose unsteadily, and brushed chunks of partly frozen mud from his clothes and face.

"That was pretty goddamn stupid, boy," Barlow said flatly. He shoved O'Hagin around and then forward. "Move on."

Dejected, O'Hagin stepped off, speculating on what was in store for him and wondering if there was anything he could do to get away from the madman and his dog, which O'Hagin was coming to believe had been spawned in hell and suckled by the devil.

Near the river's edge, Barlow ordered O'Hagin to turn left, and they continued walking. A few minutes later, Barlow had O'Hagin stop at the end of a small pier that jutted out into the river. The rushing water swirled coldly around the creaking wood pilings. As the Irishman halted, Barlow slammed him in the back of the neck with the butt of his rifle.

O'Hagin sank to his knees with a groan, his hand snapping up to gingerly rub the sore spot. He half turned his head. "What the bloody hell . . . ?" he asked, startled. Fear surged up in him.

"Just a warnin', hoss," Barlow said harshly. "It don't shine with this chil' to be shot and then left to the tender mercies of the Comanches. I aim to discourage you and your amigos from committin' similar doin's to others, and I am in no humor for discussin' the whys and wherefores of such doin's with the likes of you." He paused, letting that register with O'Hagin, then continued. "You'll tell me where them others are, hoss, and do so straight off, or I'll put you under in a most goddamn excrutiatin' manner. The more you resist me, hoss, the more pain you'll experience. Understand what I'm sayin', hoss?"

"Aye," O'Hagin said tentatively, worry coursing through him like the river rushing between its banks only a few feet in front of him.

"Good. Now get up and face me." When O'Hagin had guardedly done as he was told, still rubbing the pain at the back of his neck, Barlow said, "Now, hoss, where's your amigos at?"

"I don't know, bucko," O'Hagin said uneasily, unwilling to look Barlow in the eyes.

"Mayhap you didn't get my meanin', hoss." He paused. "I ain't of a mind to stand here and bandy words with you. Now, I'll just ask you this one more time, hoss—where's your pals?"

O'Hagin shrugged. He finally deigned to look at Barlow, but more because he wanted to see what Barlow was going to do, in part so he might be ready to fend it off.

It did no good, however, as Barlow grunted some unintelligible command and a growling Buffalo 2 charged up and suddenly tore a chunk of flesh out of the back of one of O'Hagin's thighs.

O'Hagin screamed, and Buffalo 2 backed up, the bloody mound of muscle, skin and wool pants hanging from his mouth. The Irishman bent and clapped his hands around the bleeding wound, looking up at Barlow in fear and hatred.

"Your memory gettin' any better, hoss?" Barlow asked diffidently.

O'Hagin started to retort, but Barlow cut him off. "If it ain't, ol' Buffler there would be happy to fill his meatbag with more pieces of you."

As if to prove the point, the Newfoundland dropped the bloody mess from his mouth and looked hungrily at O'Hagin. Small growls rolled up from his throat and out into the cold air, drifting toward the Irishman on the clouds of vapor.

O'Hagin looked from dog to man and back, several times. Then he slowly straightened. "I can't be sure they're still there, bucko," he said fearfully. Before Barlow could issue another warning, he hastened on, "But I can tell you where they were. I can't be held responsible if they're moved on from there."

Barlow nodded, accepting that. "Where?" he prompted.

"The two Mexicans—Sanchez and Abrego—went to Independence," O'Hagin said. "They were only here a fortnight or so before headin' back that way. I ain't seen 'em since."

Barlow nodded. He was a little surprised, but not too much. "How about Priddle and Dunsmore?"

"They said they were goin' back to Westport. I think they were plannin' to make another run down to Santa Fe." He grinned despite the pain. "I think they're lookin' for another venture, like this last one."

"You plannin' to join them, hoss?"

"Aye. We get as much specie from the next one as we did from the last, and we'll all be settled for life."

"They give you as little from the next doin's as they did this one, you ain't gonna be able to settle anything, hoss."

O'Hagin shrugged. "I'll still be better off that most folks, bucko," he said with confidence.

"Well, you might've been, hoss. But I reckon you're just gonna have to miss it."

O'Hagin's eyelids and brows shot up in horror, his bright blue eyes shocked as the meaning of Barlow's words got through to him. He looked about frantically, checking for any kind of escape or way to fight back and perhaps avoid the death sentence that had just been pronounced on him. With his size and strength, he would have normally taken his chances against the burly Will Barlow. But a hunk of meat roughly the size of his fist missing from one leg, plus the loss of blood from it, had weakened him. Plus, the blood that had run down his leg and onto the ground at his feet would not give him very good footing.

Still, he figured he had to do something. Just standing there waiting to get shot by Barlow was not an option he was willing to consider. He shuffled a little, placing most of his weight on the uninjured leg, making sure it was out of the congealing puddle of blood. He pushed off with that foot, launching himself at his foe.

Barlow, watching O'Hagin's eyes, anticipated the action, and easily slid a few feet to his left and hammered O'Hagin in the face with the side of his left fist.

O'Hagin's nose splintered and he stopped short, head snapping back. He weaved, trying to regain his balance, but the ringing in his ears and the pain of his mashed nose spreading through his head made that difficult, if not impossible.

"Stay, Buffler!" Barlow commanded. He dropped his rifle onto the dock, swung and grabbed O'Hagin by throat and crotch. He hoisted the tall, broad-shouldered Irishman up over his head and took a couple of steps, almost to the end of the pier. Barlow dipped his knees and then surged upward, pitching O'Hagin into the water as he did.

O'Hagin screeched as he flew through the air. The sound was cut short when he hit the icy water and sank. He was back up in a few moments, sputtering, several yards downriver. The current was fast and pushed him swiftly along. He shouted for help, pleading with Barlow to pull him out of the water.

But it was too late. Even if Barlow had been inclined to save the Irishman, the current had swept him well out of range already. His pleas for assistance faded with the distance and the thrum of the river itself.

Barlow picked up his rifle and turned to head away from the river. Whether O'Hagin died of hypothermia or drowning, justice had been served as far as Barlow was concerned.

He walked rapidly back to the small shack he shared with Dulcy Polzin. She looked at him in expectation when he entered. He nodded curtly. "One of 'em's paid the price," he said. "And told me where the others are."

"In Saint Louis?" Dulcy asked hopefully.

Barlow shook his head as he shed his coat and hung it on a pin by the door. He took a seat at the table and waited as Dulcy served him a plate of overdone ham slices and mushy beans. "Two of 'em's in Independence, the others in Westport. Or so that ol' hoss told me."

"So you're leavin'?" she asked, her heart sinking. She had known it was inevitable but had not expected it so soon. Indeed, she had hoped he would give up the idea.

"Yep," Barlow said as he shoveled in food. It wasn't all that tasty, but it was filling.

"When?" Her heart was in her throat.

"Tomorrow. Early. I'd leave out first thing, but I got a few things to do, and some supplies to buy before that."

Dulcy wanted to protest, but she knew better. Protest would only drive him away from her sooner. As it was, she hoped he would pay her some attention tonight, and maybe in the morning, too, before he left. That was the best she could hope for, and she did not want to endanger that.

Barlow knew how she felt, and he wanted her to be as accepting as possible of his leaving, so he was willing to give her his time and attention. Not that either was a chore. Despite her physical flaws, Dulcy was a warmhearted and attentive lover.

After he'd eaten smoked a pipe and polished off two cups of coffee—the only thing Dulcy made well—Barlow took her hand and led her to the bed.

They made love again the next morning, after which they ate a filling, if mostly tasteless, breakfast. Then Barlow went to a large mercantile store not far away. He made the decision overnight that some changes were in order. At the store, he bought two pairs of thick wool pants, two cotton pullover shirts, some socks and a pair of heavy leather boots that came almost to the knee. They would replace the moccasins he had bought just after arriving in Taos from an Indian at the pueblo just north of town. He decided to keep his thick, warm blanket coat, but he added a good pair of woolen gloves, a thick scarf and a new wide-brimmed hat.

His biggest purchase, however, was a brace of Colt Walker pistols. The six-shot revolvers were heavy, well made and powerful. He added a pair of simple holsters that slid onto his belt, some powder and ball, a bullet mold and tools for servicing the Walkers. He decided to keep his reliable old Hawken rifle, and even the small five-shot Colt Paterson.

Finally he picked up some supplies—coffee, a cone of sugar, a pouch of salt, jerky, beans, a bit of cornmeal, tea, a new small tin coffeepot and heavy frying pan, three twists of tobacco and two bottles of whiskey.

He paid for everything and had someone from the store deliver it to the house. Then he took Beelzebub to the nearest livery stable and had the man there check the mule's shoes. Two needed replacing, so Barlow told the man to take care of it and bring the animal to the house, where he would be waiting.

He walked home, where the packages from the store had already arrived. He and Dulcy spent the next two hours making love, nibbling at food in between times. Finally Barlow rose and donned a new outfit. He loaded his two new Walkers and slid them into the holsters. As he finished, the stableman arrived with Beelzebub. Barlow paid him, then loaded his sparse supplies onto the mule. At last he put on his thick coat, hooked his belt around his waist outside it, then slid the tomahawk into the back of the belt. He pulled out what coins he had left—more than he had thought—and handed them to Dulcy, keeping just a few for himself.

"You'll be fine here, woman," Barlow said to Dulcy. "Just be sparin' of your spendin'."

"You'll be back?" she asked, unable to keep the fear out of her voice.

"Just as soon as I can, Dulcy." He wasn't sure when that would be; hell, he didn't even know if he actually would return. But it was what she wanted to hear, so he said it. And, when it came down to it, he had no objections to spending the winter with Dulcy Polzin, so there was every chance he would be back.

He kissed her hard on the mouth. With rifle in hand and Buffalo 2 at his side, he turned and headed outside. He mounted the mule and rode off, not looking back.

25

THE TWO-HUNDRED-FIFTY-MILE trip to Independence was everything Barlow figured it would be in winter—cold, wet, often snowy, tedious, uncomfortable—and seemed to take twice as long as it really did. So he was relieved when he pulled into the town, but less so when he found himself a room at a shabby, run-down hotel that was little bigger or better than either of his brothers' farmhouses.

Dropping his few personal belongings and supplies off in the spartan room, he headed out and soon sat to a meal at the first restaurant he came to. He gorged himself on the less-than-succulent but fairly filling fare. Sitting back after eating, he lit his pipe and slurped down some coffee, which was at least better than adequate, then partook of plenty more of it. As he relaxed, he tossed to Buffalo 2 bits of fatty meat and gristle left over from the poor ham steaks he had dined on. The dog gulped down the hunks without chewing.

The restaurant owner grimaced in annoyance at Barlow's feeding of the Newfoundland, despite the fact that the bits were remains that no human in his right mind would have eaten. He soured even more when Barlow requested a bowl of water for Buffalo 2. The man hesitated, and Barlow, not in any mood for such irritations, said flatly, "I could have him bite your dumb fat ass and let him quench his thirst in your blood." He scrunched up one eye as he gave the restaurant owner a baleful look. "Of course, he'd likely end up

gettin' some foul disease from the likes of you, and then I'd
have to nurse him back to health, which I ain't got the time
or inclination for. So to save us all a heap of trouble, just
bring us a goddamn bowl of water, hoss."

The bony-faced man's scowl deepened but he turned and
left. He returned with a bucket half-full of water. He set it
down, some of the water sloshing over the lip of the wood
pail onto the floor.

Without waiting for his master's approval, Buffalo 2 began sloppily lapping up the water.

"Now, was that so hard, hoss?" Barlow asked the eatery
owner sarcastically.

"Bah," the man muttered and turned away.

"Hold on there, hoss," Barlow said. When the man
stopped and looked at him, Barlow asked, "You know of a
couple of Mexican fellers named Ignacio Sanchez and José
Abrego?"

"Can't say as I do." He did not seem at all interested one
way or the other, and he had answered too swiftly for Barlow's taste.

"What's your name, hoss?" Barlow demanded.

"Runnels. Claude Runnels. Why?" He tried to sound ca-
sual, but had trouble managing it. He hated Barlow, because
he feared the burly customer.

"It's like this, Mr. Runnels," Barlow said evenly. "Them
two boys're mean sons of bitches. They've kilt a number of
good men and need to pay for their misdeeds. I aim to see
that they do. Now, if you know where they are, I'd be
mighty obliged for you to tell me. In fact, it might even be
beneficial for you. Of course," he continued after a moment's pause for a puff on his pipe, "if you lie to me and I
find out about it, I'll . . . Well, hoss, when I finish with you,
your hide'll be hangin' on the door of this shit hole."

Runnels's pasty face paled even more. "I don't know
those names, mister," he said hastily. "But there ain't been
too many Mexicans in here of late. You know what these
fellers look like?"

"One of 'em's maybe my height, but a heap thinner. Probably walks with a limp in his right leg. Long, greasy hair,
hooked nose. The other's a bit taller, some thicker, with a
heap of a paunch on him. Small scar on his left cheek. Flat

nose spread over half his face. Eyes like a madman's."

Runnels stood and thought about that for a bit, then nodded. "I seen them in here a couple times," he said. He had
decided that perhaps Barlow wasn't all that bad after all,
especially if he cooperated with him. Or maybe it was just
relief that he might be able to get rid of Barlow soon, and
be done with him. "Last time was a week ago, maybe a bit
longer." He really tried to remember. If he could, he thought
that Barlow would be out of his hair soon—and hopefully
forever.

"You know where they might be stayin'?" Barlow asked,
not holding out much hope.

"No, sir." Runnels was beginning to worry again.

Barlow nodded. He hadn't expected Runnels to know
such a thing. He rose and tossed a coin on the table. "I'm
stayin' at the boardin' house run by some ol' woman named
Maples. You see those boys in here again, I'd be obliged if
you was to get word to me there. I'll make it worth your
while."

"I'll do that," Runnels said. The conviction in his voice
almost convinced Barlow that he was telling the truth.

Barlow spent two days wandering around Independence
looking for Sanchez and Abrego. There was no specific area
where Mexicans congregated in Independence, so he had to
try to scour the whole town. He stopped in at the boardinghouse at regular intervals on the off chance that Runnels
might have seen the two men he was hunting and sent a
message for him. But there was nothing.

Late in the morning of the third day, Barlow spotted his
quarry. The two were stepping gingerly down the street,
trying not to slip on the ground dotted with patches of ice,
slush and mud. Both wore Mexican boots, which, while
handsome, were not conducive to use on slick streets.

"Looks like things should get a mite interestin' here right
quick, Buffler," Barlow said as he and the dog moved into
step behind the two Mexicans, following at a short distance.
Barlow was tempted to just walk up and shoot the two, but
that would likely only land him in jail, making it impossible
for him to track down Enos Priddle and Robert Dunsmore,
once these two had been taken care of. As he walked, Bar-

low hung his rifle across his back by the rawhide sling.

Barlow and Buffalo 2 picked up a little speed as the two Mexicans turned a corner. When man and dog reached the corner, they slowed and peered around to make sure neither Sanchez nor Abrego was watching. They weren't, and Barlow was pleased to note that the small side street was deserted. He strode on, moving swiftly and with determination.

When he and Buffalo 2 were within ten feet of the two men they were following, Barlow pulled out one of the big Walker Colts and eased the hammer back as quietly as he could. Then he called out, *"Hola, los diablos."*

The two spun smoothly, moving a few steps apart as they did so, hands reaching for weapons, their actions practiced.

Barlow did not hesitate. Killers like these could be given no advantage—or sympathy. Barlow had not wanted to shoot them in the back, but as soon as they turned, he did not wait. He fired twice, the big pistol bucking in his thick slab of a hand.

Abrego went down in a jumble of arms and legs and a spray of blood, one .44-caliber ball hitting him in the chest, the other tearing through his left eye. He was dead before he hit the ground, which here in the shadows was frozen.

Buffalo 2 did not wait either. While Barlow had not given him any command, the dog knew instinctively what had to be done, and he shot forward, springing on Sanchez, sending him sprawling on his back on the icy ground. The dog went straight for the Mexican's throat, but Barlow called him off as he walked up and knelt next to Sanchez. The dog pulled his head back but left his paws high on the Mexican's chest, his two-hundred-plus pounds keeping the man pinned to the earth.

"Are Priddle and Dunsmore still in Westport?" Barlow asked harshly. His wrist rested on his knee, the pistol dangling loosely from his hand.

Sanchez tried to shrug, but it didn't work. "No idea," he gasped. He was not too afraid, but he was having trouble breathing with the dog's great weight on his lungs.

"When's the last time you seen either of 'em?"

Another failed shrug. "Week, two, maybe."

"They have plans to move on from Westport anytime soon?" Barlow's voice was growing colder, harder.

"Can you get this damn dog off me?" Sanchez asked, wheezing.

Between his accent and his difficulty breathing, Sanchez was hard to understand, so Barlow ordered, "Back off him, Buffler." As the dog did so, Barlow snatched the gun from Sanchez's waistband and pitched it. The weapon clacked off a wall and then the hard ground.

"Priddle or Dunsmore have any plans of leavin' Westport anytime soon?" Barlow repeated.

"No," Sanchez replied, grateful that he no longer had the dog on him.

Barlow nodded. "You know where they were stayin'?

"No."

Barlow remained where he was, unmoving, for a few more seconds. Then he slowly rose. He looked balefully down at Sanchez. "You made a big mistake when you took up evil doin's, hoss," he said quietly. As he turned, he said, "Kill him, Buffler."

Sanchez screamed once, briefly, before the Newfoundland's fangs ripped his larynx out, along with a chunk of throat. He didn't die right away, but he could make no sound, and the fight drained out of him instantly. It was over in seconds.

Barrow knelt beside Abrego, hoping that no one would investigate the single scream. Since no one had paid any attention to the two gunshots he used to kill Abrego, he deemed it unlikely that the scream would attract attention. He went through Abrego's possibles bag, pulling out all the money he found and transferring it to his own money pouch. He stood and headed back toward Sanchez's mangled corpse, calling off Buffalo 2 as he did. Once more he took whatever money he could find. While he was not suddenly wealthy, he would not have to worry about money for a good long time either.

He sliced a hunk off the bottom of Sanchez's heavy serape and used it to clean the blood and gore off Buffalo 2's face. "You sure do make a mess of yourself in such doin's, boy," he said softly as he wiped the dog's short muzzle with the cloth and patted the big dog's broad, thick-boned head with his other hand.

Done, he tossed the bloody rag aside and stood, looking

around for a moment. Then he stepped off, with Buffalo 2 at his side, heading down the small side street.

Within minutes they were back at the boardinghouse. It took even less time for Barlow to throw his possessions into a sack, then he and Buffalo 2 went to the clerk. Barlow made arrangements to send the money he had borrowed from Wallenbach—plus interest—to his friend in St. Charles. Then he and the dog left the shabby building and headed for the stable. Again, it was only minutes before Beelzebub was saddled and bridled. Barlow paid the livery-man, pulled himself onto the back of the mule and, without a look back, rode out of the stable and out of Independence, heading west.

26

BARLOW AND BUFFALO 2 arrived in Westport just as night was falling, along with the temperature. The air carried a threat of snow or sleet, and the wind whistled angrily through the area. With a possibles bag bulging with gold coins, Barlow decided he deserved some good living for a change, so he took a room at one of the better hotels a block or so from the waterfront where the Kansas River confluenced with the roaring Missouri River.

A restaurant was attached to the Kansas Star Hotel, and Barlow and Buffalo 2 wandered there to sit to the best meal Barlow had had since Natividad had last cooked for him. The buffalo steak was tender and ran red with juices, the turnips were done just right, the bread fresh baked, hot and doughy. The coffee, thick with sugar, had hardly any bitterness to it. Barlow ate three portions of everything, and went through two pots of coffee before he sat back with his pipe. As he had in Independence, he fed scraps to Buffalo 2, who eagerly gulped them down.

The restaurant owner—Ernst Bockner—unlike the crusty Claude Runnels in Independence, had no problem with Barlow sharing with the big Newfoundland. "You paid for the food, *mein herr,*" Bockner said in his thick German accent. "Vhat you do wit' it is your bidiness." In fact, he even went so far as to collect as many orts as he could find in the kitchen and bring out a large plate overflowing with meat scraps and set it down for Buffalo 2.

"He is big dog," Bockner explained, looking up at Barlow as he petted Buffalo 2. "He needs much food. Ya." He turned his attention to Barlow, who was busy eating, but stopped momentarily to glance at Bockner. "Isn't dot right, *herr hund?*" the restaurant owner said. "Ya!" he stood, grinning, and left, only to return moments later with a good-sized cook pot half-full of water. He set that down next to the Newfoundland. "Enjoy, *her hund,*" he said with a laugh as he headed back to the kitchen.

Barlow shook his head, pleased at the man's reaction. After finishing his pipe and another cup of coffee, he called for Bockner. "That was excellent feedin', hoss," he complimented the man.

Bockner beamed. "*Danke, Herr . . . ?*"

"Barlow." He shook the German's hand. "And you're most welcome. Ain't many folks serve up vittles as good as these—and make sure ol' Buffler there has his fill, too."

Bockner glowed even more, though he said nothing.

"You mind I ask you a question, hoss?" Barlow queried.

"*Nein,*" Bockner responded. He stopped clearing the table, standing quietly with Barlow's plates and tableware in his hands. "Vhat you vant to know?"

"You ever heard of a couple of fellers named Enos Priddle and Robert Dunsmore?"

Bockner shook his head slowly. "*Nein*. Those names are not familiar. You look for them?"

Barlow nodded, and told the restaurant owner why.

As the tale unfolded, Bockner's face grew darker and darker with anger at what the men had done.

When he was through with the explanation, Barlow added, "Priddle's a tall ol' hoss, and a mite on the thin side. Feller with a bony face and a nose that don't set nearly plumb straight a'tall."

"Ya, ya!" Bockner said eagerly, his head bobbing. "I know dot man. He comes here often. Sometimes another man is vit him. This one looks like anyvone. Or no vone. Ya?"

Barlow nodded, trying to hide his excitement. "That'd describe Dunsmore. Kind of a feller you'd never look at

twice and wouldn't be able to tell from a thousand others."
He paused, thinking, then asked, "You know where them
boys're stayin'?" he asked hopefully.

"Let me t'ink on dot," Bockner said as he gathered up
more flotsam from the table. "I vill t'ink vhile I take all dis
to the kitchen." He whisked away.

Barlow waited, outwardly patient but anxious inside. A
few minutes later, Bockner returned, smiling. "I remember,"
the German said. "Ya. I overhear them one time. They stay
at Missouri Palace. Several streets dot vay"—he pointed—
"close to the Missouri River."

"I'm obliged, Mr. Bockner," Barlow said honestly. If
Priddle and Dunsmore were still staying at that hotel, it
would save him a heap of trouble having to track them
down. He wanted this business over with. It had gone on
too long, and he had put it off more than he should have,
allowing himself to be sidetracked by foolish things like
trying to reconcile with his family. Now it was time to end
it.

"It is nottink, *mein freund,*" Bockner said. "I just hope
you catch those *kotzbrocken*—assholes. *Die typs ist ganz
schon fies*—they're pretty mean characters."

"They are that, hoss," Barlow agreed. "Or worse. Them
boys're kin of the devil himself."

It was too late now to go hunting down his quarry, so
Barlow and Buffalo 2 headed for the room in their hotel.
Barlow figured a good night's sleep would do wonders for
him. He had been up a long time, had taken out Ignacio
Sanchez and José Abrego and made the cold, though short,
journey to Westport. Some sleep was definitely in order, he
decided.

A big breakfast at Bockner's set Barlow and Buffalo 2 off
on the hunt in a well-fortified frame of mind and body. Rifle
sung across his back, holstered Colt Walkers belted around
his blanket coat, Barlow marched purposefully toward the
Missouri Palace. Buffalo 2 cavorted around him on the journey.

It didn't take long to find the ostentatious hotel—well, it
was flamboyant by Westport standards. It might not have
looked so fancy set in the better parts of St. Louis, but it

sparkled out here on the edges of civilization. Man and dog marched right inside and stomped across the plain yet somehow still elegant lobby to the desk. A taciturn clerk, his back mostly to them, proceeded to ignore them for some moments. The soft snick of Barlow cocking one of his pistols brought an abrupt change of attitude.

"May I help you?" the man asked, turning. His normal sneer dropped fast with one look at Barlow's bulk and the big, black dog who stood on back legs with his front paws on the small wood desk.

"You got two fellers stayin' here named Enos Priddle and Robert Dunsmore," Barlow said. "What rooms're they in?"

"I'm not allowed to divulge that information," the clerk said nervously. It was true, and his patrician air usually was enough to put off anyone seeking such things. But this block of a man with the big, vicious-looking dog did not seem the type to take such an answer with equanimity.

Barlow leaned on the desk and scratched his thick nose with an even thicker finger. "I reckon that's mostly so, hoss," he finally drawled. "But these're special circumstances. Now, you can either tell me what rooms're theirs, or I'll jist start kickin' in doors one after another till I find 'em."

"You wouldn't dare," Randall Casspperson said, horrified. He suspected that Barlow would do just what he had said.

"I would," Barlow said flatly.

"I'll have the constable here immediately," the clerk said, regaining some of his haughtiness.

"You won't if I put a lead pill in that fractious head of yours, hoss," Barlow said evenly, straightening. "And if you did manage it, you'd have to explain one gone-under constable—maybe more—to the leading officials of this fine city."

Casspperson believed him; he just knew that this man would do whatever he said he would, no matter how mad it might be. "One moment," he said nervously. He turned and consulted his register, flipping anxiously through pages until he found the one he wanted. He looked up. "Mr. Priddle is in Room 211, up the stairs there and to the right," he said, pointing. "Mr. Dunsmore occupies Room 212, across the hall from his friend."

Barlow nodded. "Now, how about the keys to those there rooms, boy." It was not a request.

After hesitating less than two seconds, Cassperson handed over the keys, a forced smile on his face.

"Obliged, hoss," Barlow said. Before turning for the stairs, however, he said, "It wouldn't sit well with this ol' chil' to have you callin' on the constable. Understand?"

Cassperson nodded, and tried hard to swallow his fear, but he met with little success.

Barlow and Buffalo 2 climbed the stairs, ignoring the few patrons they passed along the way. They stopped at Priddle's door and Barlow listened for a moment. He heard nothing. He slid the key into the lock and gingerly turned it, trying to avoid any sound. Suddenly he thrust the door open and charged in, one of the Walkers cocked in his hand. Buffalo 2 bounded in right behind him, a silent, dark shadow.

But the place was empty. "Damn," Barlow snapped. He eased the hammer of the Colt down and slid the revolver away. "Christ, Buffler," he continued, his irritation growing, "why don't things ever work out for us, eh, boy?"

He looked around the room, which was far more spacious than any temporary room he had used, including the one he was staying in here in Westport. It was better appointed, too, with a quality quilt on the large bed, which seemed to be mighty comfortable. There were two sitting chairs by the window that overlooked the river, with a table between them. Two empty bottles of good-quality whiskey stood on the table, as did the remains of a meal that must have been expensive. A smaller table was next to the bed, with the ever-present basin and ewer, and there was a large bureau against another wall, next to a door, which Barlow learned was to a closet. It was pretty full with clothes, of the likes Barlow could never afford—even if he wanted to wear such garments. Flocked paper covered the walls of the room, and fancy curtains framed the window.

"Looks like ol' Priddle is livin' mighty high on his ill-gotten gains, Buffler," Barlow noted.

With a last look around, he left the room, locking the door behind him. He dropped the first key into the sack at his waist and withdrew the other. He made the couple of long steps across the hallway to Room 212 and again listened at the door. This time he thought he heard the rustling of someone moving around inside.

Once more he unlocked the door silently, then he dropped the key back into his belt pouch. Pulling a Colt again, he thumbed back the hammer, turned the doorknob and shoved the door open. "Get him, Buffler!" he ordered. The dog bolted into the room, with Barlow right behind him.

Robert Dunsmore was, indeed, in the room. And he had a woman with him. Both were naked in the bed. Dunsmore froze for a second when the door flew open, then threw himself off the bed, reaching for a gun—a six-shooter, Barlow noted—holstered on his belt, which was with his pants on a chair.

The woman screamed, Dunsmore cursed, and Buffalo 2 growled as the dog leaped over the bed and landed on the floor right in front of Dunsmore. He grabbed the man's wrist in his powerful jaws and started jerking it left and right, snarls streaming from his throat.

The woman jumped up from the bed, heedless of her nudity, and headed for the door. Barlow hit her hard enough to knock her down but not put her out. He didn't want to really hurt her, but he did not want her getting out and spreading an alarm either.

"C'mere, Buffler," Barlow ordered.

The dog backed slowly away from Dunsmore and around the foot of the bed, never taking his soft, dark brown eyes off the man. He stopped next to Barlow.

"I wouldn't do that was I you, hoss," Barlow said as Dunsmore again moved, this time slowly, for the pistol.

He froze and looked at Barlow. His eyes widened in recognition. "You! How the hell . . . ? Where'd you . . . ? How'd . . . ?"

"You and your amigos really fucked up when you didn't make sure I was gone under, hoss. Nature couldn't finish the job for you, and neither could the goddamn Comanches. You won't get another chance."

Dunsmore took in the icy tone, the hard eyes and determined face and knew he was going to die. His hand darted for the pistol again. If he was going to go down, he intended to try to go down fighting.

Barlow fired once, and the bullet shattered Dunsmore's right forearm. Dunsmore gasped and fell back against the wall next to the chair. He grasped the battered limb with his other hand and looked fearfully at Barlow.

"Where's Priddle?" Barlow asked.

"Don't know," Dunsmore said tightly against the pain. Seeing Barlow's look grow even harder, he hastened to add, "He was here a bit ago. I ain't sure where he's gotten himself off to. Nor when he'll be back. I ain't his nursemaid."

Barlow nodded. "Adios, you sorry sack of shit." He fired twice, both lead balls from the heavy .44 tearing Dunsmore's head apart.

Barlow stepped deeper into the room. He figured he might as well take the money Dunsmore had. With any luck, he could find some of Seamus Muldoon's relatives and see that they got the lion's share of the cash. But before he took three steps, he heard something behind him. He whirled, crouching, bringing the pistol up.

He saw nothing, but he could hear someone running. He pushed up and charged out the door, just in time to see Enos Priddle racing down the stairs. "Get him, boy!" he commanded.

Buffalo 2 raced ahead, but was not quite fast enough—Priddle tore open the hotel's front door and zoomed out, slamming the door behind him. Buffalo 2 came to a screeching halt.

By the time Barlow got there, yanked the door open and stepped outside, Priddle was on his horse, galloping down the street, Priddle lashing the animal unmercifully with the ends of the reins.

"Goddamn, good Christ almighty," Barlow swore as he stood there on the porch, watching Priddle dash off.

He spun and ran for the livery stable, which was several blocks away. He had to slow almost immediately when he came close to falling on his ass when his still-new boots hit a patch of ice and he had to fight to catch his balance.

He cursed again and moved as fast as he dared, envying Buffalo 2's ability to travel swiftly despite the wintry obstacles littering the ground. It took more than ten minutes to make it to the livery, and almost that long for him to saddle Beelzebub. Tossing the liveryman a coin, Barlow vaulted into the saddle and galloped out of the stable, with Buffalo 2 racing alongside.

Snow has started falling, thick wet flakes tumbling down. Barlow knew Buffalo 2 could not keep up with this pace for very long, but that couldn't be helped. He just wanted to catch Priddle and remove him from the earth.

On the other hand, he did not want the faithful dog to die. Barlow slowed to a walk. "You stay behind, Buffler," he ordered, not sure the dog would understand. "Don't you try'n keep up with me and Beelzebub, boy. You understand?"

He kicked the mule into motion again, glancing back only after he was going full out, to see if Buffalo 2 had listened. Apparently the Newfoundland had; he was trotting along at a good pace, a fast one but one that would not tax him overly much.

As he galloped along, Barlow hoped his old mule could stand up to the exertion.

He was soon out of the city, pounding across the emptiness of the prairie, with the storm worsening every yard he traveled. Barlow thought the snow would allow him to follow Priddle's tracks that much more easily, but it was now snowing so hard that the hoofprints were being covered up almost as fast as they were being made. Barlow kept thundering along, hoping that Priddle had not veered off.

Barlow finally realized the wind was blowing hard into his face. So he slowed, and then stopped, sitting there, listening intently. His breathing was coming hard, as was the mule's. Still, he thought he could hear galloping up ahead of him.

He nodded and got moving again, pushing the mule as hard he dared considering the weather and the uncertainty of what was out there.

Suddenly Beelzebub tried to stop short, hooves slipping on the thick snow that covered the ground. He reared, braying wildly, almost unseating Barlow, who cursed the animal and swatted the mule with his hat. As he tried to restrain the wildly thrashing mule, Barlow saw a dark figure a few feet off in the cloud of windswept snow.

There was a flash of light, then an explosion, and Barlow fell off the mule. As he hit the ground, glad for the covering

of snow, which slightly eased his landing, he heard a shout
of victory followed by a wild laugh.

As Beelzebub raced off, Barlow rolled out of the way of
the mule's hooves and lay there, waiting. He eased out one
of his pistols and stuck it inside his coat, wanting to make
sure neither the cylinder nor the hammer would freeze.

Seconds ticked off, turning to minutes, yet still Barlow
lay there. The blasting wind made it difficult for him to hear
anything, but finally he sensed someone shuffling toward
him. He tensed, but still did not move.

A shadow moved into sight, the wind-whipped snow giving Enos Priddle an unworldly look. He had a manic grin
on his face as he approached Barlow, a pistol in hand. He
stopped when he saw Barlow lying there, uncertain if his
foe was still alive.

He shrugged. "I don't know how you ever made it back
from where we left you, Barlow," Priddle said, his voice cut
through with anger, "but I can guarantee you that you ain't
leavin' *this* place alive." He raised his single-shot pistol.

Barlow rolled from his side onto his back, trying to tug
the Walker out of his coat. It gave him trouble, and a moment of fear hit him as he worried that he would die without
a chance to fight back.

Priddle grinned wickedly, moved another step forward,
and leveled his pistol. Then he suddenly jerked forward,
arms flailing, pistol flying. As he hit the ground, Barlow
scrambled up, grinning when he saw Buffalo 2 standing just
behind Priddle. The Newfoundland was growling viciously.

"Good boy, Buffler," Barlow said gratefully. He moved
up to stand over Priddle, who lay facedown in the snow.
"Well, well, hoss, looks like you ain't about to get another
chance at puttin' me under."

Priddle pushed up on his arms a little and turned a snarling face to Barlow. "Don't be so goddamn certain about
that, you son of a bitch,' he hissed.

Barlow shot him in one thigh.

Priddle hissed with pain and clutched at his bloody leg.
"Bastard," he muttered.

"Mayhap I am, hoss," Barlow agreed, though with no
friendliness in his voice. "But at least I ain't a back-shootin'
skunk-consortin' pile of buffler shit like you."

"Piss on you, Barlow," Priddle snapped. "I ain't afraid of you, and I ain't afraid of dyin'. So just kill me and get it over with." He flopped onto his back, oblivious to the snow beginning to cover his face. He looked up and decided he did not like the expression of maliciousness that had suddenly appeared on Barlow's face.

"Reckon not, hoss," Barlow said harshly. "I ain't much of a religious man, nor do I know much of the Bible's teachin's. But I do believe in an eye for an eye." He glanced over at Beelzebub, who had sauntered back into view a few feet away. The mule stood there, front hooves pawing at the snow.

"What the hell's that mean, goddammit?" Priddle demanded, the first touch of fear reaching into his stomach.

Barlow didn't see that he needed to answer that. He simply shot Priddle in the other leg, then slid his pistol into the holster. He knelt and quickly patted Priddle down. He grinned harshly when he found another pistol—a big six-shooter much like his own. Barlow tossed it as far off into the snow as he could. Two knives and a small, single-shot pistol followed. Barlow rose, turned and gathered Beelzebub's reins, then climbed into the saddle. "Adios, hoss," he said flatly.

With Priddle's screaming admonitions ringing in his ears, Barlow rode off, leaving Priddle barely clinging to life, to die a lingering death alone here in the midst of the snow-storm that pounded the prairie.

Blood lust sated—but with his sense of loss over his daughter still fresh and hurtful in his mind, and a deep feeling of loneliness—Barlow wearily headed back to Westport. He would decide there, when he had time to rest some, whether to return to St. Louis—and to Dulcy Polzin. And as the snow whipped in a frenzy around him, he avoided with determination wondering what he would do when spring arrived.

LONGARM

**Explore the exciting Old West with one
of the men who made it wild!**

J. R. ROBERTS
THE GUNSMITH